Sharon repeated her question. "What did you say his name was?"

Confused, Nedra blinked rapidly. Had she uttered a name? "I...I...don't know. I don't remember his name."

Carla wasn't convinced. "Sounded like you said his name was Sin. Now all I've got to ask is was that a statement of fact or wistful thinking? 'Cause from what I remember of that man, a sin is something I would gladly commit with him!"

Sin

CRYSTAL RHODES

INDIGO

Indigo is an imprint of
Genesis Press, Inc.
315 Third Avenue North
Columbus, Mississippi 39701

Sin

ISBN 1-58571-017-2

Manufactured in the United States of America

FIRST EDITION

Sin

Prologue

"My mother was a junkie."

The words were said so matter-of-factly that Nedra Davis wasn't certain she had heard them. Yet, her only acknowledgment that he had spoken was a slight shift in her seat. She registered no surprise. He registered no emotion. His eyes, still focused on her, were blank. His expression was unreadable.

He continued. "She was twenty-five years old when she died. I was ten."

Simple math told her that he had been the product of a teenage pregnancy. She didn't want to speculate, but she could guess the rest of the scenario—young, pregnant, desperate girl finds escape from the reality of her dilemma in drugs. She had witnessed it too many times, and it seemed that it was the innocent ones, the children, who suffered the most. Neglected, dejected, too often abandoned and left alone to make their own way, their futures were predictable—crime, drugs, imprisonment, and, much too often, death.

There were times, however, when the outcome was different. Sometimes the lucky ones escaped the cycle of despair, using reservoirs of strength that never ceased to amaze her. Nedra studied the man sitting before her. He was one of the lucky ones.

He was strikingly handsome. Dressed impeccably in an expensive double-breasted navy-blue suit, his snow-white shirt complemented the reddish hues in his choco-late-brown skin. The silk tie he wore was conservative, navy-blue with a pattern of tiny white squares. Yet, despite his conservative attire, he wore a gold stud in his pierced left ear lobe. His hair was cut close to his head, in a wavy black sculpture, sprinkled sparsely with gray. A thick, well trimmed mustache enhanced the sparkling smile he had bestowed on her when he approached her in the parking lot earlier. Coal-black eyes beneath long sooty lashes looked at her as if they could see straight into her soul. Sharp cheekbones emphasized a broad, flat nose. Embedded in his chin was a cleft, a deep slash of a cleft, which gave his features a rugged, masculine quality. He was about six feet two inches of masculine perfection, a man any woman couldn't help but notice, even a female minister.

"Reverend Davis," he continued, "This boy is the same age as I was when my mother died. His little brother is only five. Yet, this ten-year-old is responsible for his kid brother—feeding him, clothing him, and keeping a roof over his head, and it's a job he takes very seriously."

"You say you caught him trying to steal your car?" Nedra raised an eyebrow in obvious surprise at his seeming calm at such a transgression. "Why didn't you call the police?"

"Actually, he was trying to steal the radio." He chuckled, ignoring her question. "Cursed me out good when I caught him, but he's a bright kid. Smart as hell!"

Nedra raised her brow again at his choice of words. He didn't blink, recant, or apologize, but continued.

"He by-passed my alarm system with some gadget he made himself with a piece of wood, some wires, tape, and batteries. I looked at the thing and couldn't figure out how he did it. The kid is a mechanical genius."

"You keep calling him 'the kid'. Does the boy have a name?" His obvious enthusiasm over the boy had piqued her interest.

"His name is Colin Johnson. His little brother's name is Trevor. Both of the boys are quite articulate."

"They sound interesting."

"They are, and they're good kids, good kids in a bad situation. That's why I came here to you, to your church, instead of calling the cops on Colin. I've heard that under you, this church's reputation in the community is excellent. You serve the community well—a child care center, low cost housing, an on the job training program, a food pantry, clothes closet, a drug rehab program, and a homeless shelter. You name it, Mount Peter is doing it."

"We try."

"No, you do more than try. You get the job done. When I took that boy home to talk to his mother..." He sighed, running his hand over his face in a gesture of frustration. "Nobody, nobody, should live like that. It was filthy! Dirty clothes, dirty dishes...the smell was awful! The place hadn't been cleaned since who knows when. There was no food in the refrigerator. The little one was there by himself—filthy, raggedy, and hungry. Colin was trying to steal the radio so he could sell it for money to buy food. That's what his little brother told me."

"Poor little things."

"The boys claimed that their mother was coming home soon. I knew they were lying. I suspected that she hadn't been around for a while. I was in and out of there for four, maybe five hours. I bought food and cleaning supplies and made them clean up that rat trap. I didn't see her while I was there. I took them to the laundromat to wash the clothes, and I bought them a couple of outfits."

"That was very nice of you." The more he spoke, the more impressed she was by this man. If she had passed him on the street, she would have identified him as another aimless playboy, not the kind, caring man sitting before her.

"Nice has nothing to do with it. As I said before, I was Colin at ten, and I want to see that help is available to him and his brother. I think you can help them."

Clasping her hands together on top of her mahogany desk, Nedra sighed. There was so much need for so many, it was hard to keep up.

"How can we help?"

His dark eyes shifted away from her, briefly, to the Brenda Joyce print hanging on the pale yellow wall behind her. It was a print of a mother and child, a portrait striking in its beauty and grace. His eyes shifted back to Nedra, piercing her with their intensity as she sat watching him.

Who was this stranger who had approached her so unexpected as she unlocked the door at the back of the church? He had approached her so quietly that, at first, she had not heard the deep masculine voice calling her name. Startled, the rapid beat of her heart had only accelerated as she turned and saw him standing before her. So tall, so handsome. The beat of her heart hadn't slowed since. Silently she berated herself for that fact as he spoke.

"I've been going by the boys' house for two weeks now, and I've only seen evidence once that their mother has been back in that apartment."

"What evidence was that?"

"I've been leaving her notes every day asking her to call me. She called last night, sounding high as a kite. She gave me all kinds of excuses for missing me at the apartment. She said that she needed some money to pay the rent. I knew she was lying."

"How?"

"I'd already paid the rent for three months in advance. She just didn't know it."

"So she wanted the money for dope."

"What else? When I refused to give it to her, she offered to..." His eyes wandered away from her, as he shifted uncomfortably in his chair. "Well, let's say she'll do anything for a fix. I refused her second offer, and that's when she offered to sell the boys to me."

Nedra's heart lurched. "Oh my God!"

"Like I said, that's why I'm here. The kids have to leave there. The next one might take her up on the offer."

"You're right. Where are the boys now?"

"At home. I went by there as soon as she hung up to check on them, hoping I could catch her, but I didn't. Trevor—he's the only one I can get any information from— he said she came home briefly, then left again. I stayed with them until early this morning, went home, changed, and came straight here." He sat back in his chair allowing her time to absorb what he had told her.

The sorrow Nedra felt was overwhelming. She'd read about people selling their children, but the reality of what had been said stunned her. "Why haven't you called the police about this? It's obvious that those boys need to be removed from that house immediately."

"I know, but I think it would be better if you called them. The boys are traumatized enough. I don't want them to think I betrayed them too. I thought that maybe you might have some family in the church who could take them in. I heard about the foster-adopt program you have here. A lot of your church members adopt, is that right?"

"Yes, I'm proud to say that's true."

"Then isn't there some way that you can make the process of removing them from their home easier, a way that they won't have to go into the foster care system?"

Nedra paused, her mind skirting the possibilities of how she could make that happen. "I can make a call to a friend of mine and see what can be done. She's a social worker at Children's Services."

"Great." He sighed his relief.

Nedra picked up the telephone and started dialing. "She'll need to talk with you."

"No problem."

Nedra smiled at him reassuringly as she waited for someone to respond to the ring. Nervously, she averted her eyes from his, unable to hold his piercing gaze. She was grateful when the telephone was answered.

"Child Welfare, Sharon Mays speaking."

Nedra smiled at the sound of the voice on the other end, "Hello, Sharon. It's Nedra. Unfortunately, I've got another one for you. A Mr..."

Nedra glanced up at the stranger sitting across from her, realizing that they had been talking for nearly an hour and she still didn't know his name. "A Mr..."

He gave her a crooked smile as he realized her dilemma. "Mr. Reasoner. Sinclair Reasoner." The smile deepened. "But you can call me Sin."

Chapter 1

Nedra sat with Carla watching as their friend, Sharon Mays, made her way through the lunch crowd of one of their favorite restaurants. The two women at the table had already turned the heads of most men in the restaurant when they had entered a short time before. Sharon's entrance was no different.

She was stunning. The product of an interracial marriage, her good looks usually turned heads. Although considerably shorter than Nedra's imposing five feet ten, Sharon's fair skin, gray eyes, wheat-colored hair, straight nose and thin lips were magnets for most men, but her features made her extremely uncomfortable. She identified herself adamantly as African-American and was forever proving herself as a "sister," wearing elaborate ethnic dress, and using everything from bottled tanning lotions to memberships in year round tanning salons in an effort to darken her skin.

A smile teased Nedra's large, well defined lips as she watched her friend approach them dressed in a brightly colored kente dress with matching jacket. Her untamed mass of curly hair was held back from her face with a matching scarf, twisted elaborately around her flowing locks.

"Girl! You looking good, Miss Thang!" Carla Ryan teased, as she planted a kiss on Sharon's cheek. Nedra followed suit, adding a small hug of greeting as the three women settled at the table.

"Forget you, heifer," Sharon countered, her smile of pleasure at seeing her two best friends contradicting her tone of mock offense.

Carla completed the trio, whom they had dubbed The Lemon, Chocolate, and Vanilla Brigade. Friends for over a decade, Carla, like Sharon, had met Nedra at U.C. Berkley, and since then, the three women had been inseparable. Only an inch shorter than Nedra, Carla was a caramel-colored beauty, slim and willowy, with reddish brown hair and dark brown eyes. Both women were a stark contrast to Nedra's nutmeg-brown beauty.

Ordering her lunch, Nedra sighed and sat back in her chair contentedly. It had been quite a while since she had the time to enjoy a leisurely meal with her good friends, and she wanted to savor the moment. Carla, being her usual aggressive self, was relating how she had confronted a policeman who accused her of making an illegal turn.

"Things are at a sorry state when an innocent woman is treated like a criminal because she may have made one little bitty mistake!"

Nedra and Sharon exchanged amused glances at their friend's wounded tone, sharing the knowledge that Carla drove like a maniac, and was probably guilty of making the turn.

"Anyway," Carla concluded, having exhausted her pleas of innocence, "What's up with you two? How's Mount Peter holding up, Ned? What's the Anti-Drug Queen up to now?"

Nedra frowned at the "Anti-Drug Queen" reference. A recent article in the newspaper had given her the name because of the latest crusade she was leading at Mount Peter, shutting down drug houses in the areas around the church. The church was buying the houses from their owners, usually absentee landlords, training former addicts in their drug rehabilitation program how to renovate the houses, then selling them at affordable prices to low income families. The innovative strategy had garnered a lot of media attention, which helped their efforts, but she still didn't like the name, even though the Own Your Own Housing Project, which she had conceived, had become a rousing success.

"Things are fantastic! O.Y.O. just received a major donation from the Palmer Corporation, enough to renovate two more houses and put dozens of people to work."

"Go Girlfriend!" Sharon gave Nedra a high five. "You got it going on! I am so proud of you."

"Thanks." Nedra gave her a grateful smile.

The three women had each had her dream in college, and had shared and supported each other in working toward those dreams. Carla was in marketing and wanted to own her own advertising agency. She now headed Ryan Advertising, a small firm, competing with the majors, but alive and thriving after surviving its struggling first few years.

Sharon had chosen social work, a natural for a woman with a heart of gold. Nedra, a year older than Carla, and two years older than Sharon, had majored in social work as well and had served as a mentor for Sharon when they were in college. The two of them had talked about going into private practice together, counseling children and families. Sharon was now a Department Supervisor with Children's Services. She did part-time consulting on the side. Everything was in place for her to open her own office within the next year, and it still saddened her that she would be pursuing her dream without her best friend.

After graduating from Berkeley Nedra pursued a Masters Degree at a theological seminary. Her decision stunned her two friends. Her mother was a minister but she had never mentioned following in her footsteps. Unable to believe or accept Nedra's decision her friends had actually urged her to seek psychiatric counseling.

Even now, after six years as pastor of Mount Peter, even after all the success and recognition for the miracles she had worked at what had been a small inner city parish about to close its doors, she knew that they still didn't understand the choice she had made. Yet, they did support her, and for that she was grateful.

"Well, I still say, be careful," said Carla, "These drug dealers are not to be played with. They don't like people interfering with their business, and you are interfering big time."

"Don't worry." Nedra grabbed a crunchy breadstick from the basket the waitress placed in the center of the table. "Nobody's going to bother me."

"I know, I know," Carla retorted, rolling her eyes skyward, "God's on your side."

"You bet!" Nedra grinned, nibbling the bread stick hungrily.

"Then tell him to come help the rest of us down here a little." Sharon sighed, slumping back in her chair. "I don't think he's been listening lately."

"What's up?" Although the question was asked lightly, Nedra's voice was laced with concern. Sharon was usually so upbeat, she knew it must be serious if her friend sounded down.

"You know those two little boys I put in foster care about six months ago? "

Nedra looked at her blankly.

"The ones that gorgeous hunk helped out. He came to you about them, and you called me."

Realization dawned. "Yes, Colin and Trevor Johnson."

"It looks like they'll be in foster care even longer. Their mother was found dead this morning. Overdose."

"Oh no!" A flash of pain crossed Nedra's face as she remembered the two rail-thin boys she had helped Sharon place with the Simpsons, an elderly couple in her parish who were registered as foster parents. After the initial placement, she'd had little contact with the boys other than seeing them at church with the Simpsons. Although both boys were solemn little things, they seemed to have adjusted to their new lives.

"Have the boys been told?"

Sharon bit her lower lip. "Yes, the Simpsons and their social worker told them. The worker said the oldest never shed a tear, but the little one... She said it was heartbreaking."

"Poor babies," Carla sympathized.

"The Simpsons should have called me, I might have been able to help."

"Nobody can help ease the pain when your mother dies." Sharon's eyes drifted past Nedra's as she spoke. She'd lost her mother when they were in college, and the wound of that loss still hadn't healed more than a decade later.

Understanding the emotion behind Sharon's words, Nedra reached across the table and patted her friend's hand reassuringly "I'll call them when I get back to the office and see if there's anything I can do to help."

The waitress brought their orders, and despite the fact that the sobering news about the death of the boys' mother had dampened their moods, they talked, laughed, and enjoyed each other's company for the next hour. After a sumptuous lunch, they lingered over cups of tea, reluctant to end their time together.

"Whatever happened to that hunk that took care of those boys?" asked Carla. "I know when I came into your office that day and saw him sitting there..." Carla fanned herself with her hand. "Whew! Lord have mercy. What was his name again?"

Nedra took a sip of her favorite herbal tea, enjoying the feel of it sliding down her suddenly parched throat. "Sin."

Sharon giggled, unsure of Nedra's unusual answer. "What?"

Unaware that she had said the name aloud, she was surprised when she glanced up from her cup and saw the shocked expressions on the faces of both friends.

Sharon repeated her question. "What did you say his name was?"

Confused, Nedra blinked rapidly. Had she uttered a name? "I...I...don't know. I don't remember his name."

Carla wasn't convinced. "Sounded like you said his name was Sin. Now all I've got to ask is was that a statement of fact or wistful thinking? 'Cause from what I remember of that man, a sin is something I would gladly commit with him!"

"Honey, he was fine!" Sharon crooned, remembering the chocolate-brown honey who had met them at the boys' apartment building. He had been instrumental in convincing the frightened children to go with her. "Yes indeed! And those boys were crazy about him, especially the little one. Too bad he didn't keep in touch with them."

Nedra raised one perfectly arched eyebrow in surprise. "He didn't?" She had been sure that he would check on the boys occasionally. He told her he would after seeing to it that they had found a good foster home. It was the last thing he said, before driving away. He sounded sincere, and she had no reason to doubt him. Now, knowing that he hadn't followed up on his word, she felt disappointed, but didn't know why. "I was sure he would."

"Well, not that I know of. According to the worker, though, he did send the boys Christmas presents, expensive ones."

"Well he could send me a present any day", purred Carla, "A sinful present."

Nedra laughed at Carla's antics. "Girl, you ought to quit it!" Both Nedra and Sharon knew that despite her bold declarations, she was totally faithful to Jacob, her fiancé, whom she had met on a cruise two years ago.

"No, you ought to quit it." Carla looked at her friend with a pensive smile. "You know that man was good-looking, and he was looking at you."

Sin

Nedra almost choked on her tea, coughing and sputtering as she fought for breath and to regain her composure. "You must be out of your mind!"

"So you noticed it too." Sharon leaned across the table, drawing closer to Carla, effectively shutting out the subject of their two-way conversation with one move. "I thought I was the only one who noticed it."

Recovered, Nedra frowned disapprovingly. "What are you two talking about?"

They ignored her.

"Girl, in the office when I was talking to Nedra, he couldn't keep his eyes off her."

"What?" Nedra nearly flew out of her seat.

"Same at the boys' apartment. His eyes kept straying to her, no matter what else was happening around him."

"You two are out of your minds! That man did not look at me any differently than he looked at anybody else."

Carla winked at Sharon. "Oh, so you do remember him, huh? What did she call him, Sharon?"

"Sin."

"Uh-huh. Well, all I got to say is that sin is what I saw when that man looked at Preacher Girl here."

Sharon nodded vigorously. "I believe that!" She turned to Nedra. "You know that the three of us spent almost three hours in that apartment with those boys, and I'm telling you that man devoured you with those eyes of his."

She turned to Carla. "He's got those coal-black eyes to die for."

"Uh huh, I remember. Who could forget!"

Sharon turned back to Nedra. "And they were on you for the entire three hours. I told you when we went to my office that day to put your brand on him, quick, but you didn't listen."

"Does she ever?" Carla grinned. "The girl is going to die celibate."

"You two ought to stop it!" Nedra was frustrated with herself that she was letting their innocent teasing fluster her. It wasn't the first time they had teased her about some man's admiration. Usually she ignored it, but this time it bothered her, because she knew they were right. She still could see those piercing dark eyes watching her every move, looking at her, looking through her. It had been unsettling.

Sharon and Carla were doubled over with laughter by this time, elated at having rattled the normally unflappable Nedra. Sharon was the first to recover.

"Don't take us so seriously, Nedra. Shoot, if we count all of the men who have a crush on you, we'd run out of fingers and toes. Half the men in your church are salivating after you, and you know it. The single ones and the married ones."

Sharon waited for her friend's reaction. Usually it was one of denial, despite the fact that it was true. Nedra was beautiful. Tall, shapely, with a flawless brown complexion and large light brown eyes, which stood out in stark contrast to her dark skin.

Sharon envied the large pouty lips that dominated her face. Models were paying a fortune for what God had bestowed on Nedra naturally. Yet, most of the time the woman worked overtime hiding every asset she had. It broke her heart.

Nedra sighed, how many times had they had this conversation? It was getting old. "You guys know how I constantly have to walk a thin line to keep my reputation intact, and, believe me, that's no joke. It's not funny at all. So let's drop it."

The strain of the constant effort was evident in her voice, instantly sobering her friends who, more than any others, knew how difficult it was for her being a woman minister. She had shared it with them often, and the toll it was taking on her.

Nedra could wear conservative suits, high-collared blouses, and sensible shoes, but nothing could disguise the basic fact that she was a beautiful woman. It was undeniable. She exuded sensuality, no matter how hard she tried not to, and sensuality and the ministry just did not mix. Not in the black church community. Probably not in any church community.

In her effort to pursue her profession she had made sacrifices, and male companionship had been the biggest one.

Since graduating from the seminary, she had not dated one man. Oh, there had been breakfast, lunch, or dinner with many men, but she was careful to make certain that those occasions were business. Pleasure dates were out. She never went out to social events, unless they were fund-raisers for good causes, and then she went alone, or with a girl friend. She was the soul of propriety, never straying from the straight and narrow. Self-discipline was her motto, and she practiced it religiously. She had to. People were always watching her, and she had no choice.

"I keep telling you, Nedra, if you find the right man and marry, that would solve a lot of problems for you," Carla said solemnly, her heart aching for the joy her best friend was missing without love in her life. Since finding Jacob she wanted everyone to be as deliriously happy as the two of them.

"You need to meet somebody nice and go out, have fun. You're only thirty-eight years old—"

"Almost forty!" Nedra countered, but Sharon wasn't fazed.

"And you are much too young for this pastor hermit thing!" Sharon snapped her fingers, her eyes lighting up. "I know! Richard was telling me that there's this new guy at work who just moved to the Bay Area. He and Richard have become good friends, and the guy is looking for a nice woman to date."

Carla looked at Sharon as if she was an alien, unable to believe what she had just heard. "I know you're not suggesting that Nedra date one of Richard's friends!"

Sharon stiffened at Carla's tone, instantly defensive. Richard Ryan was Carla's older brother, and the two siblings did not get along. Sharon and Richard had been dating for two years, and Richard's treatment of Sharon was not to Carla's liking. She had tried to get Sharon to break up with him a few months into the relationship, but Sharon was in love, deeply in love, and, to her, Richard could walk on water.

"What's wrong with Richard's friends, may I ask?" Sharon's eyes narrowed suspiciously.

"Don't answer that!" Nedra interceded quickly before the fight began. It seemed that, lately, anytime the three of them got together, she ended up the mediator whenever Richard's name came up. This was one person who evoked more emotion among the three women than anyone else she knew.

She had always felt uncomfortable whenever she was near him. In fact, she really didn't like Richard. She tolerated him because he was Carla's brother and she knew that despite all of her criticism of him, Carla loved him. He was her brother, her only brother. She had to love him. But Sharon, she was in love with Richard, madly in love with him, and she denied every flaw he had.

Carla complied with Nedra's request, valuing the friendship and sisterhood between them too much to pursue a petty argument with Sharon. She did love her brother, but she knew things about him that Sharon would never know. She had warned her friend not to be fooled by her brother's pretty face and smooth manners. Sharon hadn't listened, so she would have to find out the hard way how cold he could be. Perhaps, that was best.

Nedra picked up a menu, deciding to order dessert. "Let's call a truce before the fight begins. I'm going to put on an extra ten pounds in a second and order the most fattening dessert they have in this joint. Join me. Agreed?"

Tight lipped, Sharon rolled her eyes at Carla and picked up her menu. "Agreed."

Carla picked up her own menu to survey what damage she could do. "Agreed."

Ten minutes later the three women sat stuffing themselves with chocolate cheese cake, enjoying every morsel. The subject of Nedra's love life was all but forgotten, much to her relief.

Chapter 2

He had to be crazy. That was the only answer Sin could give himself for his presence at the cemetery. From the moment he heard about the death of the boys' mother, he knew that he should forget it, write these two boys off as a good deed done and not even think about getting further involved. He shouldn't have gotten involved in the first place. What he should have done was give that oldest kid a butt kicking and send him off to steal somebody else's merchandise. The kid would have survived. He was from the streets, survival was all that he knew. Sin knew that score. He was quite familiar with it.

He had been on the streets since he was eight years old. Pimps and hustlers had been his role models. After his mother died and he ran away from the last foster care home he had been shuttled to, those pimps and hustlers became the only family he had. Yes, he knew the streets, and he knew how hard and uncompromising they could be. When he looked in Colin's face that day, he'd seen the first signs of hardness that would one day claim the boy, if not kill him. Something inside of Sin had snapped, something he still couldn't explain. All he knew was that he wanted to fight for this child. He didn't want the streets to claim another one.

Behind his dark glasses, Sin studied Colin's bowed head. The boy had been stoic throughout the graveside service, showing no expression, even when Sin made his sudden appearance. Trevor's joy at seeing him had been apparent as a welcoming grin appeared on his tearstained face. The older couple sitting beside them, the Simpsons, he assumed, never having met them, had eyed him curiously but gave welcoming nods, as did the boy's social worker, Miss Charles, whom he had met. The only other person in attendance was Sharon Mays, whom he had met at the apartment when arrangements for the boys were made. And of course there was Reverend Brooks, Nedra, the officiating minister. That was it, seven attendees and the minister gathered at the graveside of a twenty-five-year-old woman to say goodbye—six more than attended his own mother's funeral. These boys were lucky.

Sin's gaze went back to Nedra as she rendered a final prayer for the young woman who had lived hard and died even harder, and for the two innocent lives she left behind. Nedra was draped in a clerical robe, accented by a flowing scarf made of kente cloth. Her black shoulder-length hair, usually worn in a chignon pulled back from her face, was piled on top of her head in a loose bun. Stray tendrils had escaped and trailed down both sides of her face. Her makeup was light but becoming. Her large eyes were hidden by lowered lids as she prayed for the soul that had been lost. Those magnificent eyes had registered shock at his appearance but quickly recovered with a welcoming gleam, which had started his heart beating double time.

It was dangerous what he was doing, and he knew it, but he couldn't seem to help himself. He was as drawn to her now as he had been in the past, a past which he was certain she didn't remember. He had known that when he went to the church that day to ask for help for the boys. How could she remember him? Their paths had crossed so fleetingly, and so much had happened to them both over the years. Yet, Nedra Davis, he'd never forgotten. Young, beautiful, eager to embrace life, she had been a breath of fresh air, a saving grace, a lifeline when he needed one.

He closed his eyes, the simple act transporting him back twenty years ago to Kansas City, Missouri, where he had enrolled in a G.E.D. class. His enrollment hadn't been a magnanimous act, motivated by wanting to do something better with his life. If only it had been. Instead, basketball had been his motivation. The community center in which he played had ruled that anyone under twenty-one, without a high school degree, could not play basketball in their league unless enrolled in a G.E.D. class, which the center just happened to offer. He was seventeen and hadn't been to school in so long, he couldn't recall the last time, but that center's basketball league was the best in the city, and he loved playing basketball. What choice did he have? His love for the game overruled his aversion to school.

Reluctantly, he enrolled. It turned out to be the best decision he ever made. It was there that he met Nedra Davis.

She was nineteen, a sophomore in college, home for the summer, and she had volunteered to tutor at the center before going back to college. She fascinated him from the moment he met her. His life on the streets had never put him in such close proximity with someone like her. She not only looked good, but smelled good. Her English seemed perfect, and she didn't curse. She carried herself like a queen and was always talking about Black Pride—a concept that was foreign to him. She excited him, and frightened him, and, as he often did when frightened, he struck out, and Nedra became his target.

His vulgarity didn't repel her as he had hoped it would. She simply flashed him a heart-melting smile. When he cursed her, she hadn't cursed back, just informed him that it was sad such intelligence was wasted. She said he was smart and could be anything he wanted to be.

Smart! Him? Nobody had every said that to him before. Nobody! He had no defense against her.

With a sigh, he opened his eyes. His gaze settled on Nedra. He didn't want to remember the street-hardened young man he used to be—all of the hatred, the anger, all of the less than honorable things he had done in his life. Yet, he knew that man had been real, that man was part of his nightmares.

The service concluded, and Sin followed the small group of mourners to the mortuary limo. It was there that Trevor, without a word, gave him an emotional hug before climbing into the limo. Still stoic, Colin offered a semblance of a handshake, avoiding eye contact with him in case he revealed his emotions. Sin was familiar with the tactic.

He watched as the boy joined his brother in the limo, leaving him alone with Nedra and Sharon Mays as they watched the huge vehicle drive away.

Sharon was the first to acknowledge him. "It was kind of you to come, Mr. Reasoner." She offered him a well manicured hand. He took it. Her handshake was firm, businesslike.

"It wasn't a problem," Sin said calmly, the evenness of his voice belying the nervousness he felt at Nedra's nearness. He shouldn't have come here. He glanced at Nedra who took a step forward and extended her hand.

"I'm sure the boys appreciate your presence, Mr. Reasoner," she said as they shook hands. She noticed that his hand was warm and clammy. Was he nervous too?

She knew that her own nervousness started when his tall, dark clad figure appeared at the gravesite. Her heart had skipped a beat. Maybe it was his attire. He was dressed head to toe in black—black turtle neck, black finely creased slacks, black tasseled toe loafers, an expensive black leather jacket hugging his sculptured frame. The only hint of color was a sterling silver hooped earring dangling from his pierced left ear. He looked mysterious, dangerous, his eyes completely hidden behind mirrored black sunglasses which kept her from seeing his eyes. She liked looking into a person's eyes, and she couldn't help but remember how mesmerizing his were. During the entire ceremony she had been aware of those eyes being fixed on her. They still were.

There was an awkward moment of silence as the three of them stood looking at each other. Then Sharon took charge.

Turning on all of the charm she possessed, she gave Sin her most engaging smile. "I'm sure the boys would appreciate it even more if you dropped by the Simpsons' place. Some of the members of Mount Peter have fixed dinner for them there."

Noting his hesitancy she quickly added, "Nedra and I are headed over there now. You're more than welcome. Isn't he, Nedra?"

Nedra could strangle her, right here in the cemetery where they wouldn't have to remove her body, just throw it in a hole. As innocent as Sharon's chatter appeared to be, Nedra knew exactly what her friend was up to and she did not appreciate it one bit! With no hint of the embarrassment she felt at Sharon's blatant efforts to "fix her up," Nedra gave Sin a smile more brilliant than Sharon's.

"Yes, Mr. Reasoner, I'm certain that the boys would appreciate you being there." She stunned herself as the words tumbled from her mouth. That wasn't what she had meant to say.

Sin was tempted. Very tempted. With deep regret he said, "I'm sorry, ladies. I appreciate the invitation, but I have a previous appointment."

Sharon didn't try to mask her disappointment. "Too bad, especially for the boys. But, let me jot down the address in case you change your mind."

Nedra watched with narrowed eyes as her friend wrote down the address. Did Sharon have any shame? She was willing to use two innocent boys as a smoke screen for a dating service. Yet, Nedra had to admit that she felt more relieved than embarrassed. She was glad that Sin declined the invitation. His presence unsettled her, and she didn't like the feeling.

Taking the folded paper from Sharon, Sin bid them goodbye. Both women watched intently as he walked toward his late-model Jaguar, climbed into the powerful vehicle then drove away.

Sharon sighed. "What a butt."

Nedra fumed. "I will kill you dead, Sharon Mays! I have never been so embarrassed in my life! How could you?"

Sharon's gray eyes widened innocently. "How could I what? Admire a fine man's butt? Child, you're the preacher, not me. I don't have to pretend that the male species doesn't exist."

Too angry to address the woman further, Nedra stomped off to her car. While Sharon, who had ridden to the cemetery with her, chuckled, discreetly, as she followed at a safe distance behind her.

Sin sat outside the two-story framed house on 62nd Avenue berating himself for the decision he had made. Why must he play with fire? The adage about getting burned had proved to be true too many times. What was it about Nedra Davis that had brought him to the Simpsons' front door? He had dated prettier women. Hell! He had dated beautiful women, women men salivated over. Yes, Nedra was pretty, actually more than pretty, but she was a minister, for God's sake! This was madness!

As he stepped out of the car, he told himself that he had business to attend to, serious business. He had been on his way to attend to that business, when he made the U-turn that would bring him to this doorstep. He had no clue why he turned around. What reason was there to madness? All he knew was that he had canceled his appointment, and here he was. With one gloved finger, he rang the doorbell.

Nedra sensed his presence before she saw him. The energy in the room had changed. All attention had shifted toward him, the stranger among them—the handsome, mysterious stranger. The reason for being there seemed to be forgotten as the sisters of the church inundated him with offers of food, drink, conversation.

Sharon rescued him, obviously delighted that he had changed his mind. She introduced him to the Simpsons, whom he had never met, and to the boys' caseworker, to whom he had sent the Christmas presents for the boys. Trevor—a handsome child of cinnamon brown, with eyes nearly the same color, planted himself firmly in Sin's arms. By the time the three of them worked their way into the dining room where Nedra sat with Colin, Nedra had calmed her racing pulse and regained her composure, praying that no one had noticed her reaction. Colin showed no visible reaction to Sin's appearance. She fought to do the same, as Sin took an empty seat at the large dining room table, shifting Trevor onto his lap.

"Glad you changed your mind about joining us." Nedra presented her best smile. She was pleased, not a quaver or a quake in her voice. She could get through this.

"I'm glad I came," Sin replied with a quick wink at the little boy on his lap, who returned the wink with one of his own. Sin turned to the solemn child sitting beside Nedra. "And how are you doing, my man?"

Colin, who was small for his age, with a complexion much like his brother's, and dark brown eyes, which slanted upward at the corners, shrugged his thin shoulders. "All right, I guess." He kept his eyes on his plate filled with food, food he hadn't touched.

"Just all right?" Sin watched him. This kid was suffering. He recognized the signs. "Well, do you think you're doing 'all right' enough to go for a little ride with me? That is if Mr. and Mrs. Simpson will let you."

Colin shrugged again, his eyes still fixed on his plate. Sin's eyes met Nedra's, each noting the other's concern for the boy.

"I'm certain if I ask them, the Simpsons won't mind if Colin goes with you. I'm sure he could use a little break, and some fresh air."

"I wanna go too!" Trevor spoke up, intent on not being left out.

"Not this time, buddy, but I promise I'll do something with you and me alone pretty soon."

The promise stopped the tears Sin was certain would have flowed if some sort of compromise hadn't been offered. After getting the Simpson's permission for Colin to take the ride with Sin, Nedra watched as the man and the boy walked through the small gathering and out the front door. She exhaled slowly, unaware that she had been holding her breath during the short time Sin had been near her.

Chapter 3

Mrs. Esther Costello could try the devil, and Nedra had no doubt that she had done so.

She had been Nedra's nemesis for years. She fancied herself the matron of Mount Peter, despite having lived on this earth only fifty-six years. Yes, Esther was certain that it was she who had been chosen by God as her church's official guardian.

She had grown up in Mount Peter, and had occupied the same second row church pew since she was brought into the church by her schoolteacher parents at six months old. She had buried her parents, married her husband, baptized and married off both her children, all at Mount Peter. She was the undisputed power in the church, before Nedra came, and had wielded her power and authority within its walls without regard to anyone. Ruthless when crossed, she had been the influence that had swayed the church congregation to vote for Nedra as pastor of Mount Peter. Nobody dared vote against her. Nedra owed her, according to Esther, and she constantly reminded her of the fact.

Over the years, Nedra had highly suspected that Esther regretted that vote, and she was right. Esther had reasoned that a female minister would be more susceptible to her control. Nedra's appearance had been deceptive, Esther would later contend. The attractive young woman had seemed quiet and unassuming when interviewed. Subsequent follow-up interviews and reference checks proved her to be more than capable of leading what was then a small flock of ninety-five members. She had discerned that the young Reverend Davis would guide their flock out of debt, quietly lead their Sunday services, and allow her to run everything else, as she had been doing for years. How wrong she had been. From the day Reverend Davis stepped into the pulpit, she had been beyond Esther's control.

Over the years the changes at Mount Peter had been too dramatic for Esther to accept. The membership grew to over a thousand, much to her chagrin. Social programs were added, to her dismay. And the accolades that were bestowed were not bestowed on Esther Costello. As the years brought more changes, her resentment toward Nedra grew.

Their conflicts gradually escalated, not having reached a crescendo, but smoldering in the heated caldron that had been created. They both knew that their mutual dislike for each other would, eventually, burst into flames. Today's disagreement was simply a brush fire.

Nedra's eyes narrowed as she looked at the portly woman standing before her. Esther worked hard trying to live up to the stereotype of the schoolteacher, her profession for the last twenty-five years. She was not unattractive. Her honey-colored skin was as smooth as a baby's, but the grimace she wore constantly made her appear older than her years. As always, she wore a loose fitting dress— usually flowers or stripe prints, neither of which was flattering. She wouldn't be caught dead in anything other than her low heeled "sensible" shoes, and adding to her stark appearance was her hair style, a graying bun wound tightly at the nape of her neck.

She had not altered her appearance in the six years Nedra had known her. She was a creature of habit, a woman disturbed by change, a suppressed personality, more to be pitied than scorned. But today, Nedra's pity quotient was limited, and so was her patience.

"Esther, all the children want is to go to Great America to celebrate the end of the soccer season. What is the problem? The money has already been approved for the trip, which, may I remind you is tomorrow morning!"

Esther sighed in frustration, addressing Nedra as if she were a child. "Let me explain to you, once again, Nedra, Mr. Simpson can't go—"

"I know that, Esther. He broke his ankle, and Mrs. Simpson can't go because she's taking care of him. Let's not go over that territory again. All I know is that these kids played their hearts out for Mount Peter this season. They were promised a trip to Great America and they're going to get it. We will not be canceling this trip!"

Esther bristled. This woman challenged her at every turn. Couldn't she see anyone's point of view but her own? "Well, my grandson is not going on a church trip that is not properly chaperoned!"

Nedra was tired of trying to be diplomatic. This woman had gotten on her last nerve, making a mountain out of a molehill.

The call about Mr. Simpson's accident had come to her office yesterday, and with it a plea from Mrs. Simpson that she take her place as a chaperone for the trip that had been planned months ago for the Mount Peter Pee Wee Soccer Team. Mr. Simpson was the coach and had made all of the arrangements.

Despite reservations and limited time, Nedra relented and volunteered. It had been she who had encouraged the church to make rules requiring an adult-to-kids ratio for field trips. The kids' safety was at stake. The rule had been strictly adhered to. She knew that if she hadn't volunteered the trip would have to be canceled, and Trevor Johnson was on the team. Only two weeks had passed since they'd buried his mother. He needed the distraction.

It was the fact that they had not found a much needed fourth chaperone with such short notice that had prompted the comments from Esther Costello. Yet, this complaint was only one in a string of complaints that she had been making all evening. They had just finished a Deacon Board meeting, in which Esther had objected to nearly everything anyone proposed. After the meeting, Nedra had hoped that she could sneak out of the church without any further contact with the woman, but no such luck. Now, cornered in the hallway between her office and the back door, Nedra listened to the woman jabbering on about denying these children a trip to an amusement park. Enough was enough!

"Listen, Esther!" Nedra made no attempt to conceal her annoyance. "If you don't want your grandson to go, fine. That's up to you. But if you want more chaperones tomorrow, then volunteer to be one. Good evening!"

Without looking back, Nedra marched through the rear door of the church, leaving Esther Costello standing open-mouthed and angry. Nedra's head was pounding as she made her way across the parking lot to her car parked in the reserved space. She was tired and hungry. What had been scheduled as a two-hour meeting had turned into a four- hour meeting, and Esther had made it seem like eight hours! Her car and the Costellos' car were the only ones left on the large parking lot. The other deacons had left some time ago. The Costellos stayed behind to lock the church.

Mount Peter had recently acquired the house next to the church, razed it, and extended the parking lot, increasing the number of cars it could accommodate by two hundred spaces. As Nedra approached her four-year-old Toyota Corolla, it looked almost abandoned on the large, newly paved lot, which at this time of the evening was illuminated by bright security lights.

As usual, she took a quick glance around the parking lot, as she swiftly unlocked her car door. She was always security conscious. It didn't hurt to be cautious. The area in which the church was located warranted such caution.

She noticed the dark-colored car parked on the street next to the lot. It was sheltered by a cluster of bushes. A small flicker of light from a cigarette indicated that the car was occupied. Its distance from her car posed no threat, as she dropped her exhausted body into the driver seat, an unidentified car was the last thing that concerned her. All she wanted was to get home, take a bath, and get enough rest for tomorrow's trip to the amusement park.

As she pulled off the lot and headed down the street toward home, the occupant of the car flipped a cigarette butt out the open window. Moments later, the car drove slowly down the street, headed in the same direction as Nedra.

The following day, Nedra was more than surprised when Sinclair Reasoner's sleek Jaguar pulled onto the Mount Peter parking lot, with Trevor Johnson in the front seat beside him. What was he doing here?

Sin Reasoner wondered about that himself as he stopped a few yards from Nedra. At the Simpson house, he had made Trevor an innocent promise that he and the boy would do something alone in the near future. While they wouldn't be alone, exactly, that future proved to be sooner than both man and boy would have guessed. How in the world did he get himself into this mess?

Glancing at Trevor, he wondered how a kid with such a sweet face could be capable of conning a grown man into doing something he swore he would never do, go to an amusement park. Obviously, he had been conned, because here he was. A smile creased his face as he watched the child, who could hardly contain his excitement as he struggled to unbuckle his seat belt so that he could get out of the car. Waiting for them was a large van ready to transport them to the amusement park.

As for Sin, his only focus was the brown-skinned woman standing beside the van. Dressed in overalls, a tailored oxford shirt, and sparkling white leather tennis shoes, Nedra looked like a kid herself. Her hair was combed into a ponytail, covered by a colorful baseball cap. Her face looked even more youthful than the last time Sin had seen her, and he liked what he was seeing.

"I was ambushed," Sin explained, responding to the mystified look on Nedra's face as she watched him saunter toward the van. "I was ambushed by a five-year-old."

Nedra smiled, trying to contain her sudden nervousness at his unexpected appearance. "It looks like we've got a much needed chaperone. Welcome aboard."

Sin thanked her, quelling his own nervousness with a smile as he took her by the elbow and steered her into the front seat of the van. He climbed into the seat behind her, vowing that this would be the last time he was involved in any way with Mount Peter, the boys, and especially with Nedra Davis.

Hours later, Nedra made the same vow about Sin as they stood, side by side, looking up at the ferris wheel that carried Trevor and a handful of his rambunctious teammates. She was enjoying herself a little too much with this man, and his masculinity was overwhelming her. Dressed casually in a pair of beige linen shorts, with a matching short-sleeved shirt, the contours of his muscular body were clearly defined, and try as she might, she couldn't help but notice. As the two of them wandered around the park with the children, she also noticed the admiring glances he received from women, but he seemed oblivious to the attention.

They had laughed at the children's antics and talked about nothing in particular when they arrived earlier; however, now, neither of them had much to say to each other as they strolled along, shepherding the children from place to place.

Sin

They had been coupled, unceremoniously, by Arnella Cotter, whose young son, William, was on the team. Arnella had the hots for Jason Rich, the assistant soccer coach and driver of the church van, and she had jumped at the opportunity to volunteer to spend the day with him. When the young charges were divided between chaperones, there was no question with whom she would be paired.

Despite their earlier camaraderie, Nedra preferred the uncomfortable silence that had descended on the two of them as she and Sin strolled through the park. By nature, she was friendly and talkative, but their earlier chatter had begun to feel too comfortable, and she felt safer in the silence. It was less intimate. She couldn't allow any intimacy to invade a casual relationship with any man.

Since she entered the seminary, she had fought hard to submerge any attraction she might have toward members of the opposite sex. To do otherwise would cause too many problems. She spurned all suitors. She did all she could to discourage even being alone with a man, knowing that any hint of impropriety could seriously jeopardize her career.

It had never been easy. She was aware that men considered her attractive. She was not oblivious to the looks of admiration coming from them. There were those, who in desperation to get her attention, had even tried to put her in compromising positions. Yet God had always smiled down on her and seen her through. She loved the career she had chosen, and felt that if and when the time was right, God would help her pick a mate. Meanwhile, her mission in life was to serve others, through Him. Of that, she had no doubt. No, any intimacy had to be avoided at all cost.

So why, did she have such unsettling feelings with this man, this stranger? Surely, Sinclair Reasoner was just a distraction, and not the man God had chosen for her. How was it possible? This man looked like a model for a magazine cover. He wore an earring for goodness sakes! He definitely was not the boy next door. Besides, she knew nothing about him. Was he a Christian? Did he go to church? Did he even believe in God?

As the children exited the ferris wheel and ran noisily, to the next ride, the two adults followed briskly, struggling valiantly to keep up. "I don't think I'm going to survive this," Sin gasped, as he caught one miniature size soccer player running helter skelter toward an ice cream wagon going in the opposite direction. He steered him back on track.

Nedra took a deep breath. "Do you go to church, Mr. Reasoner?"

Sin stopped so suddenly that a woman walking behind him ran straight into his back. Steadying her, Sin offered an apology as he looked at Nedra in complete bewilderment.

"Why?" He was cautious. "Do you plan on saving me?"

Nedra heard the teasing in his voice. Her tone remained businesslike. "Only if you need saving, Mr. Reasoner."

Sin cocked an eyebrow. He doubted if his soul was salvageable, but he might as well let her enjoy herself. "No, Reverend Davis, I don't go to church. Too busy."

"Too busy for the Lord?" Nedra's own eyebrows knitted as her expression became as serious as her demeanor. "And what is it you do that would make you too busy to attend church?"

"I'm in imports." Sin's tone no longer teased her, but warned her that the answer warranted no further discussion.

Nedra got the message. "I see. I was just curious."

He turned her words over in his head. Just curious. Did that mean interested? Because as much as he tried to fight it, he damn sure was interested in her!

After the funeral and his talk with Colin, he had dropped the boy off at the Simpson house, afraid to go back inside, afraid of seeing Nedra again. That was how he had been feeling for the past two weeks, frightened. It was a feeling that was foreign to him.

He had faced danger so often he couldn't remember all of the times. He had faced death as well; but neither was as frightening to him as Nedra. His feelings for her had been so prevalent for so long that they had become embedded in his psyche and were now a part of him. When he picked up a copy of the *Oakland Tribune*, a year ago, and glanced at the front page article about the accomplishments of a small East Bay Church called Mount Peter, the name of Reverend Nedra Davis had jumped off the printed page and rendered him speechless. A color picture of her draped in her clerical robe confirmed that there could be no mistake. She was the woman from his past, and she was living in Oakland, California.

He had cursed his fate. She lived in the very city in which he had settled, in which he had set up business. Just knowing that she was so close, yet so far from him, had renewed feelings of longing buried long ago.

He had never planned on seeing her. The San Francisco Bay Area was a place where anyone could live in total anonymity, if they chose. It was a place where anyone could hide. He had never planned on contacting her. Why would he? What would he need with a minister, except, perhaps, to bury him. Yet, he had contacted her. There were others he could have contacted. He hadn't. He wanted her, then. He wanted her now.

Yes, he was afraid. He should be, because he knew deep in his gut that this woman would be his downfall. When? Where? How? He didn't know. For now, he would ride with the tide, and enjoy just being near her, because after today he never planned on seeing her again.

Tilting his head, a smile perched on his generous lips, he was ready to continue his teasing. "Listen Reverend...

The sentence was never completed as the sound of Nedra's name being called drew their attention to a heavy-set woman rapidly approaching them. Nedra groaned. It was Esther Costello, with her grandson Evan, firmly in tow.

"I was wondering if we would run into you," Esther said, breathlessly, wiping her sweat-drenched face with a white handkerchief. "Little Evan here threw such a fit about missing the trip that I decided to bring the boy myself. After all..."

The sight of Sin Reasoner stopped Esther in mid-sentence. Consciously, Nedra had stepped a few paces in front of him, momentarily blocking Esther's view of him. Sin noticed the move but stood rooted. By the change in Nedra's demeanor he surmised that whoever this woman was, she meant trouble. He watched as a myriad of expressions crossed Esther's round face. Admiration and curiosity won.

Nedra took over. Her manner as formal with Esther as it had been with Sin. "Hello, Esther. Nice seeing you. I'm glad that you decided to bring Evan. He earned this day."

She bent down and hugged the little boy, who returned her hug. "How are you doing, sweetheart?"

The boy replied, shyly, "Fine."

Esther's eyes never left Sin's face as Nedra greeted Evan. "Yes, yes...uh, and who do we have here?"

Nedra rose to face Esther. " Esther Costello, meet Sinclair Reasoner. Mrs. Costello is a member of Mount Peter. Mr. Reasoner is a friend of Colin and Trevor Johnson. He brought Trevor to the park for Mr. and Mrs. Simpson, and he's serving as our fourth chaperone."

Taking Esther's fleshy hand into his larger one, Sin flashed his most charming smile as he squeezed her hand gently. "Nice meeting you, Mrs. Costello."

Much to Nedra's surprise, Esther blushed. "And you too, Mr. Reasoner. Are you here visiting the Simpsons?" She shot a glance at Sin's ringless left hand.

"No, I'm not." Sin offered no further information.

It didn't stop Esther. "Oh? So you live in Oakland?"

"For the time being."

"And just where do you..."

Having recovered from her shock at Esther's reaction to Sin, Nedra halted the questions before the barrage began. "It's nice seeing you, Esther. The ride has stopped, and we have to meet the kids at the exit."

She moved swiftly toward the ride exit, with Sin on her heels. Undeterred, Esther started to follow them, tugging Evan behind her. "But, Nedra! Since you're here and have four chaperones, I was wondering if—"

Nedra stepped up her pace. "Bye, Esther," she said over her shoulder as she and Sin disappeared behind some shrubbery.

Sin

Esther stood watching them thoughtfully until they faded from sight.

Chapter 4

It was the sound that startled Nedra awake—a low, mournful wail that vibrated throughout the room. Her eyes opened, slowly adjusting to the dimness of her surroundings, unfamiliar surroundings. She squinted in an attempt to focus clearly. The sound continued. She tensed, lifting her head from the pillow on which it was resting. Where was she? What was that sound? There was the slightest of movement beside her. She started and looked down. The outline of a small body lay curled in the curve of her right arm. It was Trevor. Colin lay on the other side of him, his thin arm placed protectively across his little brother. Shaking her head to clear her thoughts, she remembered. She was at the Simpson house, where she must have fallen asleep.

After the field trip they had dropped the children off at the church parking lot where their parents had picked them up. Nedra hadn't driven her car. Jason had picked her and Arnella up in the van. The ever resourceful Arnella, always anxious to be alone with Jason, had slyly suggested that Sin take Nedra home to avoid two drop offs for Jason. Neither Sin nor Nedra could come up with an excuse not to do so.

Logic had dictated that Trevor be dropped off first, given the direction in which Nedra lived, but both dreaded the moment when they would be left alone. It was a prospect that didn't appeal to either of them.

On their arrival at the Simpson house all else seemed unimportant at the sight of an ambulance at the front door. Mr. Simpson's broken ankle had become so painful that he was writhing in pain as the ambulance attendants rolled him past them, with a tearful Mrs. Simpson on their heels. Sin promised to stay with the boys while Nedra drove Mrs. Simpson to the hospital in the Simpson car. The elderly woman had never learned to drive.

It was midnight by the time Nedra returned to the Simpson house. A phone call to Sin from the hospital had informed him that Mr. Simpson had a blood clot and an operation was set for the next day. Mrs. Simpson refused to leave the hospital. Nedra would return to the house, stay with the boys, and return the next day with fresh clothing for Mrs. Simpson and supplies for Mr. Simpson. Sin had informed her that, until then, he would stay with the boys.

When she entered the dimly lit house, she had found Sin watching television, and the boys upstairs in the bedroom they shared. They were supposed to be asleep, but they weren't. They were anxious for news of Mr. Simpson. She was honest with them, told them to pray for Mr. Simpson's swift recovery, and had lain with them until they had fallen asleep. It was obvious that she had joined them in slumber.

Sitting up in the bed, careful not to awaken the two sleeping boys, Nedra glanced at the clock on the night stand. It read three o'clock in the morning. The mournful wail swept through the house once again. She got up from the bed, closed the bedroom door behind her, and cautiously crept down the dark hallway, following the sound into the lighted living room to the sleeping figure lying prostrate on the rug.

Fully dressed, Sin had stretched out to his full length during the night, his legs spread apart, one arm flung across his eyes, the other arm stretched across the carpet. He had fallen asleep while watching the television. Only the sound of the test pattern interrupted the momentary silence.

Nedra turned the TV off and returned her attention to Sin. He was sleeping heavily and was in a state of agitation. His breathing was labored, and he was sweating profusely. He began to speak rapidly, the words he uttered unintelligible, but the sounds coming from him were so like that of a wounded animal that it broke Nedra's heart.

Bending down to where he lay, she shook his shoulder gently. "Mr. Reasoner... Sinclair, wake up. You've having a bad dream."

Unexpectedly, Sin sat erect, knocking her hand from his shoulder with such force that Nedra fell back against a coffee table, hitting her arm. She winced as the pain shot through her.

Sin

Sin was sitting up, and his eyes were open, but they were not focused or aware. Leaning forward, he wiped the sweat from his forehead, then closing his eyes once again, he sank back down to the carpet, mumbling, "No!" He rolled onto his side, facing Nedra, his head mere inches from her body.

Hesitant at first, then slowly, with great care, Nedra eased his head onto her lap, caressing his face gently. He was a tortured soul in need, she kept telling herself. It was her job to comfort those who needed it. The tingle that shot through her body she ignored.

The soothing gesture quieted his restlessness, and his breathing once again became steady. Nedra smiled at her boldness as she watched his handsome face soften and he drifted into a peaceful sleep. Whatever the demons that had inhabited his dreams, her touch had made them disappear. She liked that. She liked that a lot.

It was the smell of coffee that awakened Sin. Unsure of his surroundings at first, he sat up cautiously, aware of every sight and sound until he remembered that he was at the Simpson house. The boys were asleep in their room. Nedra had come back to the house, went to check on them and... He looked down at the comforter which covered him, and at the pillow that had been placed under his

51

head. As he rose, his stiff, sore muscles could attest to the fact that he had spent the night asleep on the floor. He still felt tired, exhausted, in fact. His clothes were wrinkled, and he was wet with perspiration. When had he gotten the comforter and pillow? He didn't remember that.

The lamp he had turned on earlier was still lit, but the television had been turned off. A glance out the window through the sheer nylon curtains informed him that it was still dark. A second glance at his gold Rolex told him that it was four o'clock in the morning. He looked at the pillow and comforter that had covered him, then tensed as he heard movement in the kitchen, located beyond the dining room. Nedra.

Stretching the kinks out of his body, he picked up the pillow, placed it on the overstuffed sofa, then folded the comforter neatly and placed it on top of the pillow. Silently, he moved toward the sounds in the kitchen and, carefully, opened the swinging door leading into the room. Nedra sat at the small kitchen table placed under the window, watching him as he stood in the doorway, not surprised at his appearance.

"Good morning." Her voice was low, husky.

Sin's body reacted as if she had made love to him. He nodded, unable to speak. His senses could only take so much this early in the morning.

"I boiled some water for both of us. I took the liberty of putting a couple of spoonfuls of instant in your cup. Hope I didn't put too many."

"I'm sure it's fine. Thank you."

Sin walked over to the stove where the pot rested on the burner. He poured the water into the cup, picked up the spoon beside the cup, and stirred the steaming liquid. He didn't drink coffee, but she didn't know that. He was moved by her gesture of kindness. It wouldn't hurt to give it a try. Picking the cup up, he turned back to her, legs crossed, the kitchen counter supporting his weight.

Nedra stole a glance at him to see if she could read his mood. She couldn't. Concerned that his silence was the result of his restless dream, she wanted to ask what the dream was about. But she didn't. Instead she asked, "Is something wrong?"

He took a sip from the coffee cup. "No, nothing's wrong, I'm just tired."

"I see. Must be some of that busy work you do that keeps you out of church."

Sin laughed and shook his head. "Always the preacher, huh?"

"That's what they tell me." She stifled a yawn behind her hand.

"Looks like I'm not the only one tired. It's been a busy day."

Nedra nodded in agreement. "Yes, it has."

Sin took another sip of the steaming brew. He wasn't impressed with the taste. His eyes shifted back to Nedra. He was very impressed with her.

"It must be hard, being a minister, I mean, especially a woman minister."

"It isn't easy, but it's been worth it."

There was a moment of comfortable silence before he asked, "Do you ever have fun, Nedra?"

Her eyes flew up to meet his. The question was full of concern, not curiosity, as if he really cared about her answer.

"Of course. I love what I do. I love people...helping them, guiding them..."

"But what do you do for yourself? Who helps you? Guides you? Who loves you?"

The sound of her heartbeat began to pound in her ears as his words echoed through her. Who loves you? Her eyes met his.

"God." Her eyes returned to her cooling coffee. "And with his help I manage to do plenty for myself. As a matter of fact, I'm going on vacation soon, to Lake Tahoe."

Sin grinned. "The gambling side?"

Too nervous to register the teasing in his tone, she replied, "No. I don't gamble. My friend Carla has a cabin up there, off Burton Creek. I'm holing up there for a while, but it's a secret. I don't want my parishioners to know where I am. I really need to get away without interruptions."

"Then I'm flattered you're sharing your secret with me." Sin pulled an imaginary zipper across his lips, noting the way she had avoided his questions. "I won't tell a soul."

Silence fell over the kitchen once more as they both finished their coffee. Nedra's nervousness disappeared, and for a moment the stiffness between them slipped into a comfortable coziness that she was enjoying. It was nice.

Sin stole a look at her as she sat at the table staring into her coffee cup lost in thought. She looked almost serene. His gaze slid past her and out the window into the early morning darkness, then back to her. "I'd better get going."

Nedra started out of her contemplation. He was right. It was four o'clock in the morning. What was she thinking? After all, the man must have a home, a life. He might even be married, have a family. He'd never said. She'd never asked. She ignored her feeling of disappointment. "Oh, of course! You've done enough, more than enough helping out in this crisis. Your family must be worried."

Getting up from the table, she moved past him, through the dining room, into the living room. The kitchen had suddenly felt small and her nervousness had returned.

He followed her, watching as she occupied herself gathering the linen he had placed on the sofa. She had been fishing with the family statement. He knew that. She knew it too. She was interested. If only things were different.

Nedra turned to him, clutching the linen tightly to her chest. "I'm going to take some things to the Simpsons after church tomorrow. I'll take the boys with me to church and to the hospital. They'll be a comfort to Mrs. Simpson. They don't have any children, you know, and..."

Without a word, Sin took the linen from her hands, removing her protective barrier. Nedra flushed with embarrassment. She was rambling. She couldn't seem to stop herself. His essence simply overwhelmed her, even standing there, his clothes wrinkled, his hair mussed, sleep settled in the corners of his eyes...

A knowing smile tugged at the corner of Sin's mouth. "Where do these belong?"

Nedra collected herself. This was ridiculous. She was acting like a star struck school-girl. She took the linen back and placed them on the sofa. She was in control again. "No, I'll put them away. You'd better get going. Thank you for everything."

Leading the way to the front door, she opened it and turned to see him out.

"Mr. Reasoner...Sin...Sinclair. You have been more than kind, helping those boys. I don't know many men who would have done what you've done for them, and today has just been one more act of kindness to add to the list."

"Does that mean I can get into heaven, even if I don't go to church?"

Nedra returned his teasing smile. "It might help open negotiations."

He chuckled. She was quick. He dug his hands deep inside his pockets to keep from hugging her to him. He wanted to so badly. "Well, that's a start." He moved through the door onto the porch. He didn't want to leave. He wanted to stay, talk to her, joke with her. He made it down the steps before turning back. "Hope everything goes okay with Mr. Simpson."

He made no promises this time. He wouldn't call to check on the Simpsons. He wouldn't contact the boys again. This was it, the final act.

Standing in the darkened doorway, a mere shadow against the dimly lit interior of the house, she nodded as she sensed the finality of this departure. Sin continued to the end of the walkway, then turned back to her once again. His voice was low as he spoke. Nedra could barely hear his words. She moved to the edge of the porch, down one step, closer, aware that voices carried. The neighbors might awaken. Neighbors talk. If only things were different.

Her own voice was barely above a whisper. "What did you say?"

His voice was clear this time. Strong. Plaintive. "I said that I don't have a family. I'm alone."

Climbing into his expensive sports car, he drove away into the night.

Chapter 5

He was alone, and he was lonely. It seemed that it had always been that way. There was no one who loved him, no one whom he loved. Except...

All the way home, he forced the memory of Nedra from his mind. He would not see her again. That was it. That was final. So, he ignored the pain.

As he drove into the hills of Oakland, the brilliant lights of the San Francisco Bay area twinkled in the distance. Before him stood the house in which he lived, a stunning tribute to the artistry of architecture. Contemporary in design, it boasted lots of windows which looked out onto the magnificent view of the Bay. Built of yellow stucco, framed by towering pine and fruit trees, the house's unique angles and curves were complemented by second-and-third floor balconies. It was a dream house anyone would covet. Too bad it wasn't a home.

Avoiding the three-car garage, he parked his car in the driveway and wearily climbed the stone stairway leading to the house. Unlocking the door, he disarmed the alarm and turned on the light switch at the entrance. The interior was as impressive as the exterior. The floor plan was circular. To the right of the entrance was the living room, long, sunken, highlighted by a free standing stone fireplace in the center. A large dining area adjoined the living room and opened onto a huge patio. Adjoining the dining area was a gourmet kitchen, gleaming with stainless steel accessories. Off the kitchen was the family room, decorated cozily, and containing a second fireplace. The family room led back into the entranceway. From the entranceway, Sin took the winding staircase, two steps at a time, to the second of the three floors, which held five bedrooms between them, including the master bedroom suite into which he now stepped.

Shedding his clothing and shoes in the massive walk-in closet, he entered an adjoining bathroom, resplendent in beige marble, and stepped into the shower. An hour later, feeling refreshed, he climbed into the king-size bed occupying one side of the room. He pulled the covers over his naked body and released all thought from his restless mind, ready to welcome sleep.

It seemed that his head had just hit the pillow when the sound of the telephone ringing jerked him awake. Sitting up, he looked at the bedside clock. It was noon. He'd been asleep for hours. The telephone rang again. He picked up the receiver.

"Yeah?"

"I heard that you had something special for me."

He recognized the voice as Eddie Carter's. He didn't like the man. His voice hardened. "I've told you to not to call me at home."

"Yeah, man, I know, but..."

"There are no buts. I'll be in the Bayland office on Monday. Meet me there at ten a.m."

"I'll be there." There was a pause. Sin knew he was not going to like whatever was coming next. He was right. "Lynn's coming with me."

Sin gave a heavy sigh. He could still hear the ring of Eddie's laughter as he placed the phone back on its cradle.

Bayland Imports was located on the Embarcadero in Oakland, a group of renovated buildings on the waterfront, built in an effort to revitalize a dying area. The building occupied by Bayland was unobtrusive. Painted in muted colors, Bayland occupied the entire first floor, with various businesses occupying offices on the second floor. Sin had opened this West Coast branch of his thriving import business a little over a year ago. The location was perfect, and the contacts he'd been referred to from his East coast connections had proved to be profitable.

Arriving at the office that Monday, he greeted Mrs. Cosley, his personal secretary—the epitome of efficiency. By the time Sin had settled comfortably in his office chair, Eddie and Lynn had arrived.

Lynn Carter Williams Trellis was Eddie's sister and his business partner. Only twenty-four, she was twice divorced and made no secret that she wanted Sinclair Reasoner to be husband number three. They had dated for a few months when they first met, but what she hoped would be a fantastic relationship quickly fizzled when Sin told her that he "just wanted to be friends." She didn't need a friend, she wanted a man—this man—and she was determined to have him.

Lynn Trellis strolled into Bayland Imports as if she owned the place. She was small in stature, barely five foot one, but her stride oozed confidence with a hint of arrogance. Her honey-colored complexion was flawless. Large dark brown eyes, set in a heart-shaped face, made her appear innocent, vulnerable. But she wasn't. The short, sleek haircut that complemented her face so well and the expensive form-fitting suit she wore defined her sense of style. She was fine, and she knew it. She just wasn't sure that Sinclair recognized the fact.

Leaning back into the soft leather of his chair, his fingers stapled beneath his chin, Sin peered at Lynn beneath half closed lids as she crossed her legs provocatively. She was so obvious.

"And how are you today?" She smiled seductively.

"I'm doing fine, Lynn. Thank you for asking." His formal tone left no doubt that this meeting was going to be all business. He had tired of her flirtatious manner long ago. Dismissing her, he turned to her brother.

Eddie Carter looked like his sister, short, and honey colored, but where her compact body was shapely and well toned, he was as thin as a rail. Despite the expensive clothes he wore, they never seemed to fit him. At twenty-nine, he looked the part of a young, upcoming business man, but his manner was disconcerting. He was always in a state of continuous motion, a "nervous condition," Eddie called it. As he sat across the desk from Sin, his foot shook constantly as he placed it across his knee.

"What have you got for us?" he inquired, with a side-ward glance at his sister. He was amused at her efforts to entice Sinclair, especially since her tactics never seemed to work. For once in her spoiled life, it looked like his baby sister wasn't going to get what she wanted, and it was killing her. She had come with him today only to flirt with Sinclair, and it wasn't working. Eddie's amused eyes shifted back to Sin. The look he received was cold, hard. Eddie's amusement faded.

Sin said, "I just received a valuable shipment of vases from Egypt, old, hand crafted. The work is quite exquisite."

"Sounds good." Eddie picked up the black leather briefcase he had placed beside his chair. He set it on the desk and opened it. It was filled with money.

Sin didn't blink as his eyes slid from Eddie's face to the money and back again. "How much?"

"$250,000."

Sin nodded. Opening a desk drawer, he withdrew a plastic bag, tossed it on the desk and watched as Eddie and Lynn placed the money in the bag. When the bag was filled, he picked it up, excused himself, and disappeared behind the door that led to a small, sparsely furnished room off of his office. Closing the door behind him, he walked over to a poster on the wall, lifted it, and twirled the combination to the safe hidden behind it. Opening the safe, he placed the bag of money inside, closed it securely, then rejoined Eddie and Lynn.

"I'll make arrangements today for the vases to be shipped to you."

Eddie nodded but didn't move from his seat, despite Sin's dismissive tone. He knew the older man didn't like him, but that was all right. He still liked Sinclair. He admired his polish, his sophistication, the way he spoke and carried himself. The man was "cool" without a hint of the streets that Eddie heard he had come from. No, this man had a way about him that told the world that he had come to be the man he was the hard way, his own way. On top of it, he had a way with the ladies.

He had witnessed the way women fell all over Sinclair, including his own sister. It was Eddie who had hustled in the streets to pay for Lynn to go to college so that she could acquire all of the things in life that he wanted her to have. He wanted her to have whatever it was she wanted, and she wanted Sinclair. So, despite his amusement at her efforts to snag him, secretly he was hoping that Sinclair and Lynn could get together. This was the kind of man that he wanted for his sister.

Sinclair Reasoner was all of the things Eddie Carter wanted to be. Eddie had started out a long time ago to be more than one of the punks on the street, and he had done pretty well, having no father, no role model to follow. Now he had found one.

Sin frowned. Their business was finished. "Is there something else?"

Lynn shifted in her seat, stiffening at Sin's obvious impatience. However, Eddie seemed oblivious to Sin's cool demeanor. Rising from his chair, he began to pace the room. Sinclair leaned back against his desk, legs crossed, arms folded across his chest.

"We might have to stop doing business for a while."

"Oh?" Sin cocked an eyebrow.

"Something's goin' down on the streets, and things are goin' to get kinda hot for a while."

"And what is it that's going to make things get so hot?" Sin asked with mild interest. He really needed them out of his office. He had business to conduct.

"Well, I can't be too specific..."

"Then don't be, Eddie." Lynn's voice was ice as she rose from her seat and gave her brother a warning look. Sin caught the look. Eddie didn't. He was on a roll.

He paced the floor, his face flushed with excitement, his eyes a little too bright. His movements were a little too animated. "Hell, Sis! Soon all our problems will be over!"

Lynn's eyes narrowed. "Eddie..."

"They will! They will be! We'll be free of that bitch, and her—"

"Eddie!" There was no doubt about the warning in her voice this time. Lynn's eyes shot sparks of fire that even Sin could feel. Eddie's mouth clamped shut immediately. He stopped pacing. The wild light in his eyes dimmed as his excitement dissipated.

Lynn turned to Sin with a dazzling smile. He stared in amazement at the metamorphosis. "Sinclair, we'll have to be going now, but I do want the two of us to have lunch together soon. Come on, Eddie."

With that, she picked up her purse, threw the leather strap across her shoulder, and marched out the door, with a contrite Eddie following. The door shut quietly behind them. Sin stood looking at the closed door, shaking his head. Lynn was an enigma. Anyone who had been around her, even on a casual basis, could spot her as a chameleon. Her changes in personality were that unpredictable. Yet, Sin sensed something sinister about her. Lynn was more than a chameleon. She was a snake—a cobra—cold and deadly, and like a snake, she would strike if something got in her way.

The restaurant was crowded. Nedra and Carla had been lucky to get the table by the window. At least Nedra thought they had been lucky until Richard, Carla's brother, passed the restaurant and saw them. Now the three of them were squeezed together at a table for two, and Richard's presence had put a damper on the whole luncheon.

Nedra couldn't remember ever having heard Richard say anything good about anybody. He was determined to be miserable at all cost, and determined that everyone else be the same. It was hard to believe that Richard and Carla were even related.

It wasn't that they didn't look alike. Richard was lighter in complexion, but they looked very much alike, especially their eyes. He wore his straight dark brown hair in a ponytail and sported gold hoop earrings in both ears. Yes, he and his sister looked alike, but that was where the resemblance ended. Carla was fun and vivacious. Richard was brooding and sullen. Carla was an optimist. Richard was a pessimist. His lazy gaze looked out at the world with contempt

As the Art Director at Holden & Black Advertising, one of the most prestigious advertising firms in the country, Richard was quite successful. Transferred to the firm's San Francisco office from New York a few years ago, he was the first African-American to hold the position in that company. He was well paid, his work was highly regarded. Yet, Richard was an unhappy man. He had it all in life, but all still wasn't enough. Richard wanted more.

He was Richard Ryan III, the only son of Richard Ryan II, a state Supreme Court Judge. His grandfather, the first Richard Ryan, was one of the first black millionaires in the state of Virginia. The Ryan family was one of great importance in their state, and as the only son in the family, Richard had always been pampered and indulged. He was a man used to getting what he wanted, when he wanted it, and he wanted Nedra. He was a man unaccustomed to rejection, and Nedra had rejected his advances steadily over the years. But her rejection had only inflamed his desire for her. He wanted her, badly, and no matter how long it took, he would have Reverend Nedra Davis.

He took every opportunity to be near her. When he saw her lunching with Carla, he quickly invited himself to join them, choosing to ignore Carla's loud groan of protest. Instead, he had focused on Nedra's polite, although strained, welcome.

After a half hour of listening to Richard drone on about everything that was wrong at Holden & Black, Nedra was beginning to regret that welcome. Richard wouldn't shut up.

"Nobody in the whole place knows more about art design than me," he assured them, casually draping an arm across the back of Nedra's chair, much to her dismay. "So of course you would think that they would have checked with me before going forward with that shoe ad. After all, I am in charge of the Art Department; but, no, they can't respect a black man! He might know too much, and prove how stupid they are—"

"Richard!" Carla held up her hand like a traffic cop, stopping him in mid-sentence. She had enough. "You have been going on and on and on about how terrible it is at Holden & Black, and it's not the first time! So lay it to rest, why don't you? I've told you a million times. If you're that unhappy with your six-figure job, quit. Give us all a break. There are other people in the world who have real problems. Hell! Look at Nedra. Somebody broke into her condo last week and could have harmed her. Do you hear her complaining?"

Richard's eyes darkened as he stared daggers at his sister, before turning his attention to Nedra. "Yeah, Sharon told me about the break in. Lucky you weren't at home."

"You're telling me. I spent the night baby-sitting with the foster children of a couple in my church. The husband was in the hospital."

Carla shuddered. "Thank the, Lord. At three o'clock in the morning, they must have known somebody would be home asleep. If they had wanted to just break in to steal, they would have done it in the daytime, when chances were better that nobody would be at home. Shoot, I don't even want to think about what could have happened."

Nedra exhaled, shakily. "Me either. I was blessed."

Yes, the Lord had been with her! The alarm had gone off, and neighbors had called 911. The thieves had been scared off, thank goodness, and nothing was taken.

Carla shook her head in agreement at Nedra's statement. "Good things happen to good people. And negative people just keep on getting more and more negative." She gave her brother a pointed stare.

Richard tensed. "What do you care about what happens to me good or bad? You have never listened to a thing I say, Carla."

"Cause all you do is complain."

Richard's voice rose in frustration. "Here I am trying to tell you..."

"Tell me what?" Carla rolled her eyes in disgust. "The same thing over and over? Excuse me, but I've heard it before. Sharon might be goo-goo ga-ga over every word you say, but I'm not!"

Richard glared at the woman who had been a thorn in his side ever since her arrival in the world. She had never recognized his position of importance in the family, in the world. She thought she was queen of the universe. "Listen, Carla, I am sick and tired of..."

Nedra tensed, ready to intervene. It was starting, the verbal sparring that seemed to be the foundation of this sibling relationship.

"You're sick and tired? If you only..."

"Hi, Richie."

The childlike voice caught the attention of all three of the table's occupants. Three pairs of eyes locked with one pair of sky-blue ones. The face was pretty, but the face was also young, no more than twenty years old. The hair was blonde, with dark roots. The lips, thin and painted red, were boldly inviting, and they were definitely sending an open invitation "Richie's" way.

Leaning back in her chair, Carla folded her arms across her chest, and lifted an eyebrow at her brother. "Richie?"

Nedra grabbed her water glass off the table and quickly took a swallow, using the action to stifle the laugh that threatened to erupt. Nothing more had to be said. Two words from a stranger—at least a stranger to her and Carla—had busted him, and from the look on "Richie's" face, he had been busted. Poor Sharon.

Blood rushed to Richard's face as he tried to recover from the shock of seeing the young woman he had been with a few nights before. He didn't remember her name. Nodding, he straightened from his formerly relaxed stance, removing his arm from Nedra's chair. Of all the times for this bimbo to appear.

Averting his eyes from the young woman's he occupied himself with the gin and tonic before him with no further acknowledgment of her presence. She moved on, quickly getting the message. There was an awkward silence at the table until Carla broke it with a long, drawn out sigh.

"At least you have the decency to be embarrassed."

Nedra watched Richard closely as his head shot up. He had seemed almost humbled before Carla spoke. Now, he was angry again, an emotion she had seen in him too often. It was the source of his anger she didn't understand. It seemed to be directed toward everyone, and eventually it would destroy him. She prayed that those closest to him wouldn't be destroyed in the process.

"What about Sharon?" Nedra didn't realize that she had spoken the words aloud until Richard turned to her with a puzzled expression.

Richard gave a mental shrug. What about Sharon? He liked her. She was a good lay, but he didn't love her. He wasn't married to Sharon. He wasn't even engaged to her. She was beautiful and he liked that. Other men wanted her, envied him because of her. It was a boost for his ego. So he kept her happy. But Sharon was weak. Nedra was strong. He needed a strong woman, one who wouldn't buckle down to him, one who wouldn't do everything he told her to do. He liked strong women. He liked leaders and Nedra was a leader. So, he waited and watched for some sign of vulnerability in her that would send her running to him. Meanwhile, Sharon wasn't a bad consolation prize.

As he looked at Nedra now, he didn't see the condemnation that he had seen, clearly, in his sister's eyes. He saw confusion. He saw concern, but that was Nedra, always the preacher. He resumed his relaxed stance and, once again, draped his arm across Nedra's chair. He smiled, and lied. "I love Sharon, and I'll never do anything to hurt her."

Chapter 6

From a corner booth at Antonio's Restaurant, Sin watched Nedra as she sat eating lunch with Carla and a man. Although he had tried to concentrate on the conversation his two business acquaintances were having , it was useless. His attention constantly strayed to the small table by the window.

Who was that pony-tailed man with Carla and Nedra? A friend of Carla's? Nedra's? It was obvious that, whoever he was, he and Carla weren't getting along, and what in the hell was he doing hanging all over Nedra's chair?

Taking a sip of his water with lemon, Sin frowned. His expression didn't go unnoticed by his table mates.

"Did I say something wrong, Reasoner?"

The question brought Sin's attention back to Bob Kirk, his financial consultant. The older man was looking at him with concern.

"I'm sorry, Bob. My mind was wandering."

Bob gave him an indulgent smile. "I could see that."

Bob had helped Sin increase his financial worth considerably in the short time he'd known him, and in doing so he had grown fond of the quiet, solemn young man he had met barely a year ago. Bob's son and partner, Todd, was sitting beside him. He too was fond of Sin. He had tried to get him to hang out a couple of times, but Sin had politely declined. Now, he gave Sin a knowing grin.

"I caught the reason your mind was 'wandering'." Todd nodded toward Nedra's table. "Which one were you scoping, my brother? Lord knows, they're both fine."

Curious, Bob followed Todd's gaze. "Oh! I know one of them you can forget about. The woman in the blue dress is Reverend Davis, Reverend Nedra Davis."

"Reverend? Todd looked stunned. "A minister? A preacher? That fine?"

"She spoke at our church about six months ago. If you'd go to church sometimes, my son, you'd know these things."

Todd grinned sheepishly. "Guilty as charged. But I do know the man with them. That's Richard Ryan. He's with Holden and Black Advertising. I met him at a party they gave about a year ago."

A muscle in Sin's face twitched. Richard Ryan. He'd met Carla Ryan in Nedra's office. Could that be her brother? What was he to Nedra?

"Who's the beauty next to the reverend, Dad?" Todd's interest was obvious as he salivated over Carla.

Bob stole a look at Carla and shrugged. "Don't know, but that Reverend Davis is something." His face reddened in embarrassment as he returned his attention to Sin "I...I.. don't mean , uh, like that...you know. I mean she's interesting, being the pastor of Mount Peter, in East Oakland.

That woman has helped shut down more crack houses out there than the police. The newspapers call her the Anti-drug Queen. I've heard she's driving the drug dealers crazy."

Sin smiled and listened attentively as Bob continued singing her praises, all the while noting that across the room Nedra, Carla, and Ryan were leaving the restaurant. He didn't let his eyes linger on her as long as he wanted to. He was simply glad that he had the opportunity to see her again, if only briefly. He smiled and nodded in the right places as Bob continued to talk, zeroing in on his final words in confusion, not sure that he had heard what he thought he had heard.

"What was that last thing you said, Bob?"

Todd chuckled. "Mind wandering again, Reasoner?"

Bob repeated. "I said I'd bet a pretty penny that some drug dealers would pay a fortune to get Reverend Nedra Davis out of their hair."

Sin didn't like the sound of that. "What do you mean?"

"I mean that the dealers are losing money with every crack house she closes. You're a businessman, you know that businessmen don't like losing money, even illegal money. They're willing to go to extremes not to lose money. Ruthless people use ruthless means."

Calmly, Sin nodded in agreement, as his stomach knotted. Ruthless people use ruthless means. Bob was right. Dead right.

Sin

Nedra settled back in the bucket seat of Carla's Camero. Richard had folded his six-foot frame in the back seat, having begged a ride the mere two blocks to where his car was parked. Rather than argue, Carla had consented. As they passed the restaurant they had just left, she squealed. "Hey, Nedra, look! Coming out of Antonio's. Isn't that the hunk from your office? The one I met...the one that helped those boys? What's his name?"

Nedra followed Carla's gaze in time to see Sin standing in front of the restaurant the three of them had just left. Dressed in a suit and tie, a coat folded neatly over his arm, he stood talking to two men. He looked good.

"Yes, that's him." She smiled. "That's him."

Richard followed Nedra's gaze, looking at the tall, well dressed man on the sidewalk. His gaze shifted back to Nedra...Nedra's smile...Nedra's wistful smile.

For days after their luncheon, Sin could not get Bob's words out of his mind. They bothered him, haunted him. Ruthless people use ruthless means. He knew it was true. Nedra and her church were dealing with some ruthless people. He wondered if she knew how ruthless they could be. Human life meant nothing to those in the narcotic underworld. Profit was god. Life was expendable, all life. There was no discriminating between man, woman, or child. He knew this as fact. And there was no question that the moment she began leading her church's quiet campaign against drugs in her area, Nedra had become the enemy. How big of an enemy was the question for which he had no answer.

His restless concern had taken him to the library sifting through old newspaper accounts of Mount Peter's campaign against drugs. It had been centered in the neighborhood in which the church was located, and a few blocks beyond. The church's stand against drugs had been a quiet but determined campaign. There had never been any direct confrontation with dealers or junkies, simply the purchasing of empty properties that had been used for drug sales. No drug dealers had been named, or arrested. The media appeared to have stumbled onto the story by accident, and Nedra was dubbed the campaign's reluctant heroine. Modestly, she'd given all of the credit for what had been accomplished to the members of her church. They in turn had verified that they would not have thought of such an effort if it hadn't been for her dynamic leadership. The mutual admiration was commendable, but Sin needed to know how much all the goodwill was costing the drug world. When he saw the estimate, in the last paragraph of the last article he read, his anxiety grew. He'd known people killed for much less. That she was in danger was no longer a question, but a fact.

Saturdays were quiet in the Bayland office, so he often came in to do paperwork without the interference of ringing telephones or interruptions from his secretary. He had started early, around seven a.m.. It was now ten, and as he looked at the papers scattered on his desk before him, he realized that for three hours he had accomplished nothing.

When he was supposed to be doing paperwork, he had in fact been wrestling with his conscience, assuring himself that whatever was happening out on those streets was none of his business. If Nedra was involved, she could take care of herself. She had done so quite admirably for years before he arrived in California. Nothing had happened to her. If she posed a threat to the drug world, then why hadn't any attempt been made on her life before this? Whatever was going down didn't involve her. Why should it? Yet, Eddie had definitely been babbling about a woman being involved in whatever was happening. Some "bitch," as he so crudely put it, was involved. But it didn't have to be Nedra. Maybe it was some social activist. Some politician, but not Nedra.

Sin closed his eyes and buried his face in his hands. Not Nedra. Gently, he massaged the tense muscles in his face, then, suddenly, stilled. Why wonder, when it was possible to know for sure. Stuffing the papers into their folder, he tossed the folder back into the in basket, and pulled on his leather bomber jacket. Ten minutes later he was standing in a telephone booth outside a convenience store dialing a telephone number which he hadn't used for twelve of the eighteen months he had been in the Bay Area.

The telephone rang more than a dozen times, and he was just about to hang up when he heard a graveled voice saying "Hello." The sound reminded him of sand paper.

"Hey, man. It's Sin. How's it goin'?"

Silence greeted him. Sin pressed on.

"I need some information."

"What?" The voice was cold, impersonal.

"I need to know what's the word on the street about Moun—"

Sin hesitated. He didn't want to mention Nedra's church, her name, or anything connected to her. The fewer people that knew about his knowing her, the better.

"What do you want, man?" The voice was now cold and impatient.

Sin wouldn't be coy. "What's the word on East Oakland?" He grasped at straws trying to find more to say. What had he heard, recently? What? What? Eddie! Yes! He said something about... "Word is East Oakland is gonna get hot for a while? What's up?"

More silence.

"Talk to me, man. I need to know. If somethin' is goin' down, it could cost me some money."

Sin

"You said the magic word."

"How much?"

"$200. In twenties, mail it to me at the P.O. Box. Same address. You still got it?"

"Yeah, I've got it. Now what's the word?"

"You said the word. Money, lots of it. It's being lost in East Oakland, cause of some do-gooder crusader. Word is a contract's out."

Sin's mind raced. "Who's the target?"

"Nobody's talkin' specifics. Must be big. Politician maybe."

A politician. Yes, maybe. But a do-gooder politician? Since when?

"Do you know if the target is male or female?"

"I told you, nobody's talkin' specifics."

"When's it goin' down?"

"Don't know, and that's all I know. Mail my money today." The phone went dead.

Sin sat in his car for the next half hour musing over what he'd heard. He hadn't spoken to his contact in quite a while. He'd met him a week after his arrival, an unobtrusive man, a man of few words, most of them blunt and to the point. He was a shadow in the underworld, who moved quietly among those who chose to live outside the law. Information was the name of his game, and any information he acquired was for sale. His information had to be accurate. That was how he built his reputation. Sin had no reason to doubt him.

He reviewed what little information he'd been told, sifting the words, rephrasing them, examining their meaning in every way possible; yet, four words screamed the loudest—a do-good crusader. Damn! It described Nedra Davis up and down. Yet, he could be wrong. Maybe it was somebody else?

Sin drove, aimlessly, for an hour before he pulled up to another telephone booth, got out and made a second call. This time it was to the Oakland Police Department. Not identifying himself, he demanded to speak to whoever was in charge. He was denied the request.

Trying to calm his anger, he informed the duty officer of his suspicions that Nedra Davis was in danger, describing who she was and why the danger might exist. Hanging up, he knew that his call would be suspect, and doubted if Nedra would be granted protection. His had been an anonymous call, with no verifiable facts. There was no way he could identify himself. There was no way that he could explain how he knew what he knew. How can you explain intuition? He made a third call, providing the same information, with the hope he would be taken seriously.

Three hours had passed since the call to his contact and the two follow-up calls to get some protection for Nedra, and as he stood in line at a fast food restaurant ordering his dinner, he told himself that he had done all he could do.

If Nedra was in danger, the authorities would take care of it. After all, he wasn't even sure that she was in danger. It was just a gut feeling. But his time in the streets had taught him to never, never ignore a gut feeling.

Taking his tray to the table, he grabbed a newspaper from the bin and sat at a window table where he could see the sun setting behind the buildings. Straightening out the paper before him, he cursed silently to himself as he noted that the newspaper was a week old. Flipping through it with general disinterest, his half eaten hamburger was suspended in midair as a small headline on page ten caught his attention: ANTI-DRUG QUEEN'S HOME BURGLAR-IZED. Quickly, he scanned the article.

The hamburger remained half eaten. The fries remained untouched, and the newspaper remained open on the table as the sleek Jaguar tore out of the McDonald's parking lot, headed toward East Oakland.

Sin hadn't been inside a church since he was dumped into his first foster home. The old lady—he couldn't remember her name—forced him to go with her every night, and all day Sunday. He lasted a week there before running away. He wouldn't have been at Mount Peter today if he had been able to find Nedra last night. He'd driven by the church then, but she wasn't there, nobody was. The

Simpsons weren't at home when he drove by to see if they had her home telephone number or address, and he had no idea how to get in touch with Carla and Sharon. He had been up half the night worrying that the hit had been made, but the morning news had no report of an attack. Now, here he was sitting in the balcony at Mount Peter.

The church wasn't as big inside as it appeared outside, and it was packed to capacity. All of the seats downstairs had been filled before Sin arrived, and he had barely gotten a seat in the balcony. Others who had entered behind him had been relegated to the basement, where the service was broadcast on a wide television screen. The colors of the church's interior were warm and inviting, pale pink walls with forest-green rugs and white benches, cushioned with forest-green seats.

A trio, sitting on the floor to the left of the pulpit struck a lively chord, and the choir began to march in. Dressed in forest-green robes, trimmed in brightly colored kente cloth, the number of singers seemed endless as they marched in singing a song so joyously that most of the church came to its feet to shout and clap its approval. Sin stood too, motivated not so much by the music but his inability to see through the people who stood in front of him. He needed to see the pulpit, to see Nedra when she walked in. He watched as a line of men dressed in clerical robes walked solemnly out of a doorway to the right of the pulpit. There were four robed men, but no woman.

Nedra wasn't with them. Where was she? He felt a rush of panic.

Working his way past a line of rapturous worshippers, he approached one of the ushers standing at the top of the stairs. He inquired about Nedra's absence. She informed him that she was on vacation and would be back in two weeks. Nobody knew where she was. Sin smiled and thanked her, then bounded down the stairway, anxious to escape the confines of a building in which he'd never found hope.

As he stepped into the bright sunshine of the crisp fall morning, he took a moment to adjust the light cashmere dress coat he wore over his double-breasted suit. The street was now quiet, a far cry from an hour ago when hordes of church goers vied with each other for entrance into Mount Peter. Inadvertently, his eyes scanned the street filled with cars parked on both sides. They were all empty, except for one. It was a dark car, parked near some trees across from the church parking lot. Two men sat in the front seat. The driver flickered a cigarette butt out of the window. It joined the pile of butts lying in the street by the driver's door.

As casually as possible, Sin walked to the lot, got in his car, and drove away. He knew where he was going. He had known immediately after talking with the usher where he would be spending the next two weeks.

Chapter 7

Nedra looked in the bathroom mirror at the face peering back at her. She didn't look as though she was born yesterday, but Sinclair Reasoner seemed to think so when he expected her to believe his story that their meeting here in Tahoe was an accident.

He had claimed that he was in Reno on business and had decided, at the last minute, to come to Tahoe for a few days of rest and relaxation. It was a coincidence, according to him, that they both were in Tahoe at the same time, although she distinctly remembered telling him that she would be vacationing in Tahoe soon. It was the night when they were at the Simpson house. He claimed not to remember, but she remembered. She remembered everything about that night.

How they had bumped into each other seemed as contrived as his Reno story. She had been strolling along the trail by her cabin when, suddenly, he appeared from nowhere. Dressed in a dark sweatsuit, with a hood covering his head, he jogged past her at first, did a double take, then stopped and greeted her with a warm smile. He claimed he was surprised to see her, but she got the feeling that he wasn't surprised. He meant to see her there.

The reason why, she had yet to figure out, but something was definitely fishy.

She suspected Carla, or Sharon was behind Sin's convenient vacation in Tahoe. The thought that they would interfere with her life like this did not sit well with her. If she found out that either of them was responsible for trying to force a romantic liaison between her and this man, she'd have the head of the one responsible for this!

Even Mother Nature had conspired against her. They were snowed in, for goodness-sake! He couldn't get back to the hotel, and it was obvious that he would have to spend the night. Now here she was stuck with an unwanted overnight guest, and she was holed up in the bathroom trying to decide what to do about this situation. What a mess!

When she met him on the road yesterday morning, he had invited her to join him for dinner that evening. At first she had declined, but he had thrown on the charm, and eventually she relented. She had ended up enjoying herself, although she had to admit to being more reserved than necessary. He was an interesting man, a good conversationalist, and he displayed a quick sense of humor. Nevertheless, if she hadn't accepted that dinner invitation, she wouldn't have left those earrings, and he wouldn't have come to the cabin to return them. For some reason the dangling baubles had been irritating her, and she took them off, placing them on the dinner table with the intention of slipping them into her purse later. She had forgotten to do so. That gave him the perfect excuse to return them the next day.

It had been snowing lightly, when he trudged up to the cabin to return the earrings, and even that small amount of snow came as a surprise. It was early for snow, even in Tahoe whose economy was centered around the ski slopes. Neither Nedra nor Sin would have guessed that by the time he had eaten the dinner she invited him to share with her, and helped her wash the dishes, a full blown blizzard would be in effect. When they opened the front door, they could barely close it, snowflakes were falling so fiercely. They turned on the television to find that a snow emergency had been declared. Sin could not get back to the hotel. Nedra had an overnight guest whether she wanted him or not.

She groaned. Why had she worn those stupid earrings anyway? They weren't even hers. They belonged to Carla, who had insisted that she wear them to a function once, and she had forgotten to return them. She found them stuffed into the zipped lining of her purse and, on impulse, had put them on to go dining with Sin. She rarely wore anything like that. What had possessed her?

She moved to the toilet, closed the cover, and flopped down on top of it. Oh well, she was stuck now, so she might as well make the best of it. Anyway, this wasn't worth sweating over. It was no big deal. After all, no one knew that she was here, snowed in, alone, with a man. Even those two traitors, whom she called her friends, wouldn't have imagined this scenario. Yet, irrationally, she felt guilty about being here alone with him, although, rationally, she knew that she had nothing to feel guilty about.

Maybe it was because she had enjoyed herself with Sinclair, both yesterday and today. Dinner with him had been wonderful, both days, and he had been a perfect gentleman. Not once had he made her feel uncomfortable. He had not tried to make a move on her, either day. Nedra sighed. Why not?

She jumped, startled at the thought. Where did that come from? She liked what had developed between them, a comfort level in which two strangers were moving toward friendship. The nervousness and uncertainty of weeks ago was all but nonexistent. Friendship with him was what she wanted, not a romantic relationship. She wasn't looking for a man. She didn't need one cluttering up her life, especially not now when everything was going so well.

Yet, when she noticed the way he looked at her when he thought she wasn't looking, with that intent, dark-eyed gaze she had seen in his eyes before, her pulse would race. That look unnerved her, and she had to remind herself that this man was still a stranger. All she really knew about him was his name, not much else. He was very good at saying little when it came to talking about himself. He did tell her he was a businessman, who had moved to the Bay Area almost two years ago, and he owned an import business located near Jack London Square on the Embarcadero. He repeated, as he had that night at the Simpsons, that he had no family, and had never been married. In the two days they had been together that was all she knew about him, nothing more.

There had been plenty of conversation. Sinclair Reasoner was a master at conversation—national and world events, African American history, music, the arts. He seemed to know a little something about everything. He was also a master at evasion when it came to details about himself. Whenever Nedra asked something he didn't want to answer, he would evade it so skillfully, that she forgot she had asked the question until hours later. She couldn't help but admire that kind of skill, but it didn't foster a lot of trust.

Sighing, Nedra rose. It was time to stop hiding. She would be spending this night with an extremely good look-ing man. Something she hadn't done since... She could barely remember the last time. Nothing would happen, and no one would ever know. So, why sweat it?

As usual, she put the situation in the hands of a power greater than her own. Whispering a brief prayer about the situation, Nedra opened the bathroom door and joined Sin.

Sin

One large room made up the majority of the cabin. The ceiling in the room was high and vaulted, giving the illusion of spaciousness. The living room area was designated by a long leather sofa, a matching chair, and a coffee table that faced the huge stone fireplace which occupied one wall. The kitchen area was designated by vinyl tile and contained a small refrigerator, a stove built into the counter, a sink, and a few built-in cabinets with a maple finish. A maple dining table, surrounded by four chairs, was placed between the living room and kitchen areas. The only additional rooms were the tiny bathroom which Nedra had exited, and a bedroom located next to it. The bedroom contained a full-size bed and a nightstand. The closet had a few shelves, two built-in drawers, and a couple of hooks for clothing. This completed the entire cabin.

Nedra stood for a moment watching Sin. He was sitting on the sofa, elbows on his knees, hunched forward, his full concentration on the TV screen. The weather report was on. He turned, aware that she had entered the room. A look of concern was etched on his features.

"They're expecting up to three feet of snow."

"Three feet? Nedra wanted to cry. They'd be buried in this cabin forever!

"I took a look outside. I thought I might be able to make it down the road to the hotel, but from the look of it, nothing is going to be moving tonight. I'm really sorry, but I have no choice but to stay here tonight."

Nedra smiled and settled into the comfort of the plush leather chair opposite the sofa. She was touched by his apology. He seemed sincere. "There's nothing to apologize for. This won't be the first time I've pulled an overnighter with sin."

Sin raised an eyebrow, puzzled by her reply at first. Then it dawned on him what she was saying. The cabin vibrated with his laughter, while Nedra watched him amused.

"So the preacher does have a sense of humor!" Sin marveled, as he wiped tears of mirth from his eyes. He had sensed her resolve when she entered the room. He knew that his having to stay overnight would be awkward for her, even though she might not say it. He worried that his being here might put distance between them, just when she had begun to display some trust in him.

He had been in Tahoe three days before their accidental meeting. At the Simpson house, she had mentioned the road on which the cabin was located. He had the good fortune of remembering that and located it right away. The cabin was close enough to his hotel that his jogging story didn't seem contrived when they met. She would never know that he had been on silent watch outside her cabin since the day he discovered where she was staying.

That she had not rejected him pleased him, although he was pretty sure that she suspected ulterior motives for his being in Tahoe. She never voiced her suspicions, however, and it surprised him when she accepted his invitation to dinner. That first evening had been strained, but he had tried hard to make it as pleasant as possible. Today, their time together had been more comfortable. That Mother Nature would provide the ultimate opportunity for them to solidify their acquaintance was more than he could have asked for. As a result, he could assure himself, beyond a shadow of a doubt, that she was safe, at least for now.

"I haven't laughed that long and hard in years," said Sin, burrowing down into the cozy comfort of the sofa. "It felt good." It did feel good, being here, with Nedra. It felt real good.

The rest of the evening was spent watching the weather report and playing board games. The winner of the spirited games seesawed from one to another, until, tied, four to four, they decided to retire for the night. Nedra took the bedroom. Sin took the sofa bed. As she showered, donned her night clothes, and got on her knees to give praise to the Almighty, she gave thanks for the day, and all that it had brought into her life.

It was early the next morning when a loud yelp awakened Sin. Instantly alert, he sat up with a start and reached immediately for the revolver he had tucked carefully under the pillow. He had worn it strapped to his leg during the day, undetectable to Nedra, or anyone else observing him. Until now, he didn't think he would have to use it. There had been no indication that Nedra was in danger, but that sound brought him out of his bed and onto his feet, every muscle in his body tense. There was a second yelp, and he realized that it was coming from the bathroom. His heartbeat slowed as he recognized Nedra's voice.

"Nedra? Are you all right?"

Her muffled reply came from behind the closed door. She sounded exasperated. "I guess."

As the door slowly opened, Sin quickly pushed the gun under the pillow just as Nedra made her appearance. Dressed in a pair of flannel pajamas, her hair tousled, her eyes little more than slits, she looked less than happy as she glared at him accusingly.

"Didn't anybody teach you to put the toilet seat down after you use the bathroom?"

Nedra turned around to reveal a wide wet spot covering her derriere. Sin tried not to laugh. Nedra was angry enough already. He tried but failed and once again the small cabin was filled with his booming laughter.

Rolling her eyes as hard as she could, Nedra stomped back into the bedroom, slamming the door behind her. Men!

The rest of the day went better. After showering and dressing, Nedra exited the bedroom to find Sin cooking a large, country breakfast, complete with fried potatoes. It was scrumptious, and she devoured it appreciatively, offering a dry thank you, still annoyed by her brief swim in the toilet.

Trying to make amends, Sin insisted that he wash the dishes while she relaxed. She accepted his offer, deciding to let him eat a little more crow before forgiving him for his transgression. By the time they went outside, however, all was forgiven.

The snow had reached the predicted three feet, and was still falling. Progress was slow as they worked on clearing a path to the walkway leading to the cabin, a distance of about fifty feet. By late that evening, they had made significant progress, despite breaks for snowball fights, snowman building, and making angel patterns in the snow.

Chilled and soaked, they took turns showering, with Nedra providing Sin with the shirt and pants left in the closet by Carla's fiancé. Luckily, both men wore the same size.

After a dinner of soup and sandwiches, they decided not to continue their shoveling. Both of them were exhausted. Wearily, Nedra retired to the bedroom, leaving Sin stretched out on the sofa. He was asleep before she closed the bedroom door.

Snuggling down under the covers, she sighed, happily. Today had been fun. She had felt like a young girl again, romping in the snow. Her plans for a quiet vacation had been turned upside down by the mysterious Sinclair Reasoner, and, she had to admit, it was a development she liked. With a smile of satisfaction, she plumped up the pillow and drifted off to sleep.

Carla's frantic call to Richard had surprised him. He rarely talked to his sister on the telephone unless he happened to answer when she was calling Sharon. The sound of her voice startled him as she explained how she had tracked him down, through his office, to ask a favor. Nedra was at Carla's cabin in Tahoe. There was no telephone in the cabin. Nedra had left her cell phone in Oakland, and it was predicted that Tahoe would be snowed in. She was worried.

Richard was in Truckee, California, on business, and Truckee was not far from Tahoe. Her request that he go to the cabin and check on Nedra was more than welcome. Would he? Of course he would!

He chuckled to himself as he tucked his toothbrush into his Louis Vuitton bag, and zipped it in one smooth motion. Carla must be worried if she was desperate enough to ask him to check on Nedra. He knew that she knew it was like sending the cat after the canary. But he wasn't worried about Nedra. She was one woman who could take care of herself. That was one of the things that made her such a challenge.

Carla's call had been made the day before yesterday, and it had taken an additional day for the highway to Tahoe to be cleared of snow and reopened. He was glad to be finally on his way. Truckee had been snowed in as well, and he had been bored out of his head. There had been absolutely nothing to do in this one-horse town!

The door to the bathroom opened slowly, and a bleached blond head appeared. Glazed blue eyes glanced his way. Richard sighed. Well, there was almost nothing to do.

With a wan smile, the blond walked to the dresser and retrieved the three folded bills lying boldly on top of it.

"Was it as good for you as it was for me, honey?" The blond laughed at the cliché, oblivious to Richard's lack of appreciation at the attempt at humor. Tucking the money into a pants pocket, the blond reached for the door, started to exit, then looked back at Richard with lascivious perusal. "All kidding aside, you was good, honey. I, for one, like the rough stuff. Hope you remember to call for me if you come back here. What's your name?"

Richard's stare was cold and hard. The unsettling quiet echoed throughout the room. Getting the message, the blond hustled quickly into the hallway, hesitated, then peeked through the cracked doorway. "My name is Steve." With that he closed the door firmly behind him.

Within minutes Richard began his own exit. Checking the room one last time for misplaced objects, he grabbed his bag from the bed, and his room key from the night stand. Satisfied that he was ready for his own departure, he shut the door behind him, and headed toward the lobby, whistling. His next stop, a cabin in Lake Tahoe.

Chapter 8

It was six in the morning, but still dark, when the wailing began. Nedra sat straight up as the sound filled the cabin. It was a familiar sound, and she knew its source. Opening the bedroom door quietly, she entered the living room and turned on the light. Sin lay thrashing wildly. The blanket that had been covering him, had fallen to the floor. His long, brown body, clad in black silk briefs, glistened with sweat. Carefully, she approached him, remembering the last time she had interrupted his nightmare.

"Sinclair." Her voice was low, soothing. His restlessness waned, a little, but the moaning continued. Taking a deep breath to fortify her courage, Nedra moved forward, easing onto the edge of the sofa bed. Gently, she reached out and touched his shoulder, shaking him. "Sincl—"

Before the words left her mouth, she found herself lying on top of him, struggling for breath as she fought against his vice-like grip. She tried to scream, but the sound was a strangled gurgle as Sin rose on his elbow, drawing her closer to his body.

Alert, but still groggy, Sin, instinctively slid his free hand under the pillow for the gun. Nedra's muffled screams stopped him.

"What the hell?" Shaking his head to release himself from the last vestiges of sleep, his manhood hardened as Nedra wiggled on top of him, the heat from her soft body invading his senses. Relaxing his grip, Sin rose to a sitting position, Nedra still in his arms.

"Let go of me, you idiot!" Incensed, Nedra pounded on his hard, chiseled chest, outraged at being manhandled, and embarrassed by the heat invading her own body as she lay pressed against his half naked body. Sin released her immediately. Struggling to her feet, Nedra's fought to control her rage.

"Just what do you think you're doing?" She looked at Sin as if she was ready to strike him at any moment.

"What in the hell do you think you're doing?" he countered. "You were the one I found in my bed!"

For a moment, Nedra faltered, the question catching her off guard. She forced herself to keep her eyes focused on his face. It wasn't easy. "I...I heard you, uh, moaning. Uh, you...you were having a nightmare."

The defiant look on Sin's face quickly faded, replaced by an expression of shock and surprise. The muscles in his face contracted as his dark eyes bored into hers. Wordlessly, he rose from the sofa bed, found his pants, and pulled them on.

Nedra tried not to watch his every movement, but her efforts failed as she stood mesmerized. His body was a work of art—long, muscled thighs and legs, slim hips, a small waist, flat stomach, and muscled chest and arms, all covered by wisps of shiny black hair. There was no doubt about it, Sinclair Reasoner was built! She felt cheated when he covered his chest with the shirt she had loaned him, but he did leave it open.

As he moved into the kitchen area and started heating water for tea, Nedra shook herself out of her reverie. She expected him to say something about what she had revealed to him, but he kept his back to her as he worked in the kitchen. As she watched him, she realized that he was embarrassed by what she'd told him. Quietly, she retreated to the bedroom.

Bathed and dressed, Nedra returned to the living room. The bed had been made, and the linen put away. The smell of bacon lured her into the room. A stack of pancakes perched on a plate sat at her empty spot at the table. Sin sat sipping a cup of tea, his own plate untouched. She realized that he was waiting to eat with her. Nedra slipped into her seat, closed her eyes, and bowed her head.

"Thank you, Lord, for this meal, for this day, and for all of your heavenly treasures." She opened one eye and peered at Sin, who sat, arms folded, watching her. She had noticed, but said nothing to the fact that he had not joined her in prayer at any of their meals together. She increased the volume of her blessing. "And, Lord, please don't bring your wrath down here on our heads because this man won't pray with me! Amen."

She dug into her pancakes as Sin, rocking with laughter, said, "Woman, you're something else!" Nedra winked in agreement, as she slid a mouth-watering pancake into her mouth.

They had finished shoveling the walkway, and were back in the cabin eating what they could scrape together for lunch, before she approached Sin about his nightmares. She watched him as he finished the last of his sandwich, then sat back in his chair, rubbing his full stomach with satisfaction. She didn't beat around the bush.

"Why do you have nightmares, Sinclair? This is the second time I've been around you when you've had a nightmare. What is it that disturbs your dreams?"

His body tensed as his eyes hardened. His voice was a harsh whisper. "I don't think that's any of your business."

Everything inside of him went cold. He had hoped that she would forget his nightmares. He was hoping that the memory would melt and go away, like the snow outside this cabin would eventually. Then they could both pretend that the dreams hadn't really happened. He could hide behind his humor, his attentiveness, and his growing feelings for her, and she would never know his weakness.

Why did it have to happen here? Why did it have to happen now? He wanted her to admire his strength, not see his weakness. He had envisioned himself as Sir Lancelot coming to the rescue of the damsel in distress, even if she didn't know she was in distress.

Sin

The last few days with her had been more than he could have ever imagined. He had discovered that there was more to her than he could have guessed. Not only was she pretty, smart, and caring, but she was funny, insightful, intuitive. She was everything that any man could ever want. Everything he wanted, and his feelings for her had intensified far beyond the boyhood crush he had harbored so long. He wouldn't let her see him vulnerable, see him wanting, see him needing to share the pain he never shared with anyone before.

Abruptly, Sin began to clear the table and took the dishes to the sink. For the second time that day, he turned his back with all intentions of shutting her out, again, except, this time he couldn't.

Nedra saw it in the way his body shifted as he ran the water in the sink, added the dishwashing liquid, and began to wash the dishes. The defensive stance which he had taken, slowly became compliant, and she knew he was ready to talk. Whatever it was that had him screaming in the night was about to be revealed. She was ready to listen.

Picking up the empty glasses off the table, she followed him into the tiny kitchen area and placed them in the soapy water. She dried while he washed, neither of them speaking as she watched him and waited.

When the dishes had been put away, Nedra returned to her seat at the kitchen table. Sin leaned against the sink, arms folded across his chest, and faced Nedra. Closing his eyes, he took a deep breath, then opened his eyes, slowly, looking past her for a moment, before focusing on her face. Nedra's heart constricted at the sadness in his eyes.

"My past is something that's very hard to talk about, Nedra. It was another world, one that's hard to forget. One I really don't want to remember, and one I'm not sure you could even understand."

"Try me."

Running his hand over the sculptured waves in his closely cropped hair, he massaged his neck, then took another deep breath. "I've never told anyone this before."

He stopped, trying to force the words he was about to say back into that place within his subconscious where they had nestled comfortably for so long, but they had forced themselves to the forefront now and insisted on breaking free. He started again.

"I was a gang member." He watched her expression, expecting to see revulsion. It was blank. He continued. "Kids can be so stupid. I guess it comes with youth. It did with mine. It seems the members of the gang spent most of our valuable young lives posturing, defending our manhood, fighting over city streets that didn't belong to us anyway. But, it was all so important then. The streets and the gang were all I knew. I pledged my love, my loyalty and my life to my gang, and I meant every word."

Jamming his hands into his pockets, he began to pace as he spoke. "I told you a little about my mother when we spoke at the church that time. Like I said, she was only twenty-five when she died. I guess she did the best she could to show me that she cared about me, but it really wasn't much. Then, when the system proved that it didn't care about me at all, the gang showed me that they did. At least that's what I thought at the time. I joined when I was ten, and that gang was the closest thing to a family that I had. The boys in the gang were my friends, my brothers. The older boys were like uncles, fathers. We grew up together."

Sin stopped pacing and joined Nedra at the table. She sat looking at him intently, her hands clasped on the table in front of her. He fought the urge to take those hands in his and caress them. "I did things that I'm not proud of in those days. Things that weren't legal, things that hurt people, and I'd rather not talk about them."

Her voice was gentle, encouraging. "You don't have to."

Sin gave a half smile. He could tell that she was in her counselor mode. Good, he needed it. "Maybe some day I can talk about it."

"Maybe."

"If you know anything at all about gangs, you know that they have turf wars, and, unfortunately, when I was sixteen, my gang was involved in a vicious turf war. People were landing in the hospital daily. Eventually, the inevitable happened, some gang members on both sides ended up in the morgue."

Sin's eyes strayed past Nedra, out the window to gaze at the snow-covered trees and the beauty of nature that lay far beyond the concrete jungle in his nightmares. His voice sounded far away as he continued. "A rival gang killed one of our boys and gouged his eyes out."

Nedra cringed. Sin didn't notice her reaction.

"We sought our revenge. Guns in hand, the plan was to surprise about a half dozen of them and draw some blood. We didn't know they'd been warned and were waiting for us." Sin ran his hands over his face, as if to wipe away the memory of what he was about to reveal. "When the gun fire cleared, five of my gang brothers were dead. There had been six of us."

Sin returned to the comfort of the cozy cabin, and the warmth of the hand that had reached across the table and now lay on top of his. He succumbed to his earlier urge and took her hand in his much larger one, stroking it gently with his thumb. It was smooth, soft, velvety in texture, the long oval nails perfectly manicured, painted with clear polish. These hands had never been washed in blood. His had.

Sin

He closed his eyes once again trying to shut out the sight which had become his nightmare. His voice was barely audible as he fought the emotion welling up inside of him. "It was so quiet when I came to. I'll never forget the silence. I don't know why I lived. All I had was a scratch above my temple where a bullet grazed me and knocked me unconscious. It was a miracle. That's the only thing I can figure."

Swallowing the lump that had worked its way into his throat, he opened his eyes and gave Nedra a forced smile. "I guess that man upstairs you believe in so strongly had another plan for me."

Nedra acknowledged his words with a nod, her silence urging him to continue.

He sighed. "Anyway, I walked through the blood, through the carnage, all the way to the bus station. I caught the first bus out." Sin let her hand slip out of his. "I can still see the tracks that my sneakers left as I walked away. They were red."

Sin fell back in his chair, the power of that memory draining him. He was unable to continue. Nedra's heart constricted at the mask of pain that covered his chiseled features.

She knew that she should not have moved from her chair at that moment. Why she did move she could not explain, or rather, didn't want to explain, to herself, or, later, to others. She told herself that she was reacting to a human being who was hurting, and she had always been sensitive to anyone in pain. That's what she told herself.

She made the move, toward him, slowly, deliberately, until she was hankered down before him, taking the hands that fell loosely between his legs, into her own hands, rubbing their rough texture against the softness of her cheeks. His dark eyes lifted to look at her. Their eyes locked for a moment. Each waited for the other to deny that truth. Neither of them did. So, with all denials abandoned as lies, they let truth emerge as their lips met in a frenzy of suppressed passion.

The going had been slow, the roads were slick and dangerous, but Richard had made it, and he smiled as he pulled into the dark driveway leading up to the cabin in which Nedra was staying. He knew she would be shocked to see him, but she would hide it—she was good at hiding her emotions—and welcome him with the courtesy she always displayed. He liked that about her too. She was a lady.

From the moment he saw her, ten years ago, he had known that she would eventually be his. His sister brought her home for their mother's birthday. He approached her at the party and discovered quickly that she was unlike the other women he was used to dealing with, crude. He adjusted his approach, but she continued to reject him politely. What a turn on! He had watched her patiently as the years passed, waiting for the right time to approach her again. Yes, she would be his, and he knew that she would be worth waiting for.

As he got out of the car, Richard noted how carefully the driveway and walkway had been shoveled. It must have taken her awhile to clear that much snow by herself. Perhaps one of the neighbors helped her. He also noticed that her car wasn't in the driveway, but there was a garage about twenty feet from the house. She might have parked in there. He observed the cabin. There were no lights on. He hadn't paid attention to whether there had been tire tracks in the snow of the cleared driveway, and without the car lights it was too dark to see if there were any other than his own. Maybe she was asleep, but he doubted it. It was barely six in the evening.

He was disappointed when there was no answer to his knock. She could be asleep. He retrieved the spare key from its hiding place. Gingerly, he slipped the key into the lock, responded to the instant click, and stepped inside the cabin.

Chapter 9

She wasn't there! Richard couldn't believe it, but, she wasn't there! His survey of the darkened cabin revealed an empty closet, and a raised toilet seat. A trip to the garage revealed two sets of footprints in the snow, one small and the other larger, much larger. Both led to an empty spot where Nedra's car used to be.

At first he panicked. Had someone broken into the cabin and hurt Nedra? Frantic, he returned to the cabin to search for any clue that something had happened to her, but everything was in perfect order. As a matter of fact, the cabin was a little too clean, as if it had never been occupied. His suspicion grew. A search through the trash can revealed the evidence he hadn't wanted to find. The cabin had been occupied, by two people—two people who had shared meals, and for quite some time. His night was a sleepless one teeming with jealous rage. It was a rage that only increased as the morning sunrise revealed a lopsided snowman, and two angels in the snow-filled yard outside the cabin.

Two angels! The words echoed through his head all the way back to Oakland. Now, as he sat in Sharon's apartment waiting for her return, the sound of the door shutting alerted him that Sharon had arrived. Two angels! Who was the second one? He was determined to find out.

As Sharon breezed into the living room she started in surprise, at the sight of him. The look of surprise quickly turned into one of pleasure as she dropped her overnight bag from her shoulder and rushed over to the sofa where he lay, relaxing. In one swift move, she darted into his arms, covering his face with kisses.

"Hey, baby! I didn't know you were here?"

Richard accepted her affection with the expected kisses and caresses, until he felt her stiffen. Tearing her mouth away from his deepening kiss, she drew back and looked searchingly into his eyes. Her own eyes narrowed suspiciously. "Richard! You're high! How could you?" She got up from his lap and stood before him, her hands resting on her slender hips, ready to rail against his ever increasing use of drugs.

Richard's eyes left her accusing ones to roam briefly down her short, shapely frame. Damn! She was fine! But, she wasn't... Ignoring her accusing glare, he sat up calmly and, casually stretched his arms across the back of the sofa. He made sure that his voice was steady, the exact opposite of what he was feeling. "How was your conference?" She had been to Bakersfield for a three-day social work conference.

"Damn the conference! When did you get back from Truckee? You've been to East Oakland buying coke, I can tell! I told you if you keep using that stuff...! " Her voice had risen in anger. She wasn't ready to be sweet-talked today.

Richard maintained his conciliatory tone as he ignored her veiled threat. "I got back yesterday. I spent a night up in Tahoe." He knew that would get her attention.

"Tahoe?" She echoed. "Nedra is in Tahoe."

He would have laughed at the fear in her eyes, but he couldn't. He needed her or rather, the information she might be able to give him. With satisfaction, he turned the screw a little tighter. "Yes, I stayed at the cabin overnight."

The color drained from Sharon's face. Her voice was barely a whisper. "You stayed at the cabin? In the same cabin with Nedra? Why? Why did you go to Tahoe?"

It took everything for him to keep from laughing at the pitiful specimen before him. That defiance she had shown him so confidently a moment ago, had faded completely. He knew it would! All of that beauty, and she was so weak. So damn insecure! She stood before him now, shoulders slumped, hands at her sides, looking as if she was about to cry. She'd better not. He was tired of her tears. He'd let her stew for a while.

Getting up from the sofa, he walked across the room and picked up the TV remote. Turning on the large screen TV he could feel her eyes following him as he returned to the sofa, sat down, and crossed his ankles, placing his feet on the glass coffee table. Sharon hated when he did that.

Sharon looked at the man before her, this beautiful, sexy man. God, did she love him. He was far from perfect, but he was hers. Other women wanted him, would do anything to get him, but she had won in the end. She had chased him relentlessly, gone against the advice of her best friends, his own sister, to get him. He was hers and she planned on keeping him, anyway she could. Nobody would take him from her. Nobody!

"I asked you a question, Richard? Did you stay in the cabin with Nedra?" He couldn't have! He just couldn't have!

Richard looked past her at the TV screen as he replied. "Now what would make you even suggest that St. Nedra would ever allow herself to stay overnight with a man?"

His voice was hard, cold. Sharon had never heard him utter Nedra's name in that tone before. That was one of their problems, Nedra, but he was right about her. Despite everything she suspected about Richard's attraction to Nedra, she also knew that she could trust her friend. Yet, there was that little seed of doubt, and it was that seed that took the fight out of her now.

Richard glanced at Sharon as she picked up her overnight bag and moved toward the bedroom. He had successfully gotten her off his sojourn to East Oakland, but he still didn't have the information he needed about Nedra. He might as well put her out of her misery.

"Carla asked me to check on her because of the snow storm, but Nedra wasn't at the cabin. Her clothes were gone."

Sharon stopped before reaching the bedroom door and turned to Richard. "Not there? What do you mean, not there? Where is she?"

Richard shrugged, pretending disinterest as he kept his eyes fixed on the TV screen. He was hoping that she could answer that question. Yes, where was St. Nedra? She wasn't at home. That was for sure.

Dropping her bag once again, Sharon hurried to the telephone and dialed. "Has Carla heard from her?"

"I don't know. Carla flew to L.A. with Jacob the day she called me. She's left messages. I left her one, but we keep missing each other."

Getting no answer at Nedra's house, she hung up in frustration. "You've called Nedra's house, I assume?"

Richard nodded as Sharon turned on the answering machine. Two messages later, Nedra's voice filled the room.

"Hey, Sharon. Girl, I am out of Tahoe and all that snow. You know how I am when it comes to snow. I'm heading for the Monterey Peninsula where there's sea and plenty of sunshine. I'm spending the rest of my vacation there. I left a message with Carla too. I'll get back in touch with you about the particulars, but I'm O.K.. Love you."

The message ended.

"Well, that answers that question." Sharon's voice was light with relief as both of her questions were answered. Picking up her bag, she headed toward her bedroom for the second time as she muttered, half aloud. "Wonder why she picked the Peninsula?' Richard's jaws tightened, his breathing accelerating in anger. He stared, unseeing, at the TV screen. Sharon was no help. Useless as usual! He had heard the machine message, and he knew why St. Nedra went to the Peninsula. The question still remaining was with whom.

How had it happened? Nedra had been caught unaware, unprotected, shed of the armor she normally wore against men. When she wasn't looking, one man had pierced her armor. Now she was vulnerable.

How could one kiss send her common sense spinning out of control? How could a few caresses have her walking around in a fog over a man who was practically a stranger? What had she been thinking? There was no way that she could allow herself this indulgence! The devil was working overtime, and, unfortunately, she wasn't putting up much of a fight. She had to reverse this course of events.

Falling to her knees, Nedra clasped her hands in prayer, ready to prepare for battle. There was no way that the devil would win. "Lord, help me! Show me the light. Show me the way."

She needed to be shown the way, because, right now, she was lost. She had been lost from the moment Sinclair's lips touched her lips. From that point on, self-control had become tenuous—the self-control she had worked her entire adult life to maintain.

Nedra had melted in Sinclair's arms as what had started as a chaste kiss turned fiery with passion. Sin left no doubt that he wanted her, badly, but it had been her own reaction that had frightened her most. She was no virgin, a college love affair had put an end to that; but, in all of her experience, in her most ardent of fantasies, the depth of emotion she had offered to Sin Reasoner in that one kiss had shocked her. She had withdrawn from him, backed away, retreated to the security of the wall behind her, wide-eyed with wonder. He had apologized for his actions. She had rejected his apology, instead offering one of her own. It shouldn't have happened, she told him. Perhaps they had been caught up in the moment. He agreed. Yet, here she was, twenty-four hours later, in his beach house on the Monterey Peninsula. She was, indeed, dancing with the devil!

They hadn't discussed their errant emotions. That was a mistake, and they both knew it, because every movement they made from the moment they drew apart was propelled by the sexual tension between them.

Sin

Determined to escape any opportunity to allow her lack of self- control to be tested further, Nedra had packed her bags, locked up the cabin and climbed into her car, headed for Oakland. Sin objected strongly, declaring that it was too dangerous for her to drive back to Oakland along the snow-slick highway, alone. He declared her intentions foolish, sparking a squabble between them. Nedra was going to Oakland, and that was that!

With Sin beside her, a determined Nedra drove carefully along the road leading to his hotel. Her intention had been to deliver him there, then head home. The drive to the hotel was subdued, until they arrived. It quickly became noisy as Sin reached across Nedra, turned the car off and took the keys from the ignition, slipping them into his pants pocket. Nedra was incensed and did not hesitate to let him know exactly how she felt.

Calmly, Sin listened to her rant and rave about him being a bully, and her being able to take care of herself, but he continued to hold on to the key. Eventually, she ran out of steam.

Looking at her steadily, he quietly told her, "You are not driving back to Oakland alone. I'll leave my car here, make arrangements to have it delivered to my home, and I'm driving back with you." With that said, he had climbed out of the car and waited for her to follow him. She did.

Nedra got off her knees hopeful that her prayers would be answered. Yesterday she had been at Lake Tahoe determined to go back to Oakland. So, how had she ended up here, in his sumptuous beach house today? She groaned. Lord, she had been so easy to convince. She'd been putty in his hands. She slapped her forehead in self-disgust.

They had been driving in silence through Sacramento when he brought up the subject of continuing her vacation. She had seven days left. Why spend them at home where she would get no rest once her parishioners discovered she was back? He had a beach house she could borrow, no strings attached. He'd drive her straight there, right now. There was no need to stop in Oakland.

She had tried to resist, still angry at him for his strong-arm tactics in Tahoe. No! She didn't want to borrow his beach house. And no strings attached? Ha! She must look like a fool; but, he kept talking.

He would be returning to work, and she would have the house all to herself. Didn't she deserve some time to herself? What good would she do her congregation if she returned from her so called vacation worse off than when she left? Why look a gift horse in the mouth just to be spiteful? She had softened. He had a point.

She loved the ocean. She would take water over snow any day. She had used the snow as her excuse to leave Tahoe. But, what about her friends? They wouldn't know where she was. He was ready for that one. He whipped out a cell phone from his jacket pocket and told her to call Carla and Sharon, noting that he had the telephone at the beach house removed. Funny, but he hadn't mentioned having a cell phone the entire time that they had been snowed in at Tahoe! Despite her initial objections, she relented. Carla wasn't home, neither was Sharon, but she did leave messages for both, saying where she was going, but not with whom. Oh, yes! She had been so very easy.

They drove straight to the Peninsula, where he dropped her off at the beach house, left his cell phone in case of an emergency, and left. She wasn't sure how he got back to Oakland, since he drove her car to the Peninsula and left it with her. He simply got into a cab and disappeared.

Oh, well, why dwell on yesterday. It was time to enjoy today. She had spent most of the day exploring and relaxing in the luxury Sin had modestly described as "a cozy little beach house"— all seven rooms, including a hot tub and a Jacuzzi. It was now time to enjoy the nearby beach. Grabbing her jacket, Nedra headed out the door.

Walking along the ocean shore, she reveled in the sound of the waves caressing the rugged rock formations, the calls of the seagulls, and the beauty of the scarlet sunset. The scenery filled her with a serenity that only the ocean could bring, and to her surprise, it also filled her with sadness as she realized that she had no one with whom to share the beauty around her. She missed that.

In Tahoe, she had shared that beauty with Sin. Or rather, he had shared it with her.

She hated snow, and told him so vehemently. If she had any inkling that an early snowfall would blanket Tahoe, there would have been no way that she would have gone there. He had listened with a knowing smile, then proceeded to show her how to enjoy the wonders of a snowfall. They had built a snowman, had snowball fights, and, of course, there were the angels in the snow. One evening he had even coaxed her outside at night to marvel at the sight of the moon reflecting on the snow's perfection. He called the twinkling results, snow diamonds. She had been touched, and surprised, by his observation, and his sensitivity. It seemed that Sinclair Reasoner had many sides to his personality, she missed them all.

The thought brought Nedra to a dead stop as the realization hit her like a torpedo. She did miss him. She missed his laughter, his sense of humor, even his devilish teasing.

Oh, Lord! This couldn't happen! She had to get that man out of her mind. He was not the man for her! He was too pushy, too bossy, too flashy!

Pulling her lightweight jacket snugly around her, she retraced her steps to the house and shut the door behind her, locking it securely, as if she could lock out the thoughts of Sin.

Sin

She found that she couldn't, as she jolted awake in the middle of the night, from a dream so erotic that she blushed at the thought of it. Springing out of the oversized bed, she made her way through the house, into the kitchen, muttering to herself about the excessive life style of her host.

The beach house he had loaned her was an L-shaped structure of stone and glass with three bedrooms, including the master bedroom suite in which she slept. The bedroom provided an ocean view. There were seven rooms in all. Each comfortable in size. As a matter of fact, the living room and the three bedrooms alone comprised the square footage of her entire condo. Why one man would need so much room was beyond her. Yes, he was flashy! Not her type at all.

Warming some milk, she flopped down on a stool at the kitchen counter, feeling guilty about her criticism of him. After all, she did accept his invitation to stay here. She knew this was no "cozy little beach house" the moment they drove up. Why berate the man for being generous. She could have refused his offer up to the last minute. She hadn't.

Nedra sighed, poured the warm milk into a cup, and headed back to the bedroom. She had never been the kind of minister to tell her flock that abundance was harmful to the soul. No, she always believed that one should rejoice in God's abundance, the sin was in not sharing what one had. Sinclair was definitely sharing his. No argument there.

She crawled into bed and clicked on the TV. The cell phone rang. Nedra's heart went to her throat. It rang a second time, then stopped. She glanced at the phone resting on the night stand beside her. She could hardly breathe. If the cell phone rang again, that meant that it could only be one person. She hadn't left the number with her friends, and Sin had worked out a pattern of rings for her to know it was him calling. If there was a third ring after the pause, she was to answer the call. The phone rang a third time.

"Hello, Nedra."

She didn't want to smile when she heard his voice, but she did. "Yes?"

"I just wanted to check on you. Is everything okay?"

She wanted to retort flippantly, but she didn't. "Fine."

"You bought the groceries and stocked the refrigerator?"

"Yes."

"Good."

She sensed that he wanted to say more. She waited, breathless. There was so much more he could say, so much more she could say. Neither did.

Finally he said, "I know it's late, so I'll just say goodnight."

"Goodnight."

Sin

The line went dead. That was it, and that was as it should be. Draining her cup, Nedra turned off the TV and snuggled down between the covers. She had no time for entanglements of any kind. She had too much work to do. With another quick prayer for the evening, she closed her eyes and waited for sleep to come once again, quickly this time and, hopefully, without dreams.

Sin

The line went dead. That was it, and that was as it should be. Draining her cup, Nedra turned off the TV and snuggled down between the covers. She had no time for entanglements of any kind. She had too much work to do. With another quick prayer for the evening, she closed her eyes and waited for sleep to come once again, quickly this time and, hopefully, without dreams.

123

Chapter 10

Lynn Trellis all but drooled as she watched Sinclair Reasoner walk across the restaurant toward his table. He was, undoubtedly, the sexiest man she knew. His tall, muscular body was clad in a double-breasted black wool suit that fit him like a glove. He moved across the room like a leopard, slow, sleek, majestic. What a man!

Eddie kept telling her that Sin was too old for her, but she knew that, secretly, he was rooting for her. Her brother would be delighted if he and Sin ended up being brothers-in-law, and that was her plan. She wanted him, badly.

She knew everything about him. They had him thoroughly investigated before doing business with him. After all, in their line of work it didn't pay to take chances. She knew that he had no family, and he was very much a loner. He was raised on the streets of Harlem where he earned a long rap sheet as a teenager, and, as a teen, he had left New York City for parts unknown. Where he went was a mystery, but by the age of twenty he ended up in the army, where he wasn't very ambitious. He started out a private and was discharged a private. After his discharge, he enrolled in college at Tuskeege, in Alabama. There he earned a bachelors degree in Economics. At NYU, he earned a masters degree, again in Economics. Less than a decade ago he had started his import/export business in New York, and it was successful. He opened his California branch less than two years ago, and all of their contacts said that he could be trusted. They just never said how fine he was. She found that out herself when she met him. Oh yes, she wanted him, and he was going to be hers.

She sighed wistfully, feeling like a giddy teenager, as she beckoned the waiter over to her table, handed him a note and directed him to take it to Sin. She waited breathlessly as the waiter delivered the note, and nodded toward her table. She threw Sin a hundred watt smile, knowing by his look that he was disturbed by her acknowledging him in public. Their deal was that they keep their acquaintance as low key as possible. He was fanatic about keeping a low profile. No matter, she simply wanted him to know she was there.

At first, he seemed hesitant even to acknowledge her existence. Then he nodded, crumpled the note, and turned his attention to giving the waitress his order. Lynn noted with satisfaction the number of female eyes that strayed to his table. Well, they could look all they wanted, because only she would be touching, and when she got the opportunity to do so, she wouldn't miss an inch of that delicious body.

At his table, Sin's mind was far away from the annoying Lynn Trellis, or the cozy little out of the way restaurant in which he had chosen to eat lunch. Rather, he was day-dreaming of a beach house by the ocean, two hours away.

He wondered what Nedra was doing. It had been two days since he'd seen her. It seemed like forever. After hearing her voice, he had held the phone for a moment against his face, closed his eyes, and visualized every inch of her face. His feelings toward her had always perched on a precarious edge, threatening to explode completely out of control, even before they kissed. After the kiss, it had taken all of the strength he possessed to keep his emotions from running amuck.

He wasn't surprised when she gave the abundance of snow as an excuse to escape his presence. He knew that she wasn't ready to face the feelings she had for him, and she did have feelings for him. One kiss had revealed that. His heart had soared at the thought that she cared for him, but sunk at the thought of her returning to Oakland where it might be unsafe. Thank goodness it had worked out.

He had been surprised when she agreed to accept his offer of the beach house, but he was glad she did accept it. His only alternative would have been kidnapping her and making her go with him. He doubted if that would have worked. Nedra Davis was not a woman who could be eas-ily forced to do anything.

The hours they had spent together traveling from Tahoe to Pacific Grove had been torturous. Even their arguments had been filled with the sexual tension between them. It was imperative that they part.

Yet, what good had it done him. He'd taken a charter flight home, made some calls to get a handle on just how much danger she was still in, then spent the rest of the hours away from her thinking about her, and the time they had spent together. His midnight call to her had been spontaneous, because he couldn't get her out of his mind.

He was in love with her. There was no doubt about it. Other than his mother, he had never loved anyone before. The feeling was so foreign. Was love an emotion that would make one willing to die for someone? He was willing.

As for now, he had to regain control of his emotions, and this time away from her would give him that opportunity. He had to get a grip on himself, regain his self-control. Her life might depend on it, and so might his.

Discreet inquiries had informed him that the contract was still out on Nedra. Yet, the authorities hadn't taken his warning seriously. No crime had been attempted, no crime had been committed. There was nothing that could be done until an attempt had been made.

He had a decision to make. Nedra would be back in town in less than a week. The only chance of saving her life might be his telling her about the danger she was in. It was only fair that she knew, without that knowledge she could be a sitting duck.

She would have questions, he knew that. He would answer them the best he could without divulging too much about himself or his contacts. Despite everything, he wanted her to think well of him. He didn't want her to know about the shadows in his life. He'd already told her too much with his confession about his life as a gang member. The less she knew about him the better; but, to save her life he'd do what he had to do. Her life meant more to him than his own.

Having finished his lunch and made his decision about what he must do, Sin left the restaurant, not acknowledging Lynn as he did so. He could feel her eyes on him as he opened the heavy cut-glass door. A man was coming into the restaurant. They collided, and Sin offered an apology. The man nodded his acceptance and moved swiftly past him.

Sin looked at the retreating figure. The man looked familiar. He had seen him somewhere before. Unable to recall where, he proceeded out the door to his car.

Inside, Lynn choked on bitter disappointment that Sin hadn't acknowledged her. Looking up at the man who had bumped into Sin her mood turned sour as he took a seat at her table.

"It took you long enough to get here,' she snapped, glaring at him with hostility. "I don't like being kept waiting! Even by the great Richard Ryan."

Sin

Nedra leaned against the glass telephone booth listening to her mother on the other end. She hadn't spoken to Marva Davis in some time and she had missed the sound of her voice. Hiking down to Asilomar, the sprawling conference center located less than a half a mile from the beach house, she had used a pay phone there to call her.

Mother and daughter were close, and had been since Nedra was born. Marva had been only nineteen then, full of hope for the future with her new baby and her twenty-year-old husband. Her hopes for a bright future had been crushed the very night of Nedra's birth when her excited husband, returning home from the hospital, crossed the street between two parked cars and was killed instantly. The hit and run driver was never caught. Marva left the hospital with her newborn daughter, filled with anger and bitterness at what fate had dealt her.

She had lived with those emotions for the next three years. She was angry with everyone, especially with God for taking her husband. Putting all of her energy into raising her daughter, she disregarded everyone except her child, smothering the young girl with all of the love she could no longer offer to anyone else. Then, one day, her life changed forever.

Nedra had heard the story often. Marva was standing at the bus stop, heading home from her job as a secretary in a law firm in the black section of Kansas City. The bus stop where she stood, everyday, was located in front of a church. Each day she could hear the exuberant church service, but usually she ignored it. Yet on this particular day there was something different coming from the church's open doorway. A woman minister was preaching, and it was the sound of her voice that drew Marva inside. She was just curious, she'd explain later, but God had a different plan. Marva was saved that very day. She had enrolled in a seminary, and after earning her degree, Marva had returned to pastor the congregation of the Star Shine Baptist Church, where she had been saved. She had been their pastor for over two decades.

Her mother was a legend in Kansas City. Everything Nedra was today she owed to Marva Davis. She was not only her mother, but her mentor, her friend, and her confidante. The only problem was, she regretted having confided in her at this moment. She had mentioned that she was staying in Sin's beach house, and the interrogation was on.

"You say he's in the import business?" Nedra could almost see her mother's forehead wrinkle in an expression of concern. "How long have you known this man?"

"Oh, I met him about six months ago at the church." No need to elaborate on the circumstances. "At the church" should stop the questioning. She was wrong.

Sin

"He's one of your church members?" Marva's voice rose slightly in forthcoming disapproval.

Nedra was annoyed. She wanted to lie to her mother. It would be easier, but she'd never done so before. "No, Mama, he's not a church member. He's a friend of some of my parishioners, and he loaned me his house for my vacation. I told you, I couldn't take the snow in Tahoe. So, he was nice enough to extend this kindness."

"Uh huh." Marva sounded skeptical.

Nedra listened patiently as Marva reminded her how she had raised her only child to be a "good girl", and she had faith that Nedra would use her head about this man, not her hormones. She then recounted, meticulously, for the umpteenth time, how careful Nedra had to be as a woman minister. "There must not be even a hint of impropriety, daughter. A woman minister has a harder road to travel than a man. Always remember that!"

How could she forget it? She heard it every time she spoke to Marva. She truly believed that Marva had convinced herself that her thirty-eight-year-old daughter was still a virgin.

Nedra sighed. Let her live in her dream world. "I will, Mama. I've got to go now."

"Go where?" Nedra could hear the note of suspicion in her voice. "Are you going to be with that man?"

Nedra's temper flared. "No, Mama! What would make you say something like that? I told you, he's not even down here! How could you even think something like that!"

"Listen here child, you might be able to fool yourself, but this is your Mama. I heard how you said his name."

Nedra looked at the telephone as if it had spouted the insanity. "What in the world are you talking about? How I said his name? I haven't even told you his name!"

"I said it and I meant it. You might not want to admit it, but something's going on with you and him, and I'm telling you to be careful. You can fool yourself, but you can't fool the Lord. Just remember, evil thoughts, evil ways. I ain't got nothing else to say. Remember that I love you and so does God." With that, Marva ended their conversation.

Angrily, Nedra exited the telephone booth and stalked out of the lodge headed back toward the beach house. What in the world was wrong with her mother? She was only fifty-seven, did senility set in that young? How could she even think that there was anything between her and Sinclair Reasoner? All she had done was mention that a man had loaned her his beach house, and her own mother had her all but sleeping with him! Well, that was the last time she would tell her anything She was going to call Carla and see how things were going, but forget that. She wasn't calling anybody. If her own mother had her practically sleeping with the man, God knows what filth would be on Carla's mind if she mentioned whose home she was staying in. Forget all of them! Deciding to walk off her anger, Nedra made a sudden detour, crossed the street, and headed toward the beach, unaware of the tall, dark figure standing in the front yard of the beach house watching her every movement.

The beach was all but deserted, despite the fact that it was Friday, and the weekend crowd had been spilling into the picturesque area since early afternoon. Walking the beach had always been good therapy. Whenever she had the opportunity, she sought out the comfort of the waves lapping lazily against the shore. She'd sit for hours watching the changing tide, content with the peace mother nature could bring. Once more, she found herself sitting on what had become her favorite bench, overlooking the ocean. And as usual, the ocean was working its magic.

It wasn't often that her mother upset her, and as she calmed, she had to ask herself why she had allowed it to happen this time. Had her mother hit too close to home? Had a truth been uttered that she wasn't ready to face, a truth about Sinclair, and her feelings for him? Had they become so strong that her own mother could heard it in her voice?

It had been four days since they had parted, and each night he had called just to check on her and to say goodnight. Her heart fluttered with each phone call. After each call she would find herself lying in bed thinking about him. Last night she found herself wondering if he slept in pajamas or in the nude. Evil thoughts, evil ways. Her mother's words echoed through her head. Yet, even now, a smile tugged at the corners of her mouth at the thought of his long, muscular body stretched across the sheets of her bed.

"I hope that smile is for me?"

Nedra turned to look into the dark, shining eyes peering down at her. She smiled, and he returned her smile. His presence didn't surprise her. She had known in her heart that, eventually, he would come. She had been waiting.

Chapter 11

There were a few preliminaries to the inevitable. Nedra and Sin sat on the bench in silence until the sun set behind the horizon, then, hand in hand they strolled back to the house, each of them mentally recounting the many reasons why they should not be together.

She berated herself silently for the briefness of her moral dilemma. Could years of self control, years of moral fortitude, years of self denial be so easily dismissed? Who was this man whose voice made her pulse race at the speed of light? How could one touch from his hand make her ready, and willing, to desert the sexual morals she had been practicing for so long. Marriage should proceed fornication. That was what she had been told all of her life, although she hadn't always listened. Love should precede marriage. It was a fact in which she firmly believed. Had she fallen in love?

At the house she fixed two cups of herbal tea, and they sat in the kitchen talking. It was reminiscent of their time in Tahoe, and they looked at each other over their cup and smiled, both savoring the memory . Each of them knew, even then, that this time was coming, that as much as they avoided it, they kept moving toward the edge of a deep crevice and, eventually, they would fall. The question to be answered was would they survive the fall?

Sin lowered his cup, and placed it on the table, stirring the steaming brew meticulously. Nedra knew that he was stalling for time. He had something on his mind, something important, and whatever it was that he was going to say would change their lives. So she waited, quietly, her heart thumping wildly, while praying silently that God would give her the strength to endure whatever was coming. Sin didn't keep her waiting.

He looked up from the cup straight into her eyes, "I love you, Nedra. I've loved you for a long time, and I'd die before I would hurt you."

The breath Nedra tried to take stuck in her throat. She wasn't sure that she had heard him correctly. He loved her? How could he love her? He hardly knew her. How was it possible for him to love her or for her to love him in such a short time? Nedra stared at him, hardly able to breathe.

"Listen, Sinclair, just because we might... Well, you don't have to say..."

"I love you, Nedra," he repeated emphasizing each word. "And I know I don't have to say anything." He scooted forward in his chair, his face only inches from her face. "I'm not asking you to feel the same way about me. There's so little that you know about me, and so much you need to know, but I can't share. Yet I want to be honest with you, as honest as I can be. It wouldn't be in your best interest to get involved with me. There are things that I've done that I'm not proud of and..."

Nedra's finger against his lips stopped the flow of words, and for a moment they sat motionless, silent. Finding her voice, Nedra broke the silence. "You don't have to say any more. I go by my feelings, my gut feelings and my intuition, and there's one thing that those feelings have told me about you from the very beginning. You're a kind man, a gentle man, a good man, and that's all I need to know."

His face etched with concern, Sin took her hand into his. "But you're a minister, you have a career to think of. I've got to take that into consideration before I even think about..."

"I'm a grown woman, Sin, who takes responsibility for her actions. If there are consequences for my loving you, then so be it."

Sin was as stunned by her words as Nedra had been by his. For loving you, she had said. She loved him too?

He swallowed. His mouth was suddenly dry. "Did you say...?"

"Yes, I did."

He hesitated for only a moment as he went to her, all doubt temporarily forgotten. In one swift movement, he captured her tantalizing lips and they were as sweet as he knew they would be. Running his tongue along the inner contours of her mouth, he lingered to enjoy the taste of her before thrusting his tongue deeper into the recess of her mouth.

Nedra responded willingly, eagerly as their tongues danced in sensual union. The heat of desire eroded resistance and dispensed reasoning as Sin left a fiery trail of kisses down her throat. All thoughts of how short the time had been since she had known him became quiet echoes as his mouth covered a hardened nipple through her blouse. And as his lips continued to pay homage to her heated flesh even the echoes began to fade. She wanted him. She had wanted him yesterday. Wanted him last week. Wanted him from the first day he walked into her office.

Boldly, she thrust her tongue into his mouth, languishing in the corners, savoring his taste, his touch, savoring the feel of his erection against her body. Her moan of pleasure filled the room.

"Nedra," Sin gasped, fighting a useless battle for tenuous control. Yet, he broke contact. Weak, shaken, he rested his forehead against hers struggling to breathe. Finally, finding the strength to draw away from her he rested his hands on her shoulders, and stared into her eyes.

"Listen to me carefully. There hasn't been a day, a minute, that I haven't wanted you. But I want to know that you're absolutely sure about everything that happens between us tonight. If you have any doubts, let me know." He cupped her face, tenderly. "This is a big step for both of us and it could be a major mistake for you. You've got to understand that I don't want a one night stand. With you, I want much more. So, be sure."

Nedra swallowed her uncertainty. "I'm sure. Are you?"

Sin blinked, caught off guard by the question. Was he sure? Was he sure that the sun was a source of heat? That electricity was a source of light? That he loved and wanted this woman had been the only sure thing in his life.

He kissed her brow. No more words were needed. Nedra took him by the hand and led him into the bedroom.

It was late evening, and the sun had set leaving a large, full moon, whose rays filtered through the vertical blinds covering the windows. The light silhouetted them both as Nedra helped Sin out of his shirt and watched him as he stepped out of his jeans, socks, and sneakers. When his black bikini briefs followed, she held her breath, exhaling slowly as her eyes moved gingerly upward from his swollen shaft to his firm, flat stomach, hairy chest, and well defined biceps. He was magnificent.

He whispered. "Now you."

He unbuttoned her blouse and peeled it slowly from her body. It floated to the floor. Her jeans soon followed. With each deliberate act of removal, he replaced the discarded item with a kiss, until she was completely undressed. Then, starting from the inside of her thighs he licked his way back to her breasts, where each hardened nipple received his complete devotion.

Nedra collapsed against him, her rubbery legs unable to hold her any longer. Cradling her in his arms, he lifted her and placed her on the bed. Then, opening one of the cellophane packages he had placed on the night stand, he prepared himself for her, before joining her on the bed.

The intensity of his smoldering gaze, as he lay poised above her, caused Nedra to avert her eyes.

"Look at me, Nedra." The words were a quiet command.

She did as he asked. Sin placed a kiss above each eye. "You have the most beautiful eyes." He kissed her nose. "A perfect nose." He kissed her lips lightly. "And your lips..."

Nedra claimed his lips with a kiss that left no doubt that she wanted him. Her hands wreaked havoc in his hair, along his back, across his buttocks, as her body melded into his.

Sin moaned his satisfaction. Her skin was like velvet to his touch. Her curvaceous body writhing beneath him was hot, moist, pliant. She was driving him mad.

He had known from the beginning that being with Nedra would mean that self-control would be a forgotten memory. No one else on earth stirred his emotions so passionately.

The feelings Sin had erupted in Nedra were beyond her comprehension. No man had ever touched her with such reverence. She felt wanted. She felt desired. She felt loved.

"I want to please you," Nedra rasped, as Sin worked his way from her breast down to her awaiting womanhood.

"There's no way on earth that you won't," he answered breathlessly.

"But, I've been celibate for years."

Sin lifted feverish eyes to her in an effort to clear his mind and understand what she was saying. Years? Celibate? A triumphant smile pursed his lips before he captured her mouth in a kiss that held all of the passion emanating between them. His fingers inched into her apex, drenched with waiting. He whispered, "You please me in every way." With that he eased into her, slowly, halting at her entry so that she could accommodate his size. Then inching his way into her core, he tightened his hold on her buttocks as she wrapped her legs around him, allowing him the deepest access.

Words of endearment tumbled from his lips as he thrust gently, kissing her, caressing her with every movement. Their bodies danced in perfect unison, as Sin, with every ounce of control he possessed, held his own release until she shattered in surrender. A second later, he followed suit, as ecstasy shook him to the core.

Nedra awoke to the warmth of Sin's body wrapped around her own. His muscular arm lay draped across her waist. His face rested cozily on her shoulder, mere inches from her face. Nedra sighed, fighting off feelings of guilt and regret. They both were contradictions to the peace she felt in this man's arms. She brushed her lips against the soft locks that lay sculpted to his head. If she felt guilt she should have felt it before they made love for hours. If she had regrets, she should have had them before Sin ran a hot bath for her and bathed her sore body with titillating sensuality. After her bath he wrapped her in a fluffy towel and carried her back to bed where they made love again. They had fallen asleep in each other's arms, exhausted from their indulgence.

She loved him. She loved everything about him. And he had said, repeatedly, that he was in love with her. She felt like a teenager caught in the throes of first love. It was wonderful! She sighed again. This was no time for regrets.

"No regrets?"

His voice was silk. Nedra smiled masking any uncertainty, surprised that he was reading her mind. "I was just thinking about you."

Sin hugged her body closer to his own and gently nuzzled her neck. "I'm glad."

"I thought you were asleep." Nedra snuggled against him, unable to get close enough.

"Who can sleep with you here, lady?" He grinned down at her. "I'm surprised you let me get a cat nap, the way you've been all over me."

Feigning insult, Nedra wiggled out of his arms and swatted at him. "I was what? You take that back!"

Sin chuckled at her antics. "No, I won't!"

Nedra grabbed her pillow and held it poised above her head. "No? Don't you ever say no to me!" She smiled down at him ready to continue their merry romp until she noticed the gleam of amusement in Sin's eyes change, gradually, to one of stark desire.

He took the pillow from her. "I could never deny you anything. I love you too much."

His words raced through her like a forest fire as he lowered her body to cover his. She lay against him, still, content. If only it could always be like this.

"Oh Nedra, " he groaned. "There's so much in my life that I regret, but I know that I will never, ever regret loving you." With those words he claimed her lips, and, once again, she rode the storm of passion with him into safe harbor.

Hours later, still glowing from the power of the connection between them, they went out to a late dinner. This evening belonged to them.

They dined in a candle-lit restaurant overlooking Monterey Bay, a quiet little spot, known for its talented jazz band. Nedra had changed into an off white pants suit she had never really expected to wear, but had packed anyway for her trip to Tahoe. She'd combed and brushed her hair until it glistened, and styled it so that it hung loosely on her shoulders, framing her face and accentuating her beige colored-eyes. Sin was entranced.

Before going to the restaurant, they stopped by the quaint hotel in which Sin was staying. He changed from jeans and turtle neck into a custom-tailored suit. The creamy beige color against his chocolate skin was striking. As she gazed at him against the flickering candlelight she smiled appreciatively. This man was truly fine. Surely, he was living up to his nickname this night.

Sin was in heaven at last. From the moment he jumped into his car and headed toward the Peninsula, he had berated himself for coming here. There were so many reasons not to be with Nedra that he couldn't remember them all. Yet, the sound of her voice each time he spoke to her overshadowed all of those reasons. He had forced himself to stay away from her for as long as he could. She was safe, that was the important thing. But the urge to see her, to be with her, had been so overwhelming that he had finally stopped trying to fight it. Now, he was here. So was she. They had found the elusive connection that he had longed for so long. At this moment, nothing else mattered.

After dinner they joined the other patrons on the dance floor. Any pretense of being anything but enamored with each other had been totally abandoned. As they danced, every touch of Sin's hand on her body sent Nedra's heart-beat spiraling. He stroked her back and pressed her to him boldly, fitting her form snugly into his body's nooks and crannies as if that was where she belonged.

Her arms encircled his trim waist. She laid her head against his chest. His heart beat uncontrollably, leaving no doubt as to who was causing its rhythm. She smiled, enjoying her newfound power.

She tilted her head to look up at him, as if seeing his face could hold the answers of the universe. Sin planted a tender kiss on her lips.

"What was that for?" Nedra asked.

"For you." He smiled pleased that she appeared com-fortable with his public display of affection. "I want you to know how much you are cherished."

Nedra snuggled closer, choked with emotion. What a man!

The song ended, and the band went into a second song as slow and romantic as the last one. They continued to dance, the heat radiating between them. Sin sighed. Never had he felt like this before. This was as good as it got. He could think of only one thing that could make it better.

Glancing down at Nedra, he looked into beige eyes that returned his look. She raised a questioning brow. He grinned sheepishly. "Wishful thinking,"

"Uh-huh." Nedra laughed knowingly.

They left the restaurant at midnight, eager to continue what they had found between them. Outside, a patient line of patrons was still waiting to enter the restaurant. As the valet brought Sin's car to the front, Nedra climbed in. She didn't hear her name being called from the back of the waiting throng.

The woman who had vied for her attention from the back of the waiting line turned to her dinner companion. "That looked like Reverend Davis. My next door neighbor, Esther Costello, goes to her church." She watched as the car drove away and disappeared into the night.

Chapter 12

Nedra awakened before Sin and slipped from his arms without waking him. As she made her way to the bathroom for a shower, her legs still felt shaky and her body tingled from their evening of passion. After returning home from the restaurant, they had made love until they both fell into a stupor, simply too exhausted to continue. According to the clock radio sitting on top of the marble sink, it was ten o'clock in the morning. They had fallen asleep at six.

After saying her morning prayer, she peeked into the mirror that stretched across the vanity, wondering if she looked as different as she felt. She felt rejuvenated. She felt alive! She also felt like a hypocrite. It was amazing how the light of day could make everything appear so different.

She had indulged, luxuriously, in the pleasures of the flesh without the sanctity of marriage. In her position she knew that she couldn't condone that for herself.

As a minister she had never condemned couples for the ways in which they showed their love. Instead, she had counseled them to love wisely, to love responsibly, to understand that love was a gift not to be treated lightly. God's gifts were to be treasured, and the gift of love was the greatest gift of all.

Her views were not shared by everyone in the church. She had been chastised more than once by church elders for her less restrictive views. There were those who felt that she should rain fire and damnation on those in the church who committed sexual indiscretions. She had respected those opinions but held to her convictions. She was not put on this earth to judge others. That was God's job. It was Him whom others would have to face. It was Him whom she would have to face.

She could only guess what the church elders might say about her indiscretion. Would they forgive her? Could she forgive herself?

Nedra lifted her eyes to gaze past her own reflection in the mirror to that of the man standing in the doorway behind her. His long, naked body rested casually against the door frame, a sexy smile on his ample lips.

"Good morning." His voice was an octave lower than usual, still husky from sleep.

"Good morning," she replied, removing her robe from the hook near the sink, acutely aware of her nudity. She slipped into the robe as Sin continued to stare at her through the mirror.

Pushing himself away from the door frame, he sauntered up behind her and snaked his arms around her waist. He planted a kiss against her temple. "I wish you hadn't done that. You were quite a sight for sore eyes standing in here naked. I nearly had cardiac arrest."

Nedra could feel his arousal pressing against the small of her back as she tied the robe more securely before turning in his arms. "And so might I, Mr. Reasoner. I'm not used to a naked man standing in the bathroom first thing in the morning. It's a shock to the system." And much too tempting. She took a step away from him.

Sin followed her. Burying his face in the crook of her neck, he whispered seductively, "And what do you want to do about that shock?"

Nedra grabbed a large towel from the rack and wrapped it snugly around his waist. "There." She turned to exit, noting the puzzled look on Sin's face.

He caught her arm before she could leave the room and looked from the towel to her. "What's this about?"

"Modesty." With a quick peck on his lips, Nedra left the room.

Sin looked after her. Modesty? It was a little late for that. He scowled. Something was wrong, and it didn't take a genius to guess what that something was. He had hoped that they would have more time together before the guilt and regrets began. It looked like he was wrong.

It was noon by the time they both showered and dressed. Sin had fixed large, fluffy pancakes for breakfast, dripping with butter and blueberry syrup. They ate in silence, each with a section of yesterday's paper propped in front of them. Each keenly aware of the other's presence, their camaraderie reminiscent of their time spent together in Tahoe.

But this wasn't Tahoe, the time spent there was long gone, and Sin would give anything to have that amount of time back. This was Saturday, and tomorrow would be the last day of her vacation. By Monday she would be back in Oakland, where her life was still in danger.

He stared at the words on paper before him, seeing nothing, succeeding at his effort to appear calm. In reality his anxiety had heightened. Where before he made love to her, before he voiced words of love to her, he had been willing to die for her. Now, he was willing to kill. There was someone out there who wanted her life, and he would not let them have it.

The problem was, he did not have a plan. He had known all along that hiding her away was only a temporary solution. No progress had been made in finding out who was after her. His contacts had been of no help, and his call to the authorities had proved fruitless.

There had to be a solution. Maybe they could go away somewhere. Maybe to one of the islands, Fuji or Tahiti. There he could keep her, with him, safe, loving her with everything in him. He wouldn't have to share her with anyone, not her friends, not her congregation. There she would feel no guilt or regret. It would just be the two of them, living, loving, making love as fervently as they had last night.

He could start a whole new life, become the kind of man she deserved, the kind she could be proud of. He would confess all that he had been about, and she'd forgive him for his deception. She had a kind heart, a gentle spirit. She would forgive him, absolve him of his sins. Convert him, make him new again. He had been told that ministers could do that, wash away a person's sins. If anyone could wash him clean again, Nedra could.

Glancing up, he expected to find her preoccupied with her reading. Instead, she sat draped in her seat, her arms folded across her chest, looking at him pensively. He raised his eyebrows in silent question.

Her gaze was piercing. "Okay, what's wrong?"

Sin's brows creased in resignation. Was he that transparent? If so, he owed her honesty, as much as he could give. "I don't want you to go back to Oakland."

Her face softened. "I know how you feel. I could stay here with you, like this, forever. But—" She shrugged. "I've got responsibilities."

He had known that she would misunderstand his meaning. But he understood hers clearly. First things first. He had to tell her. But would she believe what he had to say?

"I believe that your life is in danger in Oakland."

She thought he was joking. She joked back. "Everybody's life is in danger in Oakland." Her eyes shifted back to the paper, dismissing the subject with one gesture.

He tried again. "About two weeks ago, I received some information that made me believe somebody's trying to kill you."

That got her attention. She looked up from the newspaper.

"Kill me?" she echoed.

"Yes, the work you've done in East Oakland, to remove drugs from the area around the church, I heard that it's made some drug lord very unhappy."

Nedra gave a nervous laugh. He had to be kidding. "I bet." She returned to her teasing tone, and to the newspaper.

Sin frowned in annoyance. "I'm serious, Nedra. The information I've received indicates there's a contract out on your life."

Nedra looked up at him once again. Two weeks ago. She folded the paper neatly and laid it aside. Her heartbeat increased as she examined his expression. It was as serious as his tone. Two weeks ago. She remembered her initial feeling that their meeting in Tahoe had not been an accident. That had been almost two weeks ago. Was that the reason he came to Tahoe? To protect her?

"How do you know there's a contract out on me? Who told you?" She still wasn't sure that he was serious. She hadn't put a dent in Oakland's drug trade. The dealers had just moved to new locations. What he was saying didn't make sense.

Sin could still hear the doubt in her voice, could see the denial in her stance. How much should he tell her? "I heard that some drug dealers—I don't know who—had put a contract out on some do-good preacher who was making them lose business in your area."

Nedra relaxed, unaware that she had even been tense. "And you assume that I'm the 'do-good' preacher?"

Her tone was skeptical. Sin fought to keep a rein on his temper. Didn't she understand? He could lose her! Sin leaped from his seat and stalked across the kitchen, the very thought of living without her tearing at his heart. "Nedra, all signs point to the fact that you are the preacher in question, and you are in danger. This is not a joke, and I don't find anything funny."

The anguish on Sin's face propelled Nedra out of her seat. She walked over to where he stood, leaning against a counter, glaring at her. True or not, it was certain that he believed what he was telling her. A tremor shot through her body at the possibility that it was true.

"Well, if that's really the case, why didn't you go to the police?"

Sin hesitated. How much could he tell her without telling her too much. "I did call the police, but I don't think they believed me. I've checked and nobody seemed to take my call seriously." He left out the part about calling anonymously. It would raise too many questions.

Nedra nibbled on her lower lip, a habit when she felt unsure of herself. "I'm not the only minister in Oakland who has interfered with the drug traffic. Not that my church has done much to stop anything. If they didn't say my name, how do you know they were talking about me?"

Sin reached out and took her into his arms. She sounded less doubtful but he could tell that the possibility of truth frightened her. That hadn't been his intent. He rubbed her back comfortingly. "It was pretty clear that it was a woman. What other woman preacher in Oakland is raising hell?"

His tone was a teasing one. Yet if what he was saying was true, how fearful should she be? Sin was there for her. He had been there from the beginning, watching out for her, protecting her. It dawned on her that she was here, in this house, because of his belief that she was in danger. That meant that he had cared for her long before Tahoe. His caring had started...when? At their first meeting?

"So, if it is me, what would you suggest that I do? Hide out forever?"

Sin's hold on her tightened. "If I could keep you safe with me, forever, I would; but, if you could stay here a little longer..."

"Sin..."

"One more week at least."

"But, I've got too many—"

"I know, responsibilities."

"It's true. I can't stay longer."

"Can't or won't. Please, Nedra. I know I'm asking a lot."

"Yes, you are." She tried to draw away from him, but he wouldn't let her. Taking her face in his hands he drew it close to his. "Are you sure that your responsibilities is the only reason that you won't stay?"

Nedra lowered her eyes, unable to hold his gaze. "This is unreal, like some TV show, or dime store novel. What can you do in a week? You're not the police."

Sin relaxed his hold on her. She wasn't ready to face his question. "If I can find out who's behind this, then maybe I can get the police involved." With their dead bodies, he wanted to say, but how could he tell her that he was willing to kill for her?

Fear crossed her face. "No! That's too dangerous. I'll go to the police myself."

"And say what? That you heard that I heard somebody say there's a contract on you? Even I've got to admit it sounds vague; but, as long as there's the possibility, I want you safe. Stay here."

She shook her head. "I can't."

"Why not?" He was impassioned. "I asked you to be sure."

Her eyes flew to his face. The heat emanating from his eyes singed her. "I'm sure that I love you."

"Then prove it and stay here." He kissed her brow. "Please" He kissed both eyelids. "For me." He kissed her mouth and her resistance began to wane.

It was on the Monterey Boardwalk that all discussion about her prolonged stay on the Peninsula ended. As she and Sin strolled along, hand in hand, playing tourist, she recited a list of calls she would have to make if a prolonged stay was to be possible. The first call was to Carla whom she hadn't contacted since leaving a message about her whereabouts the first day of her arrival. Even then she hadn't offered details.

Assuring Sin that she wouldn't share the real reason for extending her vacation, she found a pay phone and placed her call, watching him fondly as he sat perched on a nearby bench, enjoying an ice-cream cone. Carla answered on the third ring.

"Hey, Girl!" Nedra smiled, warmed at the sound of her voice. "What's up?"

"Nedra! Nedra! Thank, God!" Carla's voice bordered on hysteria.

Nedra snapped to attention instantly. "What is it? What's wrong, Carla?"

Sin

Across the way, Sin noticed the change in Nedra's demeanor and dropped the unfinished cone in the trash as he started walking toward her.

"It's Sharon. She's in the hospital." Carla started crying. "It was that bastard brother of mine! I could kill him! Richard hit her."

Nedra gasped. "Hit her?"

Sin reached her side, disturbed at her distress. "Who got hit?"

Nedra mouthed Sharon's name.

"Yes, he hit her!" Sharon repeated. "He beat her! She told him about the baby, and he hit her!"

Nedra frowned in confusion. "Baby? What baby?"

"Sharon's pregnant. She told me the day before yesterday. I told her she was crazy. Richard's too irresponsible to take care of himself, let alone a child. She told him she was pregnant, and he went crazy. She said he started breaking things, cursing her, accusing her of trying to trap him."

"Is she all right?" A chill ran through Nedra. Sin pressed closer to her, rubbing a hand up and down her back, offering his support.

"No, she's not all right. Her lip is swollen. Her face is bruised. She's got a broken rib! And..." Carla's voice broke. "He could have killed Sharon. That bastard! He could have killed his own baby! I told her to put him in

157

jail! You should see her, Nedra. You should see her! Jacob was so mad he went to find Richard to kick his ass!"

Nedra took a deep breath, trying to calm herself. She never did trust Richard. She didn't even like him! The only reason she had tolerated his attention, his presence, was because of Carla. Now, she could dislike him openly. She would pray for him, but she still didn't have to like him.

"We need you, Nedra. Sharon needs you, and so do I, because the Lord knows I have hate in my heart today, and it's against my own brother. Oh, God!" Carla's sobs intensified. "I can't believe this!"

"Okay, Carla, I'm coming home. I'll be there today." She saw Sin visibly tense but turned her back as she gripped the telephone and reassured her friend. "You hold on. I'm on my way."

Hanging up the telephone, she turned back to Sin, ready to defend her decision if necessary. It wasn't. The look on his face showed his concern, but it also conveyed his understanding.

"I'll drop you off at the house and go fill the tank while you pack. We should be there before dark."

Without another word, they hurried to the car, both mentally preparing themselves for what they would face in Oakland.

Chapter 13

Despite his calm demeanor, inside, Sin was a raging torna-
do. Nedra drove her car back to Oakland. He followed
her, right to the entrance of Kaiser Hospital. He left her
there after she promised to spend the night at Carla's and
to call him on his cell phone as soon as she could manage.
She also promised not to reveal their newly formed relationship to her friends.

It was almost midnight when he pulled up to an all
night convenience store and dropped coins into the pay
phone on the outside of the building. He was determined
to get some answers to his questions, before Monday, no
matter what he had to do to get them. It could be Nedra
was right. Maybe he had jumped to conclusions too quickly. Maybe Nedra wasn't the target. There really wasn't any
definite proof. The break-in at her house could have been
a simple burglary. Burglaries happened often enough.
That car that he spotted outside her church the Sunday he
attended, it could have been explained in a million different ways. Perhaps he had been living his life in shadows
for so long, he saw a boogieman around every corner. Yet,
years of fine-tuned intuition told him that he had been right
initially, and he could not bear the consequence of misread
intuition.

He dialed the number rattling through his brain. The same number he had dialed two weeks ago. He couldn't rest with this uncertainty.

The phone rang three times before a groggy voice answered with a less than friendly greeting.

"It's Reasoner. I need an update on the East Oakland situation."

"What the hell! Man, what time is it?"

"Time for you to give me the $200 worth of information I paid for two weeks ago."

A strong expletive singed his ear. Sin was unfazed. He wanted answers, and he wanted them now. This wasn't a request. It was a demand.

"I've given you plenty of time to find out the name of the 'do-gooder' marked for the hit in East Oakland. If you don't have the name, get it, before midnight tomorrow."

There was silence on the other end. He knew the little weasel was weighing the level of danger he heard in his voice. The man was wary, and he should be. The silence was short-lived. "That subject is dead in the water, man. You late. The shooters got wasted Friday night."

"Wasted? Friday night? What kind of game are you playing?"

"No game, man. Word is they was the ones in the shoot-out Friday night."

"Shoot-out? What shoot-out?"

"The one with Eddie Carter's people."

Sin

Sin's body went numb. "Eddie Carter's people?"

"Yeah, man. Where you been? It's all over the papers. Two young bloods tryin' to move into his territory hit Carter and some of his people. It happened Friday night. Carter and four others got wasted. Word is the shooters was two of them."

Eddie? Dead? The shooters? Wasted? Sin's mind raced to comprehend. How were the shooters related to Eddie? Was he the one who put out the contract on Nedra?

Closing his eyes, he visualized the round, youthful face of the man who, like himself, had grown up with no childhood. The filth in which they wallowed had sullied them both and wouldn't allow Sin even the luxury of liking the man. Eddie had liked him and looked up to him with admiration. It was all crazy! Too crazy! Who knows, under other circumstances they might have been friends. Now, all he felt was a sense of relief.

Eddie was now a memory, and Nedra was free. If the bastard had been responsible for a contract on her life, there wasn't a spot in hell hot enough for him!

"You sure about this?" His tone warned the snitch he had better be.

"Yeah, man. Ninety-nine percent."

It was the one percent that still bothered Sin, but the odds were the best he had heard yet.

"And did you get the name of the hit?" He had to know for sure.

"Not guaranteed, but I know it was a woman."

Sin's heart skipped a beat.

"Say man, why you so uptight 'bout this? They hit yo' kin folk or somethin'?"

Sin ignored the question. "I'll keep in touch."

Long after he had disconnected, Sin stood with his head against the receiver, listening to the rapid beat of his heart. The end of the danger had come as swiftly as the beginning. He trusted the reliability of the information the contact had given him. The man knew that inaccuracy could mean his life. He felt relatively sure that Nedra was safe. His love was safe. But what about tomorrow? She was playing in flames that could consume her. Yet, so was he.

Getting into his car, he drove toward the house in the Oakland Hills, his mind still swirling with the events of the weekend. He recalled Eddie and Lynn in his office, and that it was Eddie who had first mentioned that things would get "hot" in Oakland, bragging about how all of his "problems" would be over. Yeah, they were over all right. Completely over! And what about Lynn? Where was she in all of this? Did she have anything to do with this contract? He knew she was aware of what her brother was doing, but there had never been any evidence that she was deeply involved in his business. Men and fashion seemed to be her preoccupation. Yet, that day in his office, he had sensed something in her tone...

The ring of his cell phone disrupted his train of thought. "Hello."

"I miss you, already." Nedra's voice washed over him like a spring shower.

"I miss you too. How's Sharon?"

On the other end, Nedra fought to contain her emotions of rage and contempt for Richard. She'd found Sharon weeping, with black and blue bruises covering her upper arms and torso. Nedra had been angry enough at Richard to kill him. Her feelings toward the man were way less than Christian, and she had done some hard praying to keep from cursing his very existence on earth.

"She's doing better. They're releasing her tomorrow morning, but, God help her, after all she's been through she's still defending that man."

"Where are you now?"

"I'm at Carla's. We're bringing Sharon here when she's discharged. Nobody can find Richard, and Lord knows what he'll be up to next. It's safer for Sharon not to be at her apartment right now."

"Is she pressing charges against him?"

Nedra bristled, her anger and disappointment aimed at Sharon this time. "No. As a matter of fact she's defending that...that...scum. It doesn't matter though, because what he did was still assault and battery and the authorities are going to bring him in for questioning."

"Good." He'd only seen Richard Ryan once. He couldn't say that he would remember him if he saw him again, but he'd never forget the way Richard had draped himself, a little too intimately, over Nedra's chair. That alone was enough to color his opinion of him. "Now, how are you?"

Nedra smiled That was why she loved this man. He was not only kind, but thoughtful.

"I'm tired, but I'm fine. Carla and Jacob went to bed about fifteen minutes ago."

"Did you tell them about us?"

Sin sounded a little too anxious, and Nedra frowned in confusion. "No, we agreed that I wouldn't. What's wrong? Why is this such a problem for you?"

Sin hesitated. What could he tell her? That he did have a problem, but not one she could solve. Rather, it was one that could destroy her, and he'd do anything to keep that from happening. He knew that their relationship would have to be short-lived. The life he had chosen left little accommodation for deep involvement. His was a lonely existence. Love had been an illusion for most of his life, and to have found a love like this was more than he had ever hoped for. He just wanted to hold on a little longer, if it was no more than a few more days, even hours. He'd take what he could get.

"As I told you before, I think we should keep a low profile."

Sin

She had heard his hesitation, taken note of how he had evaded her question, and the tug of apprehension that had been a pin prick when he first suggested not revealing their budding relationship increased a little. There was something definitely wrong with this picture. She had jumped into deep waters with Sin feet first. She now had to know whether she was going to drown. She was blunt. "Are you married, Sinclair?"

He didn't hesitate. "No, I'm not married, although I can see why you might think I would be. Believe me, Nedra, it's best that nobody knows about us right now. Please, trust me on this."

Trust him? She loved him. She trusted him with her life. As a matter of fact, she was trusting him with it. So much had happened in so short a time. "So, when can I come out of hiding?"

Surprised by the sudden shift in conversation, but glad it had been changed, Sin explained the most recent developments as honestly as he could, skillfully avoiding the name of Eddie Carter, and her question about how he got the information he was sharing. "Just let me make a few more phone calls and confirm what I've heard, and if I'm satisfied with the answers, you're home free."

Nedra chuckled nervously. Somewhere in her subconscious she still was not totally convinced that the intrigue against her was real. "Well, that was quick."

Sin sensed her unspoken doubts but didn't address them. He knew the reality of the streets, where everyday the impossible became possible. It was a reality that she never had to know to survive, but he knew that lack of knowledge could be costly. "Not quick enough for me. I just want you to start watching your back, Sweetheart. Believe me, every snake out there might not be poisonous, but those that are can be deadly."

Richard was still angry. The fight with Sharon had sent him out into the streets of Oakland in search of some blow, and his usual supplier was nowhere to be found. Hell! The bitch had dumped his good stuff down the toilet demanding that he stop snorting, then threw that pregnancy bomb on him. What did she expect to happen but an ass kicking? Now, word was he was in trouble! Where was the justice?

He cruised another corner, and had no better luck finding a supplier. Eddie Carter's death had temporarily caused a shakeup in the ranks.

Making a U-turn, he headed his bright red Beamer in the opposite direction. He knew where he could get his supply, and from the main source too, not some street jockey.

A burly bodyguard with whom he was familiar answered Lynn Carter's door, and after patting him down, accepted Richard's explanation that he came to offer his condolences. After the bodyguard checked it out with Lynn, he was led to her.

Her appearance was shocking. Usually impeccable from head to toe, he found her dressed in a loose flowered silk robe, devoid of makeup, her hair unkempt, and her eyes swollen from crying. It was obvious that she was taking her brother's death hard.

She looked up at Richard with large, vacant eyes as he offered his condolences, all the while wondering how he was going to talk her out of the dope. He already was in deep debt to the Carters for past purchases, and Lynn had pulled no punches when they met for lunch some weeks ago. She had informed him that the time for payment on that debt was long overdue.

He had gotten angry at the less than veiled threat of harm if he didn't pay up. They had gall! After all the favors he had done for them, making sure that their dope was distributed in the highest places, he felt that his overdue debts had been paid long ago. Sure, he'd chipped a bit off the top for himself, but it was he who was risking his career and his reputation to satiate the drug appetites of a class of people the Carters only wished they could break into. Even Lynn's little degree from UCLA couldn't buy her way into the circles he was born into, and she was jealous of that fact, and he knew it!

Neither one of the Carters liked him, and the feeling was reciprocated. At their meeting, that day, the little slut had looked at him with contempt on her face and had railed at him about how he had everything. She said that she couldn't understand why he would jeopardize it all for money he didn't need, and a high that didn't matter.

Hell! Of course she didn't understand. The little ghetto rat came from the sewer, she wouldn't recognize a good time if it hit her in the face, which was exactly what he wanted to do that day. Instead, he had sweet-talked her into an extension, agreed with her that the next favor she asked would be a big one in exchange, and had been provided with enough dope to last him for a while. That was, until Sharon dumped it!

His blood boiled whenever he thought about how selfish she had been. She never considered him, only herself. Telling him she was pregnant. The last thing he wanted was a kid! Well, maybe he took care of that matter when he showed her who was boss.

Faking his best look of concern, he turned his attention back to Lynn who was nearly incoherent as she lamented over the death of her brother and vowed revenge, blaming his death not only on rival drug dealers, but on the situation in the East Oakland territory that the Carter organization had once ruled. They had been pushed out of that territory as if they were nothing and forced to invade areas of the city that had caused dissension and dispute. The result had been Eddie's death. She vowed revenge on the "do-gooder" who had forced their move from East Oakland.

Sensing her present state of vulnerability, Richard took advantage of the opportunity and worked his sympathetic musing into a request for more dope and more credit. Adding hastily that he still intended to pay his previous bill.

Lynn's state of mind proved not to be as susceptible as he suspected. She looked at him through narrowed eyes, and Richard tried not to recoil at the hurt and anger he saw in them as she studied him long and hard.

"You are a piece of work, Richard, but I'll tell you what I'm going to do for you. I've been saving the little favors you owe us, adding them up until I could come up with one that could wipe out your debt completely."

Richard sat up, interested. Wipe out his debt? He could live with that! How big of a favor could it possibly be?

"I've go a little job that my brother had a couple of peo-ple on, but circumstances being as they are now, they're no longer available. I need somebody else to take over for them.

She stopped again, looked at him, her eyes narrowing further. "And you're the perfect person for this little job."

Richard gave her a smug smile. "What's the job?"

"I need somebody wasted."

Richard's smile vanished.

"That do-good preacher has been costing us money for much too long, and now she's cost my brother his life."

Richard nearly choked. "She?"

A deadly smile transformed Lynn's expression. "Yes, she."

Richard could hear his heart pounding. "She who? Who do you want wasted?" He closed his eyes and waited, but he already knew. East Oakland. Drugs. A "do-good" preacher. She. He heard the name in his mind before the words left Lynn's mouth.

"Nedra Davis. I want Reverend Nedra Davis dead."

Chapter 14

It was Sunday, and Nedra sat in the chair next to Sharon's bed, reading the bible. Sunday had always been special to her. Being a preacher's daughter, how could it not be? It was the Lord's day. A day of worship, fellowship, and prayer.

Each day she read a passage from the bible, followed by a prayer, but on Sundays that daily ritual always seemed special. It was as if, on his special day, God could hear her words more clearly, grant her request more quickly. She knew it was a foolish thought, God heard prayers everyday; but, she closed her eyes and whispered her prayer a little bit more fervently this day, asking God to move her friend past this pain.

Earlier, she and Carla had taken Sharon home from the hospital and whisked her to the large, sunny house in the Berkley Hills that Carla and Jacob shared. Sore and emotionally scarred, Sharon had spoken very little as they tucked her into bed and tried, unsuccessfully, to feed her breakfast. Now she lay sleeping peacefully; but, Nedra knew that she was not at peace. What Richard had done had injured more than her physical body, it had injured her spirit, and it took longer to heal a wounded spirit.

"How is she doing?"

Nedra opened her eyes. Carla stood in the doorway.

"She hasn't stirred. You go on, Carla, I'll take your watch and stay with her a little longer. You've had a long weekend. You've got to be tired."

Tightening her arms across her chest, Carla sighed deeply. "It's been a long weekend for all of us." She managed a wan smile. "Come on down and get a cup of tea. There's nothing either of us can do for her right now, and you didn't eat breakfast. At least I've had something to eat."

Minutes later, settled in the cozy kitchen nook bathed in sunlight, Nedra watched as Carla poured hot water into the cup placed before her, then took a seat across the table. She looked tired. Dark rings lay beneath her eyes.

Nedra dunked her tea bag, laid it aside, and relished the warmth of the liquid as it slid down her throat. "Is Jacob still upstairs?"

"Would you believe he went downtown to the office?"

Nedra raised a questioning brow. "On Sunday?"

Carla chuckled at what she described as Nedra's preacher voice. "Yes, he's working on some big case the Prosecutor's office is putting together against this Carter Group, or something like that. They had a big shoot-out this weekend, drugs, rival gangs...you know the story."

"Oh, Lord."

"Bodies all over the place. Jacob's office has been tracking them for a while, and they're about ready to lower the boom. A lot of people are going down on this one. The shoot-out may speed things up a bit, and with all that happened with Sharon and Richard..." Carla's shoulders slumped noticeably. "Well, Jacob hasn't had time to take care of the business he brought home with him, so he went down to the office where it's quiet."

Nedra nodded. A comfortable silence settled between them but it was interrupted by a small voice from the doorway.

"He loves you."

Nedra's eyes flew to the speaker. Beige eyes met gray ones. There was no need to pretend, all three of them knew to whom Sharon was referring. Carla jumped to her feet and hurried over to Sharon.

"What are you doing up? The doctor said you need rest!"

Eyes still trained on Nedra, Sharon shook Carla's hand from her shoulder and moved with some effort across the kitchen. She slid into the space abandoned by Carla.

Nedra held her friend's eyes. "I never encouraged him."

"I know that, but that doesn't matter to him. That's the attraction."

Carla began to pace. "Richard's not in love with Nedra. He's obsessed with her. He has been for the longest."

Two pairs of eyes shifted to Carla, whose agitation increased with each word she spoke. "He used to come to me, even before he met you, Sharon, begging me to talk to Nedra for him. I didn't want to get involved. She made it clear that she didn't want him, but my dear brother doesn't take rejection easily. He thinks he's God's gift to women!" Her face etched with anguish, she stopped in front of Sharon. "I told you not to get involved with him! I told you he meant you no good. All of this should have been out in the open years ago."

Nedra added quietly, "I didn't want to hurt you, Sharon, so I thought if I ignored his feelings for me they would just go away."

Carla stopped pacing. "I chose the same tactic, and look what it's come to. You love him too much, Sharon, more than he deserves, and now you're pregnant." Carla dropped her face into the palm of her hand as a sob tore through her body. "Oh God! I never thought that anything like this would happen!"

Nedra went to Carla and hugged her, then settled her into a chair. Across the table silent tears slid down Sharon's bruised face, while Nedra's own tears also flowed freely.

Carla's shoulders heaved as she wept, pain filling each word. "My brother is sick, Sharon. There has always been something wrong with him. It was never something I could put my finger on, and my parents ignored it. He's the light of their life, but something is definitely wrong. He needs professional help. If I had insisted that he get some earlier, maybe all of this wouldn't have happened. Maybe... Oh, Sharon, I'm so sorry."

Reaching across the table, Sharon took Carla's hand. "You have nothing to be sorry for. I'm grown. I've got to take responsibility for my own life."

"And he has to take responsibility for his." Carla sniffed. "Press charges against him."

Sharon recoiled. "It would kill your parents."

"They'd survive. You've got a child to think of now."

Sharon blanched. "No. No, I don't."

"What!" Nedra and Carla reacted simultaneously.

"They took a test in the hospital. I'm not pregnant. The home pregnancy test I took was wrong."

Carla looked surprised. "But you said your period stopped!"

"The doctor said it might be stress. It's definitely not a pregnancy." Sharon looked at Nedra and attempted a smile. She failed. "I guess it's like you always say, God always knows best."

Nedra nodded as her hand covered Sharon's. "That's right, He does."

Outside the two-story stucco house, nestled near a grove of flowering trees, a red BMW was parked. Fortified by a head full of dope, Richard was feeling no pain. It had taken him the entire night and much of the morning to convince himself that there was a way out of this mess. He knew Sharon well enough to know that she wouldn't press charges against him. She loved him too much. All he had to do was talk to her a little, tell her he loved her, and put a little overtime into some good lovemaking.

He'd gone to her apartment and found her car parked in its stall, but letting himself into her place, he'd been surprised not to find her there. The place was still in shambles, and there was blood here and there. The possibility that he'd hurt her worse than he thought crossed his mind, but he dismissed it. He hadn't hit her that hard.

He figured she was at Carla's, hiding from him. She was so predictable. She always went there after they had a fight. Of course this was the first time he had hit her where bruises were visible, so he'd have to hear it from Carla before he got Sharon out of there.

He was surprised to see Nedra's car parked in Carla's driveway. He thought she was still shacked up on the Peninsula with that lover of hers. He couldn't believe his luck.

Lynn's directive had shaken him, and he had put her off by telling her he'd think about it. She'd given him twenty-four hours to make his decision, or make full payment on his debt. He had until midnight Monday.

He'd snorted coke for hours trying to figure some way out of this. He had borrowed so much money from

Sharon, she was practically bankrupt. His mother would give him some money, that was if she could get it from his cheap father. His Dad had put his foot down the last time he called and asked for a loan. He had reminded Richard that he made a good living, and he was way past the age where he had to borrow from his parents. He suggested he learn how to budget his money. Richard had hung up on the old man. He vowed to cut out his tongue before he asked him for anything else. But, it looked like he might have to go back to the folks anyway. At least that was how it looked before he came up with the perfect solution to his little problem.

He really didn't want to kill Nedra. He loved her. If she could have a little accident that would put her out of commission for a while, he would take credit for her mishap. That should satisfy Lynn, or at least be some payment on his debt. He could get the remainder of the money from his mother. That should do it. Nedra would still be alive, and he could show her how attentive and caring he could be while she was recuperating. After that, they could be together.

It was the perfect solution. Sharon was old news anyway. Who wanted to be saddled with a whining woman and kid.?

Nedra might not be as pure as he thought she was, but that could prove to be even better. She had a little experience behind her now, and she wouldn't have to be taught from scratch.

With determination in each drug-laden step, he approached Nedra's car. Then demonstrating a skill that would have amazed those who knew him, he made the adjustment appropriate to drain fluid from her brakes. Within fifteen minutes he was back in his car and driving out of the hills of Berkley.

Nedra was despondent. After having a good cry, she and her friends had sat at the kitchen table discussing subjects that they had avoided for years. For the first time since they'd known each other, Sharon confessed her long harbored jealousy of Nedra, whose brown-skinned beauty she craved. She was shocked to discover that her friends weren't surprised by her confession as the three of them explored its source. More tears were shed, tempers flared, and old resentments surfaced, but the result was a step toward healing, and the strengthening of a friendship. It was a catharsis for all three women, but it left them emotionally drained.

Nedra needed her own healing. She needed strong arms around her to restore her equilibrium and reassure her that everything would be okay. In the privacy of her bedroom at Carla's house she called Sin. He listened to her pain and said, "Come to me."

Borrowing Carla's car, which blocked her own, she followed the directions he had given her to his home. She found him standing at the front door, waiting. Silently, she slipped into his arms.

She talked, he listened, offering little comment as he went about fixing dinner and lending his support. Sin gave Nedra a tour of his beautiful house before he served a dinner which turned out to be a culinary delight. He added candlelight, a linen table cloth and napkins to enhance the baked Cornish hens, wild rice and squash. He'd worked hard to make the evening special.

Stuffed, Nedra folded her hands under her chin and leaned across the table, offering him a sensual smile. "You're just full of surprises, aren't you, Mr. Reasoner. You live like a king, cook like a chef, and dress like you stepped off the cover of GQ magazine. Is there anything you can't do?"

Sin smiled and struck the same pose. "I can't preach a sermon."

Nedra laughed. "Who knows...you might want to try it someday. I bet you'd be good at it."

Sin shrugged and grinned, happy that she was here with him, and that he could make her laugh. She had been so depressed when she came to him that he'd do anything to make her happy.

What she had related to him about Sharon and Richard had angered him, especially the part about Richard's obsession with her. Used to hiding his emotions, he gave her no indication about how he felt about Richard Ryan. But if the man made any attempt to approach Nedra romantically, Sin vowed silently that it would be his last attempt. Nedra was his.

He reached across the table and took her hands into his. "I've got good news for you. You're out of danger. I've made some inquiries, and I've been told that the contract on you is no longer a factor."

Nedra's face was a mask of confusion. "Wait a minute. One second you're telling me my life is in danger, the next second you're saying that the hit out on me is no longer a factor. Do you know how that sounds?"

"Like the script from a bad movie."

"To put it mildly, and what's this about making inquiries? Do you have some underground network of informers who let you know about all of the people on hit lists?"

Nedra stood and walked to the window, putting distance between them. That inkling of doubt about him that had surfaced before began to prick at her subconscious again.

"Be straight with me, Sinclair. What is all this about? I'm almost sure that you didn't just happen to be in Lake Tahoe the same time as me. And that little trip to the

Peninsula, the more I think about it, the more suspicious it gets. You told me that you heard my life was in danger. So you've been protecting me, haven't you? And now, all of a sudden everything is just fine. It's all a big mistake. You have to admit all of this sounds kind of strange. What am I supposed to believe? How can you play games with my life like this?"

Her words hit him like a battering ram. How could he play games with her life? He moved, quickly, closing the distance between them, then crushing her body to his. His heartbeat vibrated against hers. His voice cracked with emotion. "How can you believe I would play games with your life? You're the most important thing in this world to me. Your life means more to me than my own life."

His lips covered hers, hungry, demanding, stifling further discussion. Nedra's body ignited. He broke the kiss to whisper hotly against her mouth, "I love you, Nedra. Don't ever believe anything else. Stay with me tonight."

Nedra stiffened. "Sinclair, I—"

"I know. I know. We don't have to make love. Just let me hold you. You need that."

Yes, she did.

"And I need you."

How could she argue with that?

Chapter 15

Nedra looked at Sin sleeping peacefully beside her and thought what a beautiful man he was. It wasn't just physical beauty that made him the man he was. It was more than that. His heart and his soul were beautiful, although he sometimes tried to conceal both. He had tried to protect her. He had loved her before loving her. He had been willing to put his life on the line for her. The details of all of this she wasn't quite sure of, but she was humbled by the depths of such emotion.

She knew that she had tried to live a good life. She served the Almighty, tried to help others, tried to treat others as she wanted to be treated. She had never expected a reward on earth, but surely this man must be it. Never before had she felt such an unquenchable yearning for one person as she felt for him, and she knew that those feelings were returned. But was it right? Was marriage between them even a possibility?

She had already declared her love for him, but this need for him, this insatiable desire when she was with him was so new, so different, so overwhelming. Their relationship was still in its infancy, still fragile in its present state. Where would it lead? Could it lead to marriage? Only time would tell. Until then, was she strong enough to deny herself the luxury of making love with him again? She could only hope.

She caressed his face, encircled the gold stud in his ear, smoothed his moustache, let her fingers trail lovingly down his cheek to rest on his dimpled chin. Lord, he was beautiful. He stirred in his sleep, and she snuggled closer to him. What a test of strength self-denial had been. As he promised, they had not made love during the night. But God forgive her, she had wanted to, badly.

They had gone to bed around midnight. She was dressed in a pair of his oversized pajama bottoms and one of his t-shirts. He wore a pair of pajama bottoms, although he told her that he preferred sleeping in the nude. Nedra lay curled against Sin's chiseled chest while he gently stroked her back. She felt such contentment that she smiled.

"What are you smiling about?" he asked, kissing her ear lobe.

"I was just thinking how happy I am. What a great range of emotions I've experienced in one very long day. And all on Sunday, my favorite day of the week."

It was Sin's turn to smile. Her words meant more to him than she would ever know. "Are you happy? Are you really happy?"

She nodded, whimpering in delight as his hands glided lazily down her body.

"Then I'm happy too, because that's all I want for you, for both of us, a lifetime of happiness."

But she wondered if complete happiness was possible. Or, would this love break both their hearts?

It was then that she looked into his eyes and declared, "I love you, Sinclair. I don't know where this love comes from. I don't know where it's going, but I love you. I'm putting my trust in you, and my heart in your hands."

Monday morning they shared breakfast and toyed with the idea of ignoring all of the day's responsibilities to be with each other, but reason prevailed. The weekend was over. It was time to face a new day. But this day was different. For the first time, in a long time, neither one of them would face it alone.

Nedra had called Carla the night before to inform her that she would not return to her friend's home. Now she called her for an update on Sharon.

"She's better," Carla stated, sounding more encouraged than she had yesterday. "And what are your plans for the day? You coming back here? Going to work? By the way, where are you, at home?"

Letting the latter go unanswered, Nedra informed her that she would be calling the church secretary, have her gather the work that had piled up in her absence, and she'd go by the church and pick it up. "Then, if you'll drive my car to your office, I'll drop by and we can exchange. I'll bring the work to your house and keep Sharon company today."

Carla agreed. "Sounds like a plan to me."

Nedra was reluctant to bring up his name, but it was best to know what they were up against. "Have you heard from Richard?"

Carla's upbeat mood disintegrated. "Not yet, the rat should be too ashamed to crawl up from his sewer. But, he'll surface. I'm surprised he hasn't come by to sweet-talk Sharon out of sending his butt to jail."

"Did she agree to press charges?" Nedra sounded hopeful.

"She's weakening. Why don't you work on her while you're here?"

Nedra heard a voice in the background.

"Jacob's getting ready to leave," Carla said. "He's blocking your car. Got to go. See you around ten?"

Nedra agreed and hung up. She had a million things to do today.

Humming a familiar love song, she stood before the full-length mirror in Sin's bedroom and began brushing her hair. Moments later he rushed through the bedroom door, dressed for his day at the office. As usual, he looked good. She followed his reflection through the mirror as he looked absently around the room while patting his jacket pockets for his keys and checking his inside pocket for his wallet, all the while muttering to himself. He was action in motion until he noticed her watching him. He stilled.

Nedra gave him a questioning smile. "What?"

"You." He came up behind her and planted a kiss in her hair. He took the brush from her hand. "I like the idea of your being here with me in the morning getting ready for your day." He began raking the brush, slowly, through her tresses. "How's Sharon?"

Nedra closed her eyes and leaned back against him enjoying the tingling sensation this simple act was causing. The scent of his cologne teased her senses.

"She's fine. Richard hasn't shown up yet."

"And he better not show up around you."

Nedra turned, concerned by the harsh tone in his voice. "Don't worry, I'm not afraid of Richard. As much as I love Sharon, I know that she's weak in at least one area, and that's when it comes to him. She never would stand up to him. When confronted with anyone who stands up to him, Richard's a coward. Believe me, he's harmless."

Sin placed the brush on the dresser and looked at her, not bothering to hide the skepticism on his face. "Nedra, there's one thing that life has taught me: any dog with teeth will bite."

Sin

Shut in his office for over an hour, Sin tried to concentrate on the papers before him. It proved to be an impossible task. Nedra loved him. She had looked him in the eyes and said the words. I love you. He had wanted to pinch himself to see if he was awake or dreaming.

Since the day he had met her, so many years ago, he had hoped for, wished for this day to come. He didn't believe in miracles. He had asked for a miracle when his mother was hooked, and she died. He had asked for a miracle when he was moved from house to house, but he found no home, no family. He stopped believing in miracles long ago, but to receive Nedra's love—this was as close as he could possibly come to a miracle.

Earlier that morning he had made several more calls that confirmed Nedra's safety. That chapter was now behind them. A new chapter in his life was beginning, and what a chapter it would be.

He had everything a man could want, a career, prestige, money, and now, above all else, Nedra. He loved her beyond reason. He had to stop himself from shouting with joy whenever he was with her. She stayed on his mind, constantly. He could hardly concentrate on anything else when he wasn't with her, or think about anything else when he was. Having her in his home, in his arms, had been more than he could ever have conceived. It had been perfect. His whole world was different now, and some changes had to be made.

The sound of his name on the intercom shook him from his musings. His secretary said, "Mr. Reasoner, I know you asked me not to disturb you, but Mrs. Trellis is on line one, and she sounds very upset. Do you want to speak to her?" Her voice lowered to a compassionate whisper. "It might be about her brother."

Sin sighed. His mind had been so filled with Nedra, he had forgotten about Eddie's death. He took the call.

"Hello, Lynn. I'm sorry to hear about Eddie. How are you doing?"

He could feel Lynn's sadness, even separated by the telephone. She sniffled. "I don't know how I'm going to get through this, Sin. He was the only family I had. I loved him so much."

Sin's heart went out to her. He knew just how she felt. He'd been there.

"Is there anything I can do for you?"

There was a moment's hesitation before she continued. "I'm so alone. I need someone, someone to be with me, badly, while I make his funeral arrangements."

She paused, as if waiting for a reply. He offered none. How could he?

"I know it's a lot to ask. I mean, I know we don't really have any kind of relationship, beyond business, that is, but, I was hoping..."

Sin

He had to put an end to this. He spoke as gently as he could. "I understand, Lynn, and I'm sure that one of Eddie's friends would be more than happy to help you."

Her voice rose to a childish whine. "But I don't want them to help me, I want you to. You're more mature. You'll know what to do, and Eddie was crazy about you. You asked me if there was anything you could do for me!"

Sin remained calm, recognizing the hysteria caused by her grief. "I'm sorry, Lynn, that's something I can't do. Again, please accept my condolences. I've got to go." He disconnected before she could continue, then buzzed his secretary.

"Please find out which funeral home has Mr. Carter's body, then make arrangements to send flowers."

"Okay, Mr. Reasoner, and how should the card be signed?"

"Sign it, with condolences from Bayland Imports."

"Yes, sir."

There would be no personal gestures, no attending the funeral, and from now on, no contact with Lynn Trellis. Eddie was dead. A lot of changes were going to be made.

Nedra stopped by the church office to pick up the pile of work left stacked in her in-box after her long absence, then headed over to Ryan Advertising. It was past ten now, and

189

Carla still hadn't arrived at her office, neither had she called. This was unlike her, and Nedra wondered at her delay. She sat in the waiting room, sipping the tea the receptionist had offered her, anxious to get to Sharon. She had spoken with her earlier and Sharon was still in a lot of pain, emotionally and physically, but she was ready to talk to Nedra.

Glancing at the clock once again, Nedra laid the magazine she had been flipping through aside, and decided that Carla was out of luck. She had too much on her plate to delay any longer. She'd drive Carla's car back to the house and later give her a piece of her mind for her tardiness. But, she did wonder why she was tardy.

Outside, the answer became obvious. Down the street from the office, she saw Carla and her fiancé, Jacob, pressed against his car, engaged in a very passionate public display. Nedra smiled, remembering her own hormones raging out of control only a short while ago. She approached them, clearing her throat loudly.

"Okay, you two, break it up! This is a public street, you know."

They both looked up reluctantly and ended their kiss, flashing her sheepish grins. Carla turned in the arms of the man who was to be her husband six months from now, the glow of love radiating on her face. Nedra raised a brow at the hair that was still slightly mussed, and the blouse that had been misbuttoned. She folded her arms across her chest and glared at them accusingly, trying to hide her amusement as she spoke. "Where's my car?"

Carla didn't pretend to look embarrassed. "Oh! Your car. It's at the house. Jacob said he would bring me to work, and you could leave my car here. He's going to take you back to the house."

"I've got a meeting about five minutes from our house," Jacob added.

"Uh-huh. So it took you two over an hour to make a twenty-minute drive to the office?"

Jacob's boyish looking face broke into a naughty grin. "We stopped to attend to some, uh...some business." He tightened his hold on Carla as he planted a quick kiss in her hair. The gesture reminded Nedra of Sin.

"Yeah, I got your 'business'." Nedra chuckled and shook her head at the two love birds. "Come on, Romeo, let's go. I've got some business of my own to attend to."

After one last lingering kiss for Carla, Jacob helped Nedra into the car, and they headed toward the Berkley Hills. He bopped along to the music coming from his CD player, occasionally singing off key.

Nedra liked Jacob Belle. They had grown close over the two years since he and Carla had been involved. Six feet tall, he was a handsome man, a light, toasted brown, with an array of thick curly black hair framing his square-jawed face. Jacob was fun loving, full of jokes and lots of teasing when socializing, but he was a brilliant, astute attorney when in the courtroom. Nedra had seen him in action, and he was dynamite. A star in the Prosecutor's office, he was destined to move to the top. She loved hearing him talk about his cases. It was fascinating.

"Sharon told me that you're working on a big case involving these people who got shot this weekend."

Jacob groaned. "Don't you women keep anything a secret? I told Carla that this was hush, hush."

Nedra felt guilty for having opened her mouth. "Oh, oh. She didn't tell me that."

Jacob chuckled. "Obviously. I guess it doesn't matter though. In a few days, maybe a week, things will be going down anyway. Maybe we'll be able to make at least a dent in this drug war. God knows, anything is better than nothing. I don't need to tell you how much drugs have cost the Black community."

Nedra nodded. She knew all too well.

Jacob continued. "I hate the bas—" He glanced at Nedra apologetically. "I hate the leeches making profits off other people's pain. We're going to get some of the hypocrites in suits this time, instead of just the small-time street hustlers. Eddie Carter was one of them on the list, but that was taken care of for us. We're going after some of the so called 'legitimate' businessmen and women. The ones who sit in their ivory towers and pretend to be innocent, while they make it easy for people like Eddie to move all that dirty money. They move it through the system so that it looks clean, and in doing it, help keep this whole drug thing going. We've got a whole lot of big fish going down this time. They're hiding their misdeeds behind legitimate businesses, from Oakland's Waterfront to City Hall, but..."

Sin's Bayland Imports flashed through Nedra's mind as Jacob continued talking. His business was located on the waterfront. She hoped it wasn't too close to where Jacob was describing, or he might be in danger. Maybe, she should say something...

"But, I don't expect this information to go any further than this."

Nedra jumped, her mind drifting back to the conversation. "What? What did you say?"

"Hey, aren't you listening to me, Ms. Preacher ? I said you're to hold what I've told you in confidence. I've already said too much, and, obviously, I shouldn't have said anything to Carla."

"I know you share everything with her."

"Yeah, but promise me you won't share this little secret with anyone else."

"You can trust me."

Arriving at the house, she thanked Jacob, retrieved her briefcase, and headed for the house. Jacob stuck his head out the window before driving away.

"Hey, will you do me a favor?"

"Of course."

"We drank all of the milk at breakfast today. Would you mind going to the store and buying some more? I'll pay you back."

Nedra agreed, rejecting the offer of reimbursement. As Jacob drove off, she started toward the house, halted, then glanced down at her briefcase, weighing the options. With the amount of work she had to catch up on, and the time she wanted to spend with Sharon, there might not be time to run to the store later today. It was best to go now.

Tossing the briefcase into her car, she jumped in after it, and put the key in the ignition. The engine purred to a start.

Chapter 16

Inside the house, Sharon wandered to the front window in time to see Jacob drive off and Nedra get into her car. She had been waiting for her. She had a lot to talk to her about. She had decided to break up with Richard. It was time to take control of her life, but she knew she was weak when it came to him and she needed the advice and strength of her friends to help her through this. Concerned that Nedra wasn't coming into the house, she wrapped her robe tightly around her and shuffled out the door, calling to Nedra as she backed out of the driveway. She caught her attention.

Nedra turned the car off and rolled down the window, greeting her friend with a warm smile. "Hey, Lady, what's up? You certainly look better than you did yesterday."

Self-consciously, Sharon's hand flew to her bruised face. Nedra noticed the gesture. "No, Sharon, you really do look better, and by the end of the week your bruises will probably be gone."

Sharon gave a forlorn shrug. "I guess. Listen, where have you been? I missed you last night, now you're going off again without saying goodbye. I thought you were coming inside so we could talk."

"Oh, I am. Jacob asked me to get some milk for the household. I'm just running down to Safeway. I'll be back in a minute. Do you want something from the store?"

Sharon shook her head no. Once again, Nedra started the car. This time there was a click, then nothing. She tried again. Again, a click, then nothing.

Nedra frowned in annoyance.

"Try the radio," Sharon suggested.

Nedra turned it on. Nothing.

"Try the lights. Let me see if they come on."

Nedra obeyed. Sharon shook her head as the obvious became clear.

"It's the battery," Nedra grunted in disgust. Setting the parking brake, she retrieved her briefcase, and followed Sharon into the house.

It was Tuesday morning when Nedra returned home. It seemed like an eternity since she had been in her own house, among her own things. She had purchased the condo on the island of Alameda, near Oakland, as a refuge. When she still lived in Oakland, the small house that served as a parsonage was like a subway station, with her parishioners feeling free to come in and out any time of the day or night. She had absolutely no privacy. There was some grumbling when she purchased her own place and abandoned the parsonage, but it didn't matter. She had the right to privacy, just as her parishioners did, and she made it clear that she meant to have it. Everyone at Mount Peter was aware that if they needed her all they had to do was to call and leave a message if she was unavailable. She would get back to them. Uninvited guests to her home were not appreciated. Over the years her parishioners began to respect that declaration.

Her home wasn't spectacular, a simple two-bedroom apartment, located in an unassuming building about ten years old. The living room was spacious, with an adjoining dining area and a small kitchen. A hallway led to the master bedroom suite, with a private bath. The bedroom opened onto a balcony. A second bathroom separated the master suite from the smaller second bedroom, which Nedra had turned into an office. Overstuffed sofas and chairs in colorful floral prints dominated the decor. Limited edition prints by well-known Black artists adorned the walls. Her place was cozy and comfortable. Most of all it was home, and she was glad to be back in it.

Unpacking her suitcase, she tossed two weeks worth of clothing into the washer, then went to her office to retrieve messages off her machine. She had decided to avoid going into the church office at least one more day. So much had happened in these two short weeks she needed time alone to absorb it all and time alone to think about Sinclair.

Sinclair Reasoner. Who would have guessed that the sound of a name could send her heartbeat into a full gallop. She hadn't spoken to him since leaving him Monday. Sharon had occupied most of her time. Her friend had flatly refused to press charges against Richard, but some progress had been made. Sharon had declared that she was breaking all ties with him. Finally, she seemed to understand that real love brought joy, not pain.

Settling at the rolltop desk in her home office, Nedra pressed the playback button and began writing down messages. Her pen halted in midair at the voice of Esther Costello. This was the second message she had received from her. She had left one at the church, yesterday. Nedra hadn't bothered to return it. That message had been a written one, leaving Nedra unaware of its tone. This recorded message left no doubt. "Reverend Nedra Davis, return this call as soon as you return from your vacation. " Her emphasis on the last word in the message was caustic. Nedra was on instant alert. What was that woman's problem now?

Dismissing Esther once again, she continued to collect her messages, until another one caught her attention. It was from Mrs. Simpson. She had never called her at home before.

"Reverend Davis. I'm sorry to call you at home this late. I thought you were back from vacation. It's Monday. Anyway, I'm beside myself. My husband's back in the hospital with his ankle and I can't take care of the boys no longer. I had to call their worker. She came and got them a little while ago. (sigh) I feel so bad about all this. Them boys done been through so much. Well, anyway, I just needed to talk to you. If you can call me when you get in, I'd appreciate it. I usually stay up late."

Nedra called her at once. There was no answer. Calling the same hospital Mr. Simpson had been in before, she found him there, and so was Mrs. Simpson. She was very remorseful and described the boys as sad and solemn when they left. Colin was especially quiet, and she was worried about him. She informed Nedra that Trevor had called Sin before they left, and begged him to take them in. She asked if Nedra could help the boys in any way. Nedra made no promises, but said she would do what she could.

Sin had asked that she make all phone contact with him outside his home on his cell phone. She dialed the number. He answered on the second ring, his voice crisp and formal. It softened at the sound of her voice.

"I just heard about Colin and Trevor. Mrs. Simpson left a message on my answering machine here at home."

"You're back at your place?" His voice registered concern.

"You said it was safe."

"Yes, but I feel better when you're around other people."

Nedra was touched by his concern, but enough was enough. "I'm fine, Sin. It's those two boys that I'm calling you about. Mrs. Simpson said that Trevor called you. Do you know where they are?"

On the other end, Sin sat back in his office chair and recalled the hysterical child who begged him to come for them last night. He hadn't cried since he was a baby, but it had been hard swallowing the lump that had lodged in his throat. His voice conveyed the pain of having to reject that request.

"I called Family Services this morning and talked to the caseworker assigned to the boys. She said they've been put in the Children's Center until they can find another foster home for them."

"The Children's Center! That's like an orphanage! They don't belong there." Sin ran his fingers through his hair in frustration.

"I know, but maybe a foster home will open up soon."

Sin heard the tears in her voice. "Are you going to be all right?"

She swallowed the lump in her throat. "Yes, I'll be fine. How about you? That phone call from Trevor had to be hard on you."

Sin closed his eyes and savored the essence of this woman. This was why he loved her so much, her awareness, her kindness, her concern for the feelings of others.

"I'm fine. The worker said that I could visit the boys after they get settled. I'm going to take her up on that."

Nedra knew that he would. That was Sinclair. That was her love. "I'd like to see you tonight," she said, surprised at her boldness.

"Me too. Can you come to my place?"

"I'm not sure. My car might not be ready."

"Your car? What's wrong with your car?"

Taking the cordless phone with her, Nedra moved to the bedroom and stretched out on the four-poster bed. "Oh, the battery went dead yesterday, so I had my mechanic go over the whole car, so nothing else would break down on me. He found out that the brake fluid had drained out somehow."

Sin, who had drifted over to one of the love seats in his office and draped himself across it, sat up straight at this bit of news. "What? That could have been dangerous!"

"I know. God was watching over me. Anyway, my mechanic said I need new brakes. He's installing them. I won't be picking my car up until tomorrow. So, I don't have a ride. Why don't you come over here?"

Sin was hesitant. He still was uncomfortable with them being seen together. Under any other circumstances he would shout his love for her to the world, but there was so much he had to attend to before he became worthy of publicly calling himself her man.

"I...I don't know."

His continued hesitancy caused the seed of doubt to sprout once again. Nedra was growing tired of this. She knew that he wasn't married. There were no signs at all in his home that there was another woman in his life. As a matter of fact, other than the art on the walls, there were no personal pictures anywhere in his house that she had noticed. So, why was this continued secrecy so important to him?

"I'll tell you what, Sin. I do have a lot of work to catch up on, and since your coming over here seems to be such a problem."

"Nedra..."

"I'll just stay here, and you stay at home. Maybe we can get together later."

She hung up the telephone with firm resolve. She was going to get to the bottom of this. What was it? Because he had some trouble with his faith, was he ashamed to be seen with a preacher?

The telephone rang. She answered on the first ring.

Sin's voice caressed her like satin. "What's your address?" She told him.

"I'll be there by six."

He brought Chinese food for dinner, and slices of cheese cake for dessert. They sat at the table in her small kitchen dining, but food was the last thing on her mind. There were matters that needed to be settled between them, and this was a good time to settle them.

"Why do you want to remain so secretive about our relationship, Sin? You said my life was no longer in danger. So what is it?"

She watched him closely as he put down his fork and sat back in the chair. He looked thoughtful for a moment then addressed her. "Why is it you don't want to make love with me anymore, Nedra? You answer my question, and I'll answer yours."

"W...what? Well, I..." she stammered. The question was totally unexpected.

"I'll answer it for you. It's because you're a minister. You've had sex outside marriage and your conscience is bothering you."

She remained silent. She couldn't deny the truth.

He continued. "When we were in Monterey I told you that I would be as honest with you as I could be. I have been, but have you been honest with me or with yourself?" He leaned across the table drawing closer to her. "You assured me that you were ready for my love and for its consequences. I don't think you are."

Nedra sat as still as stone. Every word he said was true. "I'm sorry, Sin, but I feel like a hypocrite preaching one thing and practicing another." A tear worked its way down her cheek.

With the pad of his thumb he wiped it away. "Don't be sorry for having a conscience. You wouldn't be the woman I love if you didn't have one."

"I'm not ashamed of having made love with you."

He smiled. "I'm glad to hear that. But?"

"I've got to show more control in the future."

"No, sweetheart, we have to show more control. You're not in this alone." He pulled her up and around the table and settled her on his lap.

It was her turn to smile as she gave him a quick kiss of gratitude. "You're wonderful."

"Humph, no actually I'm horny."

Nedra laughed. She could feel the evidence of that fact beneath her.

Sin hugged her to him. "I won't lie. I want you. Every time I'm near you, hear your voice on the phone, I want you. But if we never make love again, that won't stop me from loving you."

She was touched by his declaration.

He continued. "This will all work out, Nedra, I promise you. I just need a little more time to take care of some things. Then we can shout it to the world what we mean to each other." He lifted her chin with his finger. "Just a little more time is all I need."

Hours later, after Sin had left, reluctantly, and she had gone to bed , the ringing of the telephone aroused Nedra from her sleep. She answered it with a drowsy, "Hello."

"Good evening, Reverend Davis. I can hear that I may have awakened you. I must say I'm surprised that you're in bed this early."

Sin

It was Esther Costello. Nedra rubbed the sleep from her eyes and sat up.

"What is it, Mrs. Costello? Has something happened?" The clock read ten.

"That's what I want to know, Reverend Davis, what is happening?"

Nedra's head was clear now, and she could hear the censure in the older woman's voice. "What are you talking about?"

"I'm talking about telling a lie, Reverend Davis. I'm talking about a minister telling her congregation that she was going away, alone, on a quiet vacation, and, instead, is seen running around Monterey with some man. No wonder you didn't return my calls. I shouldn't be surprised; but, as a deaconess in Mount Peter church, I believe, Reverend Davis, that an explanation is in order."

Chapter 17

Nedra had never been a cursing woman, but if she had been she would have cursed Esther Costello out that very evening. Instead, she coolly informed her that whatever she did with her private life was her own affair, and hung the telephone up.

She decided that she wasn't ready to share the conversation with Sin. She could handle Esther and anyone else who meddled in her business.

Wednesday morning and afternoon at the church office went smoothly. There was no mention of Esther's accusations from anyone she spoke to. Wednesday evening prayer meeting was another story. There was everything from indirect, teasing references to the possibility of Nedra having a man in her life, to Esther's bold demand that she reveal the name of the mysterious man. It was a demand Nedra didn't bother to dignify with a response.

Esther had been astute enough to make her demand out of earshot of the others in attendance, but as Nedra walked to her car in the parking lot, Esther followed her, confrontation in her every step.

"You know, Reverend Davis, you are supposed to be a moral example to the members of this church, and I am

appalled that you should take your responsibility so lightly."

Nedra bit her tongue and kept walking. She had said
what she had to say.

I feel personally responsible that you, as a woman minister, fail to provide the moral guidance that is so badly
needed these days. After all, do I have to remind you that
it was I who persuaded the others to give you the privilege
of leading our flock here at Mount Peter."

Continuing to ignore her, Nedra unlocked the car door,
and got in. Esther held the car door firmly, keeping it from
shutting completely. Her controlled demeanor suddenly
transformed in front of Nedra's eyes as her face contorted
with hate. Nedra stared at her in fascination as the woman
went on a tirade.

"I knew that you weren't all you pretended to be.
Everybody has been fooled by that pretty face of yours, but
I had your number from the start. All of the men panting
after you, thinking you're something special. You're
always getting the credit for everything that happens
around here. But, I knew there was another side. You run
around here like you're better than everybody else. Won't
listen to anybody. You know it all. Now, look at..."

Tired of looking at and listening to her, Nedra used the
door as a lever to push the woman away from her car.
Then slamming the door firmly shut she drove away while
Esther was still in mid-sentence.

Sin knew something was wrong. When he last spoke to Nedra Wednesday evening he could tell that something was bothering her. For a scary second he thought that she might have changed her mind about loving him, but that thought was quickly dismissed. He had never been as happy in his life with any woman and she seemed happy with him. Yet, there was definitely something bothering her, and he was concerned.

He had questioned her. Had she been threatened in some way? She said no, so he hadn't pressed the issue. He didn't want to renew old memories about when her life had been in danger. Yet, he was uneasy. What about the brakes failing on her car? He hadn't forgotten that. She said the brake fluid had drained. Was such an occurrence unusual? He didn't know much about cars except how to drive them. He'd have to check on that.

Although he was certain her life was no longer in danger he still remained cautious where Nedra was concerned. When he went to visit her he had observed the surroundings carefully looking for suspicious cars and any suspicious people. His radar had been on automatic, but he had spotted nothing. Could he have been wrong?

The disturbing thought was with him all day as he went about the duties at his office. His secretary reminded him that the Carter funeral was that afternoon, and informed him that she had sent the flowers. Sin thanked her for the follow up, and answered in the negative about attending the funeral. All ties with the Carters were now officially cut. However, Lynn Trellis seemed to have other ideas. She called the office just as he was calling it quits for the day.

Lynn's voice was choked with tears. "He's gone, Sin! He's really gone! And you didn't even come to the funeral."

He felt sorry for her, but there was nothing he could do. "We at Bayland sent our condolences with flowers."

"Yeah, I saw them. Condolences from Bayland Imports. How cold can you get? I thought you were Eddie's friend?"

"No, Lynn, we were business acquaintances. Nothing more."

"Then why can't we be friends?" She sniffed. "I need somebody, Sin. I need you. I buried my brother today!"

This was going nowhere. Even sympathy went only so far. "Like I said, I'm sorry about Eddie. I'm sorry about any young life that's uselessly wasted, but there is nothing further I can do to help you, Lynn. All I can do is wish you well. I have to go now. Good luck to you in the future." He hung up before she could say another word.

Lynn Trellis was angry. The whole world was against her. Eddie was dead. Sinclair was treating her like she didn't exist. Even Richard Ryan wasn't giving her the respect she deserved. She'd given him an ultimatum with a deadline that he missed two days ago. She had been so preoccupied with Eddie's death that she hadn't followed up on that. It was unfinished business she had to take care of.

She had to get a hold of things. She had to pull herself together. If she let Richard get away without paying his debt, she'd lose control of the business that Eddie had worked so hard to build. She had to earn respect within the organization, and fast.

Few people knew how deeply she was involved in the organization, or that she intended to control it. It had been she who had used her business expertise to help Eddie turn his street operation into a million dollar business. She had been the one to talk Eddie into wasting the preacher. It was about economics, nothing personal. However, it was Eddie who had garnered the respect of his people. These were the same people who viewed her simply as his pampered little sister.

Richard Ryan was one of the few people who knew how deeply she was involved in her brother's business. The two of them had been sleeping together for a couple of months before she recruited him to use his contacts in the advertising business to help expand her brother's business. Richard was hooked on coke, anyway. It really had-n't been a challenge to get him to sell his soul.

Now, he was just a nuisance. He couldn't pay his bill. He couldn't even kill a preacher! What good was he any-way? She knew he was probably in hiding, on the run because his days were numbered. Even if he did waste the preacher, she'd still have him killed. Oh well, one thing at a time. There were priorities. Her brother's murderers were the first on her list. After that, she'd return her atten-tion to Reverend Davis. Meanwhile, there was still Sin. She wanted him despite his continued reluctance. But, he would come around, and she would do whatever it took to have him. There was nothing he could do about it.

By the end of the week Sharon's physical scars had healed to the point where she could cover them with makeup, but the emotional scars weren't so easy to hide. She still wouldn't press charges against Richard, to the frustration of her best friends. For her own peace of mind, and to escape the pressure they were putting on her, Sharon extended her emergency leave of absence from her job and flew to Seattle, where her father was waiting with open arms.

The drive back from the airport was a solemn one for Nedra and Carla. Before leaving, Sharon had revealed that Richard was hooked on crack.

He hadn't been seen in a week. His secretary had contacted Carla to see why he hadn't reported for work. She was running out of ways to cover for him. It was through his secretary that Carla discovered that Richard's job had been in jeopardy for months. His work was erratic. He was late for meetings, missed others altogether, and he had altercations with fellow employees. He was on his third written warning and had been put on probation. This disappearance act should get him the pink slip he had been trying so hard to earn. That he was hooked on drugs came as no surprise to either Carla or Nedra. Nothing that Richard did surprised them anymore.

Carla hit the steering wheel in frustration. "I don't understand why everyone covers for Richard. Sharon, his secretary, our parents, all the other women he's screwed over the years! When will people demand that this grown man grow up!"

Nedra wondered too. But she didn't see it happening soon.

On the patio of a four star hotel in Sausalito, a tourist hamlet separated from San Francisco by the Golden Gate Bridge, Richard sat gazing at the scenery before him. In the distance, beyond Alcatraz prison and the lush greenery of Angel Island, San Francisco rose majestically amid a shroud of fog. The scene was postcard perfect, but Richard saw none of it. Instead, he sat wrapped in a dingy hotel robe, unwashed, unkempt, his mind in a drug-laden fog.

He had scoured the Bay Area newspapers since Sunday looking for information about Nedra's auto accident, but he could find nothing. Finally, he had called the church and asked whether she would be delivering the sermon this coming Sunday. He was told that she would be. What in the world had happened?

Without Nedra's dead, or, at least, injured body, he was a man on the run. He had missed his deadline, and Lynn had a bullet with his name on it for sure. The bitch was crazy! Look what she had driven him to!

He was not used to living like this. He had two hundred bucks in his pocket, no money left in the bank, and because he had messed up with Sharon, nobody reliable to borrow money from. If Carla was any kind of sister, he could count on a quick loan from her. He knew she had it, or if not, that big-time lawyer boyfriend of hers sure did. But, forget that. She was probably turning Sharon against him this very minute. She had always been against him. On top of it all, he had probably been fired. He'd have to cut down on the dope for a while. He'd been so stoned he forgot to call in to work. There was nowhere to turn. If it wasn't for the two credit cards Sharon had gotten for him in her name, he more likely than not would have been forced to stay in some two-bit motel these past few days and eating in fast food restaurants. There had to be a way out of this!

Moving from the patio to the king-size bed that dominated the bedroom of his suite, Richard lay down and folded his arms over his bloodshot eyes. He had to think!

The only solution he had come up with to redeem himself in Lynn's eyes was to follow through with the contract and take Nedra's life. Even the thought of that pained him. Yes, she had disappointed him with that little stunt of hers in Tahoe, but he could forgive her that. If he could get to her, let her know that her life was in danger, maybe he could get her to go away with him, even if he had to take her by force. Eventually, she'd forgive him, especially after he explained everything.

Yes, that was it! This was a better plan than the last one. With that settled, he snorted a line of coke off the night stand, plumped up the pillows supporting his back, and waited for his high to take him to the place he longed to be. Oh, yeah, life was beginning to look good again. He'd let things settle down a bit, sneak back into Oakland, and get Nedra. That would get her out of Lynn's reach. She would still be alive, and the two of them would finally be together.

Chapter 18

It had been one week ago, exactly, that Nedra and Sin first greeted the morning in each other's arms. Since that time, a lot had happened, and each could sense the force of the whirlwind that threatened their relationship. Yet, they held on.

Nedra looked across the room at the man she loved. Dressed in a pair of worn jeans and a T-shirt, both of which fit his well-toned form splendidly, he was conducting a scavenger hunt to find the TV remote. She smiled. This was the man who had changed her whole world, and she liked living in that world. Even Esther's veiled threats didn't bother her. She had a right to a life outside of Mount Peter. She had earned the right to this bit of happiness, and Sin did make her happy.

He made her feel more like a woman than any man had before, and she had noticed that it had begun to reflect in her appearance. She had always been careful about her appearance. Her profession did not dictate that she had to look dowdy. Yet, this evening she had taken extra care. She'd spent the morning at the hair dresser and the afternoon shopping. The result was the mock turtle neck sweater and black leather pants, which were different and daring for her. She looked chic and stylish, from head to toe and felt that way as well. The looks Sin had been giving her told her he appreciated the effort. The heat between them had been smoldering all evening.

"All right!" Sin's triumphant shout raced across the room as he held the remote unit high up like a trophy. He pushed the power button. The wide-screen television in his entertainment center flooded the dimly lit room with light.

Sin joined Nedra on the sofa, and shifted her lithe body to fit snugly against his own as he burrowed her in his arms, ready to enjoy the video he had rented for their evening together. His eyes swept briefly down the shapely contours of her body.

"Did I tell you that you really look good tonight?" I like that outfit, especially those pants."

"Thank you." Nedra grinned, pleased by the compliment and stirred by the fire she saw in his eyes. The evidence of his admiration was pressed firmly against her back. She cleared her throat as flames shot through her body. "So what is this mystery video that's supposed to be 'right up my alley'?"

Sin winked mischievously. "You'll see."

The words, "The Preacher's Wife," flashed across the screen.

Nedra groaned. "You have got to be kidding! No violence? No gratuitous sex?"

Sin laughed at the disappointed look on her face and planted a quick kiss on her cheek. "I'm afraid not, preacher lady, but it does have Denzel."

She grinned her approval, then reminded him that the movie also had Whitney. Sin grinned an approval of his own.

Between munching on popcorn, tickling each other until breathless with laughter, and stealing quick kisses that left promises of turning into a whole lot more, they managed to see the entire movie. At its end, they lay on the sofa, cuddled in each other's arms, contentment covering them like a blanket.

Nedra sighed. The time was right to ease the conversation around to the subject she wanted to discuss.

"I spoke to the boys' caseworker yesterday. She told me that you visited them in the Children's Center. She said that she talked to you and suggested that you take foster parenting classes so you could take them into your home."

Sin tensed. "Then she also told you that I said no."

Nedra shifted in his arms so that she could see his face. "Well, I can understand the reasons for that. You're a single man, two little boys would be a lot of responsibility. But I was thinking, considering your own experiences with foster homes..."

Setting her aside gently, Sin rose to his feet and went to the entertainment center to retrieve the tape. "Yeah, I'm quite acquainted with foster homes."

Nedra could hear the bitterness in his voice. He kept his back to her as he put the tape back in its case. "I thought you were going to find another foster home for them with some of your parishioners?"

"I'm going to try."

Sin turned at the uncertainty in her voice. "What do you mean you're going to 'try'? I was positive that you could find a family for them."

Nedra chose her next words carefully. There was such hope in his voice, more hope than she could offer. "I can't guarantee that I can find another two-parent family for the boys. All I can do is try."

"But it doesn't have to be a two-parent home. You've got what...a thousand people in your church, and you're telling me not one of them wants to take in two orphan boys? So much for Christianity!" He spat.

"Don't blame Christianity, Sin. Life is responsible for this situation. Just like you, people know that it takes a lot to care for two growing boys. I've seen people in our church with much less than you have take strangers, old and young, into their homes."

"Oh, I see, so you're trying to make me feel guilty about not taking the boys in?" Sin's stance had become defensive as he glared at her. "I can tell you right now, you're a little late. It was hell leaving those boys in that so-called Children's Home. It looked more like a prison than a home. There they were putting on this big front saying it was no big deal, they could take it. All the while I could see the pain, the fear in their eyes. And they've got the right to be afraid. I know what they'll be up against if they put them in the foster care system. Even if they're lucky enough to stay together it'll be hell. If they're separated it will be double hell!"

The pain in his voice was wrenching. Instantly, Nedra regretted her contribution to what had to be one of the hardest decisions he ever had to make.

"Sin, I didn't come here to make you feel guilty. I would never do that." She went to him, burying her face in the curve of his neck. "I love you."

Sin's stance changed from defensive to defenseless as he tightened his arms around her absorbing her strength. "Oh, baby, leaving those kids there was so hard."

"I know. I know." She ran her fingers through his hair absorbing his pain. "You don't have anything to feel guilty about."

"I don't know what else I can do for them."

"Baby, nobody could have done more for those boys than you have."

His face hovered above hers. "I need you Nedra. You'll never know how much." His voice broke as his lips met hers hungrily. The smoldering flame was ignited.

Nedra's body pulsated, responding greedily to each delicious demand until rapture replaced reasoning. Sin stripped them both of their clothing as his hands, his lips, his tongue worked pure magic. Every lick, every nibble, each stroke, each caress was maddeningly potent. The fire between them was lethal. Nedra was lost in the flames.

Trembling, doddering on delirium, Sin covered his shaft to protect her then lifted Nedra to meet him. "Hold onto me," he whispered. And she did.

Their lovemaking was frantic and frenzied, as if parting were an impossibility. Sin chanted her name like a mantra. She responded wildly to each powerful stroke. As the haze of released passion descended upon them, all questions, answers and doubts were forgotten in a fog of insatiable desire.

It was late when Nedra retrieved her clothing and dressed to go home. Sin lounged on the sofa watching her, the fire of desire still threatening to reignite. He could never get enough of her. Yet, he consciously doused the flames. The silence between them told him that they were flames that should have been extinguished hours ago. They hadn't been.

"Don't blame yourself, Nedra," he said quietly. "It was my fault. I could have stopped what happened between us. I was selfish. I didn't want to."

She looked at him appreciatively. "Thanks for trying to give me a way out, but you know better and so do I. We're not kids, Sin. We're both responsible for our own actions." She gave a heavy sigh. "I always thought of myself as a strong woman. I took pride in the fact. But it seems when it comes to you, I'm not as strong as I thought."

Touched by her words, Sin rose and tried to take her into his arms. She pulled away. He didn't insist. It was best.

"You are a strong woman, Nedra. Intelligent, strong and beautiful, three of the qualities I love most about you. Never doubt yourself or my love."

"I have no doubts about you, Sin. I did have doubts about the reasons you've given me about why you want our relationship to remain secret. But after tonight, after this week I can understand why."

Sin snapped to attention. After this week? There was something about the way she said those words. A knot began to form in his stomach. "Why do you say that?"

"We were seen in Monterey last weekend. Half of my church knows that I'm seeing someone, and by Sunday the other half will know."

The knot tightened. "Do they know who?"

"No, I don't think so."

He could feel her watching him closely as he got up from the sofa and crossed the room giving them distance. Leaning against the fireplace he tried to appear casual, undisturbed about her news. He kept his expression blank.

She tested the water. "It looks as though our emergence as a couple might be made public sooner than we thought." She joined him at the fireplace, her eyes never leaving his. "You know I didn't understand all this secrecy at first, but with what's happening it's become clearer. Being with a woman minister isn't easy. Being a woman minister isn't easy. There are members of my church who will be all in my business if I brought you around. But that's inevitable. " She gave a sad smile. "Yet, it would have been nice to have enjoyed our privacy a little longer."

Sin knew that she was registering his reaction to her words closely, and he had always been a master at controlling his emotions, except when it came to Nedra. It took great effort for him to retain his impassive expression and mask his anxiety. He had hoped against hope that he would have more time to settle the complications in his life. One week certainly wasn't long enough, Eddie's unexpected death had helped a bit, but...

"So, it looks like the jig is up?" He tried to make light of the moment. He moved away from her again, back to the sofa where he sat down and settled against the plush pillows, stretching his long legs out before him. He grinned at her.

Nedra noticed that the grin didn't quite reach his eyes. "And you're not upset that our little secret came out before you wanted it to?"

"Things happen when they're suppose to happen, Nedra. There are some things we just can't control." Eddie Carter was dead. His primary contact in the drug trade was no longer a factor. It was time to get out of all of this business!

Nedra's smile was brighter this time. She liked his answer. "You're sounding like a minister now, Mr. Reasoner. Your philosophical evaluation of this event more than meets with my theological approval."

Sin laughed at her antics hoping that it didn't sound forced. Unable to resist touching her any longer he planted a kiss on her forehead. "Everything is going to be fine, baby. You'll see." Everything was going to be fine!

The Sunday morning headline read, Drug Bust Nabs the Cream of the Crop, but it meant nothing to most Bay Area residents. The authorities were always touting the success of one drug arrest or another, but nothing ever changed. Yet, this bust was different, Carla mused, as she read the article over her morning cup of coffee. The handsome, brilliant attorney, Jacob Belle, would be handling this case. It was as good as won.

With a satisfied sigh, Carla continued to scan the article. She recognized some of the names mentioned. There was Eddie Carter, mentioned as one of the men killed recently in the drug war. And there was Lynn Carter Williams Trellis, his younger sister. Carla remembered seeing a picture of the attractive young woman in the newspaper not long ago. She had been weeping over her brother's casket. The names of the others who had been indicted, along with Mrs. Trellis, were less familiar. She expected that they were mostly young street punks, devoid of hope, preying on others like locusts.

Then there were the names of those under investigation for involvement in various aspects of drug trafficking. There were a couple of judges who had accepted bribes. Their names were familiar in the city's social circles, but she didn't know them personally. They were joined by three prominent attorneys who, reportedly, had sold their souls for a price. Thank God neither she nor Jacob had come in contact with any of them. Then there were the businessmen who were suspected of being involved in this sleazy business. Almost every name was known and respected in the Oakland community, all except one businessman mentioned.

According to all accounts, he hadn't been in the Bay Area very long—a little over a year. Yet, he was highly successful. His business concerns spanned the two coasts, under the name Bayland Imports. His name was Sinclair

Reasoner, and he was suspected of laundering drug money.

Carla's coffee mug froze in midair. Sinclair Reasoner! It couldn't be! Not Mr. Fine! Immediately, she reached for the phone.

Nedra heard the telephone ringing as she darted toward her front door. If she answered it she would be even later than she already was. So, depending on her trusty answering machine to do its job, she closed the door behind her as the machine clicked on.

Esther Costello sat in her usual spot at Mount Peter, satisfied that she had done her Christian duty. She didn't know who this man was that Ms. Davis was cavorting with, but she had informed her fellow churchgoers of the goings-on of their precious minister. She had been shocked by some of the responses.

The newer members, the young ones with loose morals, seemed delighted that the pastor of Mount Peter was sleeping around with some man. Obviously, they thought nothing of the church's good name. It was important that their minister be a good example to the flock she was leading, and Nedra Davis certainly was not! Hadn't she done enough to try and run Mount Peter into the ground? Who was this man anyway? What did he do for a living? Was he a Christian? A man of good character? Whoever Nedra chose as her mate must meet certain requirements, certain moral criteria, ones that would reflect well on Mount Peter. Well, Ms. Davis might think she could hide her little affair from some less persistent members of this congregation, but not from Esther Costello! She planned to find out the name of this man, and she planned to find it out soon!

Chapter 19

Sunday had always been Nedra's favorite day of the week. Only good things happened on Sundays. Today was her first Sunday back in the pulpit after two weeks off, and she was looking forward to it.

She delivered a well-received sermon on love and tolerance. Esther had been on her mind when she wrote it, and she knew that she would need lots of both to continue tolerating that woman. No one in church said anything directly to her about the rumor Esther had made a point of spreading about her vacationing with some "strange man." Most of the reactions were sly smiles that clearly indicated it was about time. Nedra was encouraged. Maybe something she said in her sermons over the years, about judging others, had gotten through.

After visiting a few hospitalized parishioners, Nedra swung over to visit Carla. She had been feeling guilty not having shared with Carla and Sharon her relationship with Sin. Sharon had so many problems right now that Nedra's secret seemed trivial; but, she was in love, and she wanted at least one of her best friends to share in her happiness. It was a minor miracle that Carla hadn't already heard the rumor about her "cavorting" from someone at Mount Peter, but she hadn't attended services today, and Nedra couldn't wait to see the look of surprise on her face when she broke the news. Nedra loved surprises, especially on Sunday.

Sin hadn't read the Sunday morning paper. After his morning run, he returned to the house, showered, then answered the urgent message left with his service by his secretary. It was she who told him the news. He soothed Mrs. Cosley's concerns, thanked her for calling, then sat in his second-floor office waiting for his world to end. The sun had set, and the evening shadows had filtered into the darkened room when the doorbell rang. On mechanical legs, he went to answer the summons. He didn't bother to ask who it was. He knew.

The look of hope in her eyes was overwhelming. She was here to hear the words that would confirm that look of hope.

"Do you have faith in me?" he greeted her at the door.

"I have faith in God. I believe in you." Nedra stepped over the threshold and headed straight for his arms. His arms remained at his sides. The pain on her face shot straight to his heart.

She followed him into the family room, where they had cuddled together only hours before. She sat on the sofa. He sat on the matching love seat. There were only inches between them. It felt like the Grand Canyon.

Sin

Sin

Nedra waited. She waited for Sin to erase any doubt.

Carla had reminded her that he was only being investigated, but she could hear the concern in her friend's voice. She knew that Carla was privy to information that even reporters didn't know. Jacob shared everything with Carla. So, to soothe her fears, to strengthen her belief, she went to him. Now, she waited.

Sin knew her expectations. He knew what she wanted from him. He also knew that he might not be able to give it to her. In time he might have been able to, but time had run out.

From the beginning, his greatest fear had been to have her and then lose her. He knew that he would do anything to keep that from happening. She meant too much to him. Yet, she meant so much to others as well. She had been chosen to smooth the way for those with no hope. He knew this to be true. He had been one of those without hope, until she entered his life.

If he lost her, it would destroy him. If she stayed with him, she'd be destroyed. He couldn't let that happen, no matter how great the sacrifice.

"I told you once that there were things that I've done in my life that I'm not proud of." His voice was quiet, controlled.

"Is what they're investigating one of them?" She tried to sound in control herself.

She hoped that he would deny it. All he had to say was the word no, and she would fight heaven and hell to stand by his side. He remained silent.

They stared at each other across the distance they had created, and even now, their repressed passion permeated the room, filled the silent spaces.

Sin wanted to memorized everything about her so he'd never forget her. But he doubted if he ever would. This was the kind of woman any man would die for. With her by your side, there was no battle that couldn't be won. But this was one battle that he wasn't going to ask her to fight. She would lose.

"If you'll remember, I told you once that if there were consequences to loving you, then so be it," said Nedra.

"But, those consequences could bring too high a price. If you love me, I want you to do as I ask."

Her heart thundered in her chest. "No."

"Nobody can connect us by name."

"Carla knows. I told her."

"I want you to cut your losses, before this gets out of hand."

"Explain to me if you have a part in this, that's all I'm asking."

"We won't contact each other again. See each other." He swallowed the lump in his throat. "I never want to see you again."

Nedra was angry. There was no way that he was making this decision as if she had no part in it. "No, Sin. You're not listening to me!"

Sin wanted to go to her, take her by the shoulders and shake some sense into her. But if he touched her he knew that he would never let her go.

"You're mistaken, Nedra, I am listening, but what I hear I won't accept. I'm being investigated for suspicion of dealing in the drug trade. Something your church has fought a battle against for years, and Mount Peter is one of the few examples that can be pointed to that has a record of success. Deny it or not, people are following your lead. If there's even a hint of your being tied to me, everything you've done will be suspect."

"But you were willing for us to be together publicly before all of this happened!" She hated the way she sounded, wounded, desperate. She hadn't meant to sound that way, but she did. That was how she felt.

Sin's tone didn't change. "I wasn't willing, I was resigned, but even then, reluctant. You've got enemies, and our being together would be all of the ammunition they need to make sure you don't make any more progress with the things your church has been doing. Tell me I'm lying?"

She couldn't and he knew it.

Sin felt sick. His heart constricted in his chest. Why shouldn't it. It was breaking. "This was a mistake from the beginning."

Nedra bit her bottom lip, struggling to maintain control of her emotions. She was determined not to cry. They could get through this. "God doesn't make mistakes."

"If that's true, then he placed you in the right place, at the right time, and he placed you there for a purpose."

Nedra couldn't argue. Right now she couldn't even think straight. She had to get away. Now! If she didn't leave, she would collapse. She had to have time to think clearly, so she could plan. After she devised a plan, she would return. That was, if he let her. From the look on his face, from the set of his jaw, she knew he wouldn't.

She didn't recall walking to his front door, or the drive home. She didn't remember opening the door to her condo or entering. She did remember falling to her knees in the bathroom and vomiting. She remembered crawling to her bedroom, and onto her bed, where she lay, unmoving, staring into space. She also remembered the last words he uttered as she walked away from him: "Thank you for stopping the nightmares."

The only problem was, hers were just beginning.

Sin

Sin was a zombie. He became one the moment Nedra walked out of the door. The tears that had followed her departure, the tears that had streamed down his face, soaked his skin, and seeped into his heart, went unheeded. Tears were foreign to him. So was pain. He ignored it. It didn't matter that it invaded every pore of his body, or settled in each bone, or that it rushed through his bloodstream like a raging river. He had mastered the skill of not feeling anything, long ago. That was, until...

The next day, on his way to the office, Sin shook her out of his head. He had been given a few weeks with her, weeks he would always cherish. That was more than he had ever asked for, more than he ever hoped for, and they would be the only memories in his life he would want to take to the grave. It was over. That was it. She was safe, and uninvolved in all of this. Now, he must brace himself for whatever lay ahead.

He had hoped it would never come to this. He had hoped that he could get out before he was discovered. Unfortunately, luck had not been kind in this instance, but at least he had been prepared. He knew what to say. He knew what to do. The only thing about it was that he no longer cared. He was the master of not feeling. That was, until...

The news reporter stood in front of some place called the Bayland Imports office, jabbering away on the evening news. That blasted noise was getting on her nerves, and Esther turned the sound down as she stood at the kitchen counter preparing the evening meal. Her next door neighbor, Jane, had dropped by to make her miserable day even more miserable. She was chattering away about something or another. She was worse than the TV set. When would the woman go home?

It was bad enough she had to spend her day battling a room full of fourth graders who didn't want to learn anything. Then she had to come home to a worthless husband, too lazy to carry his share of her heavy load, supposedly because he had a bad heart. It sure didn't stop him from running around on her. How many had it been? She had lost count. Thank God he had sense enough to be discreet. Then there was those children of hers. The ungrateful brats! After all of the sacrifices she had made for them, they never appreciated anything. They both lived close enough to visit, but when did they ever come by? When they wanted something, that was when! She regretted the day she gave birth!

Now, when she wanted to come home to some peace and quiet, here comes Jane, and her big mouth, crying to her about her husband, Marty. The lush! Everybody knew he was a drunk. She knew it too, so what was she whining about now? She drew her attention back to the woman sitting in her kitchen chair.

"What did you say, Jane?"

"I said, that's him!" Jane's face was flushed with excitement as Esther followed the woman's gaze to the television screen.

Two black men, impeccably dressed, were walking hurriedly from a building toward a late model car as the reporter pursued them relentlessly, trying to stick the mike into the face of one of them. Esther frowned as she turned her attention back to Jane. "Who are you talking about?"

Jane pointed to one of the two men as they reached the car. He kept his head averted, preventing a good view of his face. "That's the man I saw with Reverend Davis in Monterey. The one I told you about, remember? The reporter said that the other one is his lawyer."

Moving swiftly, Esther drew closer to the small TV set, all interest in anything else forgotten. "Are you sure?"

Jane gave a reassuring chuckle. "Am I sure? Honey, do you think I could forget anything that fine?"

As she spoke, the man turned his head quickly enough for Esther to see his profile. She gasped. She knew that face! Where had she seen it before?

Jane caught the sign of recognition. "Do you know him?'

Esther shook her head in the negative. "No, but... What did they say his name was? What's this report all about?"

Esther endured Jane's sigh of reprimand and the scolding she gave her about never listening to people. Those ticking moments gave her just enough time to recall where she had seen that face before, and with whom! She nearly shouted at Jane as her patience with the woman's chatter ran out. "What's his name, Jane?"

Jane told her, and repeated what the news report was about. She watched in fascination as Esther's dour expression changed into one of triumph.

It was the night desk at the newspaper that received the anonymous telephone call. According to the woman, the anti-drug minister whom the media had dubbed the "Anti-Drug Queen" was romantically involved with a "Drug King" and someone needed to look into it. She gave the man's name. The caller was given assurances that someone would do just that. The assignment was made the next morning.

Chapter 20

Carla was worried. Nedra had left her house Sunday evening. It was Tuesday morning now, and she had not seen or spoken to her. She knew that she had gone to talk to Sinclair Reasoner, against Carla's better advice. She expected a call from her after that, but she had yet to receive one. Her calls to Nedra went unanswered.

When Nedra informed her of the secret affair with Sinclair, Carla was hurt. She shared practically everything in her life with Nedra and Sharon, how she could keep something like this from her was beyond her comprehension. Yet, in retrospect, considering what was happening, maybe it was best she hadn't known. Jacob had never provided her with any names, but if she had known in advance she might have been tempted to say more than she meant to. Nedra loved the man. There was no doubt about that. From what she told her, Sinclair Reasoner loved Nedra. But if that man hurt her friend... No, it was best that she hadn't been confronted with the dilemma of knowing about the affair.

It seemed that everybody in town knew about it now, or at least thought that they did. Her telephone had been ringing off the hook. It seemed that "somebody" had spread a rumor that connected Nedra with that "Bayland

Imports man" the newspaper named as being under investigation. People were calling her asking what did she know about it. She chose to remain silent.

Sharon had called earlier from Seattle, and Carla was reluctant to tell her about the developing events. Richard still hadn't been seen, and now, neither had Nedra. Sharon had enough problems. So, Carla had faked happiness and sunshine, and dismissed Sharon's concern that she had tried to call Nedra several times in the past two days, but had yet to get a response.

Carla had informed her, truthfully, that Nedra left a message with the church secretary that she would be unavailable for a few days. Then, after talking to Sharon, Carla jumped into her car, with the key to Nedra's house in her pocket. If she wasn't home, she would find out where Sinclair lived, and God help him if anything had happened to Nedra!

Checking the garage, she was relieved to find Nedra's car parked in its stall, and even more relieved to find Nedra in the living room of her condo. What she wasn't happy about was the state she was in—clad in pajamas, crying. She barely looked up from where she sat, huddled on her love seat, as Carla let herself into her home.

She had never seen her friend like this, depressed, dejected. This wasn't Nedra. She was always in good spirits, full of life. She fought the urge to take her into her arms and comfort her. What was called for, now, was tough love.

Hands on hips, she walked over to her. "Girl! If you ever pull a disappearing act like this again, I'm going to kick your butt from here to L.A. I have been worried to death about you! I'm getting ready to run some bath water so you can wash your stinking behind, then I'm going to fix you something to eat. After that, we will sit and we will talk." She rubbed her hands together. "Now let's get to it!"

An hour later, Nedra sat in the kitchen nook of her condo, still listless, but feeling much better. It was ironic. She was the one trained to comfort others, but it was Carla who seemed to know, instinctively, how to comfort her.

Since leaving Sin's house, she had felt like she'd been hit by a truck. She had cried until she had no more tears to shed, then she had made an attempt to begin functioning normally. She couldn't. Depression had settled upon her like fog on the bay, and she found it difficult placing one foot in front of the other. All she'd been able to do was sleep. The meal before her was the first she had since Sunday and, even now , she picked at it as she informed Carla about her talk with Sinclair. The end of her story brought silence from Carla.

Nedra frowned. "So, you don't have anything to say?" Carla had an opinion about everything. Her silence was unnerving. "Or maybe you have too much to say.

Whatever it is, I deserve it. I deserve everything that's happening to me, after all I'm the one that did wrong. He never mentioned marriage. He never said that we'd be together until death do us part. And I never asked him. I made love to him without benefit of marriage and now I'm being punished for it." Silent tears began to flow.

Getting up from her chair, Carla took her empty plate to the sink, washed it, then placed it in the drainer before returning to the kitchen table and her seat.

She looked thoughtfully at her friend and picked her words carefully. "You don't believe what you just said, and neither do I. Every sermon you've ever preached has spoken of God's love, not his vengeance. So I won't even go there. Where I will go is when you told me about you and Sinclair. I really didn't know what to think about the whole thing. I know Sharon and I teased you about him, because we were looking at him, physically, and Lord knows we liked what we saw. In light of his possible involvement with drugs, I really didn't like what I heard from you about being involved with him, even though I know people are innocent unless proven guilty. But there was something I sensed about the man that one time I met him, something you've sensed too. It was something you learned to love."

Carla sat back in her chair and observed her friend closely. "You might not like what I'm about to say, Nedra, but you know I'm going to say it anyway."

Sin

"Like I didn't know that." Nedra pushed her plate away, and braced herself for the frank opinion Carla was more than capable of giving.

"Sinclair was right to do what he did."

Nedra leaped from her chair, knocking it over in her anger. "How can you say that? He has no right to make a decision like that for both of us."

Carla remained calm. "I don't disagree with that. But, like I said, the decision that was made was the right one."

"The decision never to see him again?" Nedra's temperature was rising as she stood glaring at her friend.

"No, the decision to protect you so that you won't be destroyed by the fallout."

"To protect me? I'm not some child who needs to be looked after!" Carla was going too far. She had never been so angry with her. "I am a thirty-eight year old woman with a mind of my own!"

"And a God-given talent to help and lead others. You've been locked up in here for two days, you don't know what just the hint of a scandal is doing to Mount Peter."

"Mount Peter is strong enough to get through it."

"I don't disagree with that, but it needs a strong leader to help it through, and Sinclair is seeing that the church gets it. Until the cloud over him is lifted, he's got to let you go."

Too angry to look at Carla or speak to her any longer, Nedra stormed into the living room, and plopped down on one of two matching love seats. Snatching up the remote, she turned on the TV, choosing to occupy herself with any-thing except dealing with Carla, who followed her into the room and took a seat opposite her.

Nedra stared at the screen, determined to ignore her, hoping that she would go away. The news report on the screen was nothing but background noise, ignored by them both until a picture of Sinclair was flashed on screen. Another man was with him and they were walking out of a building. Both women snapped to attention. Carla grabbed the remote and raised the volume.

"Mr. Reasoner, a prominent businessman, seen here with his attorney, reportedly used his legitimate import business to launder illegal drug money. It is rumored that Mr. Reasoner, a bachelor, has been linked romantically with Rev. Nedra Davis, pastor of Oakland's Mount Peter church, which, supposedly, has been in the forefront of fighting the drug trade in East Oakland."

Nedra sat stunned. She hadn't looked at TV, read a newspaper, or listened to the radio for days, but two things were clear. Sin had been identified, and Mount Peter's motives were now suspect just as he had warned they would be.

"The newspaper and TV reporters have been snooping around questioning anybody remotely connected to Mount

Peter, " said Carla. "And I'll bet you a million dollars we both know who's behind the media knowing about you and Sinclair!"

Both looked at the screen again. Sin's face could no longer be clearly seen, but his broad shoulders, usually held so proudly, were now hunched, and the catlike gait with which he walked now seemed to drag.

"He looks so tired."

Carla's eyes flew to Nedra, noting the sadness in her voice and the look in her eyes as she watched him. She knew the look well. It was the same look she had for Jacob.

As Sin and his attorney vanished from the screen, Carla clicked the set off and joined Nedra on her love seat. Grabbing her by the shoulders, she turned her to face her. "Now, you can hide in here, feeling sorry for yourself, if you want to, or go out there and take care of business. There are things that need doing, and you're the one to do them. Remember, you didn't get this far by faith for nothing. "

One hug between them was all that was needed to mend their differences. Nedra was re-energized. She was so mad that her first thought was to storm over to Esther's house, and forget all of her Christian training. She wanted to kick some serious behind, but Carla's cooler head prevailed.

Carla stayed with her the rest of the night, and they talked until the early morning. They planned strategy to combat the rumors and innuendoes, talked about Sharon and Richard, about Colin and Trevor. They talked about everybody and everything, but Sin. He was the one subject that, for Nedra, was too painful to discuss.

After breakfast, as Carla left to prepare for the rest of her day, she turned to her friend with a look Nedra recognized. She was about to impart some of her famous unsolicited advice. Knowing Carla's frankness, she might not like what she had to say. She was wrong.

"I don't know this Sinclair Reasoner at all, but there's one thing I can say about him. Considering all that you've told me, and judging from what's gone on so far, you are one lucky woman for having him in your life, no matter how long it was. Because, girlfriend, I can say this with no reservations, he loves the hell out of you."

"No comment! No comment! That's all both of them can say!"

Richard crumbled the newspaper and tossed it across the room where it bounced off the television screen. "Well, I know I've got plenty to say! How about how they whored around up in Tahoe! I bet y'all didn't know that one!"

He was furious! After all he had done for Nedra.
Damn! He saved her life, and here she was screwing
around with one of Eddie and Lynn's lackeys.

For the last couple of days, the media had been filled
with reports about the Carter drug bust and the relationship
between the "Anti-Drug Queen" and an alleged member of
the Carter drug ring. Speculation as to how much Nedra
knew about the drug ring was rampant. There were even
some who insinuated that she might be involved with
drugs. Her character was questioned from every quarter.

There was one report, from some neighbors of a couple
named Simpson, who belonged to Mount Peter church.
The neighbors related how they had spotted this Sinclair
Reasoner's fancy car parked overnight in front of the
Simpson house some time ago. According to the report,
Mr. Simpson was laid up in the hospital and his wife was
taking care of him, while the great St. Nedra was supposed
to be baby-sitting two orphan children. Instead, she was
doing some laying around herself.

Some big-mouth woman, who called herself a "concerned parishioner" told another TV reporter that she had
seen them "all hugged up together" at some amusement
park, when they were supposed to be chaperoning a group
of church children. The lady's next door neighbor,
prompted by Mrs. Big Mouth, added that she saw them in
Monterey together, getting into the same fancy car that the
Simpson neighbors had described. Mrs. Big Mouth added

that her neighbor had informed her they had been propped up against a wall, outside a Monterey night club. She reported, with a look of righteous indignation, that she'd been told they had their tongues down each other's throats, kissing, making a public spectacle of themselves. The neighbor tried to interrupt her, but Mrs. Big Mouth hastened to add that she thought that it was a disgraceful sin that a minister, a servant of the Lord, should carry on in public like that, without regard to her Christian calling.

Richard agreed. He had loved her. He had worshipped her from afar. She was good. She was pure. He had even forgiven her for a moment of weakness. It showed that she was only human. But this! This whoring around like some street slut! And with a common drug dealer, and all the while she was rejecting him! This really pissed him off.

He had saved her life and jeopardized his own. He had planned to go for her, take her away. She had played him for a fool. What a fool he had been! Probably everybody in the Bay Area knew she was a whore, but him. Everybody had been laughing at him for thinking she was some kind of saint! Well, nobody played him for a fool! Not Richard Ryan III, the son of Judge Richard Ryan II. No, he didn't play that!

Richard took another snort of coke to ease his irritation. Yeah, he had to alter Plan Number Two just a bit, but that shouldn't be a problem. He didn't have to worry about Lynn any longer. The papers said that she was in a psycho ward. It seems she went whacko when they arrested her and bugged out completely behind bars. They said that she was a psychopath and was locked up for evaluation. Hell! They didn't have to do an evaluation, he could have told them, up front, that she was crazy.

Now, he was free to return to Oakland and take care of this Nedra business. He wasn't ready to kill her for Lynn Trellis, but now it was personal. She had played him! She had everybody laughing at him.

Richard reached into the night stand drawer and withdrew the pistol Lynn had given him to kill Nedra. It was untraceable, and he had been given instructions about where to dump it after the hit. It would never be found, and, no one would suspect him of pulling the trigger.

He ran his hand slowly along the smooth edge of the pistol's barrel, then aimed at a spot on the wall opposite the bed.

He grinned. "Yeah, it looks like Plan Number One is back in effect." He pretended to pull the trigger. "Pow! Gotcha! Goodbye, Reverend Davis."

Chapter 21

Attendance at Mount Peter Baptist Church was usually good on Sundays, but the Sunday following the news reports linking Nedra with Sin there was standing room only. Ushers had to turn potential worshippers away. The media was banned altogether from attending, although numerous newspaper reporters donned their Sunday best to pose as pseudo worshippers.

Nedra was ready. She had faced the onslaught of aggressive media, questioning parishioners, irate deacons, and the accusations and condemnation of some of her fellow male ministers with her head high. Jacob had referred her to one of his fellow attorneys if she needed legal advice. She had thanked him, but declined. She had done nothing legally wrong. As far as she knew, there was no law against loving someone.

When she stepped into the pulpit that morning, she did so with confidence. Esther was in her usual seat, a smug smile of victory planted firmly on her lips. She had managed to split the congregation into two warring factions and felt close to seeing her major goal accomplished, removing Nedra Davis from the pulpit of Mount Peter.

Esther's own faction averaged fifty and older, married couples, widows and unmarried, longtime members of the church. They were the church leaders, the deacons, the head of committees. Those who contributed heavily, financially, to Mount Peter. They held power and they had money. The faction that supported Nedra was younger, mostly single professionals and some married couples with young children. The teenagers were one hundred percent behind Reverend Ned, as she was affectionately called. They were delighted that she had found herself a man! Though vocal, most members of this faction did not hold the power in the church that their counterparts held, and Esther was quick to dismiss them. An emergency Deacon Board meeting was scheduled for the coming week. Nedra would be asked to explain herself, if she could, but Esther was certain she couldn't. Some members of the Sisters of Help had personally asked Nedra about Sinclair Reasoner. They reported to Esther that they were told, with no sign of shame whatsoever, that she owed them no explanation, and didn't mean to give them one. Nedra informed them that she had done nothing in public to embarrass the church. The arrogance of the woman was unbelievable!

The great Reverend Davis had been caught red-handed engaged in immoral behavior that had put a cloud of suspicion over Mount Peter. It was practically guaranteed that after next week, Nedra would no longer lead the church down the road to ruin!

So, it was with this in mind, that Esther met Nedra's eyes. Neither woman exchanged greetings. Neither woman blinked. The battle lines were drawn.

After the announcements were made, the greetings were given, and the singing was completed, Nedra took her place in the pulpit and looked out into the crowd.

"The topic of today's sermon is one that is dear to my heart. The title may be an old one but the subject is as new as the day. I'm calling today's sermon, "Bearing False Witness Against Thy Neighbor," subtitled, "Judge Not Lest Ye Be Judged."

Nedra had never been a fire and brimstone preacher. She preferred to get her point across subtly, but the events of the past week didn't call for being subtle. She preached the good sisters out of their seats and had them shouting up and down the aisle. She had grown men weeping and children rocking in their seats. Without taking her eyes off Esther Costello, she gave no explanations and offered no excuses. She simply challenged anyone who was without sin in Mount Peter to come stand before her and cast the first stone. When, drenched in sweat and breathless from her delivery, she finally took her seat, she did so to a standing ovation. Everyone stood except Esther Costello. But when Nedra met her eyes this time, Esther blinked.

Sin

Sin tossed the last pair of socks into the suitcase and closed it with a snap. Gripping it firmly, he pulled it off the bed and placed it beside the other two already sitting at the door. He was ready to go. All he needed was the word. He didn't know when it would come, or if it would come, but arrangements had been made for him to be taken safely out of the state, and possibly the country. Soon, he would be a man on the run if the legalities didn't turn out to his advantage.

Sighing, he settled onto one of the chairs in his bedroom and stared into space. He had been doing a lot of that lately, sitting and staring at nothing. His eyes wandered to the discarded newspaper lying on the table in front of him. He tried to force himself not to reach for it again, but he did so anyway. Nedra's eyes stared back at him. She was dressed in her clerical robe, posed sedately for an official church photo. His finger slowly traced the outline of her full lips and caressed the contour of her delicate cheek bones. Why he kept torturing himself he didn't know. Maybe because he deserved the pain—a pain he thought he was immune to, but was finding more and more difficult to ignore.

His eyes strayed to the headline to the right of the picture. Anti-Drug Queen Fighting Rumors of Drug Connections. It was worse than he had imagined. They were hounding her unmercifully. If only he had left her alone. He knew he should have. He had told himself over and over to do just that. If he had left her alone, this never would have happened! It was all his fault.

Placing the newspaper back on the table, he wandered across the room to stare out the window, once again staring at nothing. Maybe his leaving would reduce the pressure on her. Things would die down, people would forget. Things could get back to normal for her. Sin drifted over to the bed and, listlessly, flopped onto it.

Would things ever be normal again? How bad was it for her? How was she holding up? He wanted to see her so badly, he ached. But seeing her was impossible. If only he could find out how she was doing.

Crossing a forearm over his eyes, he found the dark welcoming. Lately, he hadn't felt like facing the light, but even in the darkness he found that he couldn't shut her out of his mind.

"Girl! I thought Esther was going to fall right out of her seat, our girl, Nedra, was so bad!" Carla gushed, pacing the living room with the cordless phone pressed to her ear. Sharon was on the other end, enjoying Carla's blow-by-blow description of Nedra's sermon.

Carla had insisted on picking Nedra up that morning, and escorting her to Sunday morning service for moral support. After church, they had come to Carla's house to fix

Sunday dinner. Carla had spent the remainder of the afternoon calling everyone she knew to tell them about Nedra's triumph.

As she lay stretched out on the sofa, recovering from the heavy meal, Nedra tried not to enjoy Carla's enthusiastic praise, but she found that her humility went only so far. She had to admit feeling pretty good about the day's events. Carla's voice interrupted her thoughts.

"Hey, Nedra, Sharon wants to talk to you!" Carla thrust the receiver into Nedra's waiting hands. "Tell her I said kiss, I've got to get to the Oakland Airport, Jacob's flight lands in twenty minutes." She picked up the coat and purse she had discarded when they entered. "Don't forget, Mrs. Wilson next door baked us one of her famous lemon pies. She's going to drop it off. We can chow down for dessert. See ya!" She whisked out the door at a run.

"That girl makes me tired just watching her." Nedra laughed into the telephone. "Hey, my friend, how are you doing?"

"Much better since I heard about how you cleaned house today." Sharon's voice echoed her pride.

Nedra smiled at the colorful description. "Well, I haven't cleaned house thoroughly yet, but at least I swept up a bit. But Carla's bent your ear enough about me. How are you doing? When are you coming home?"

There was silence on the other end as Sharon gathered her thoughts. "I'm doing better, Nedra, a lot better. Carla told me that Richard still hasn't been seen or heard from. She didn't seem to be worried though."

"Sharon, believe me, Richard can take care of himself."

"I know, but with his problem and all..."

"You mean his drug addiction."

"Yes, his addiction. Well, I was thinking that something might have happened to him."

Sharon's need for reassurance was apparent. Carla wouldn't give it to her. Nedra did. "I'm sure he'll be all right, Sharon. We would have heard something if he wasn't."

"Yes, that's true." There was another pause. "I know you might not be able to understand this, Nedra, but love isn't something easily dismissed."

It was Nedra's turn for silence as her friend's words wrapped around her heart. "You're wrong, Sharon, I do understand. I know exactly what you mean."

Richard parked his car up the street from Carla's house, approximately where he had parked it the day he tampered with Nedra's brakes. Carla's car was in the driveway. Good, he could get the information about Nedra's whereabouts from her.

He had driven by Nedra's condo. Her car was in its stall, but when he managed to get into the building, there was no answer. Some woman coming out of the apartment next door said that she had seen her getting into some fancy car earlier that morning. He didn't have to ask, she was probably with that Reasoner bastard. He was here to find out. Carla would know where she was. She'd know her entire itinerary. The two of them were thick as thieves.

Patting his jacket pocket to check on the gun, he got out of the car and headed toward the house. Yeah, his beloved sister was just the right person to lead him to his prey.

The door chime rang just as Nedra was ending her conversation with Sharon. "Hon, Mrs. Wilson is at the door with one of those finger-lickin' good pies of hers."

"Lucky!"

Nedra laughed, remembering all of the girl talk the three of them had here at Carla's, topped off with one of Mrs. Wilson's pies. "Eat your heart out, but come home soon. Got to go! Love ya!"

Disconnecting, Nedra dropped the phone and went to the door, opening it with an expectant smile. Her eyes widened in shock at Richard standing at the front door. He looked equally shocked. She was the first to recover.

"Richard! What are you doing here?" She moved aside as he eased past her, whispering a quick, silent prayer for the Lord to give her the strength to be civil to the man. She'd need all of the help she could get to maintain her composure. Just seeing him brought back the memories of

Sharon's battered body. She followed him into the living room.

Richard, reeling from the shock of coming face to face with Nedra so soon, took a seat on the sofa she had abandoned. "I came to see my sister."

"Carla's not here." She took a seat in a chair opposite him, noting that he was making himself at home without an invitation. "She went to pick up Jacob at the airport."

"Her car's outside." He sounded dubious.

"She must have taken Jacob's car."

A slight smile pursed his lips. "So, you're here alone?" He looked around as if seeking confirmation.

She nodded. "Carla and Jacob should be back soon, maybe in an hour or so."

He did not respond but got up and started walking around the house, peeking into the dining room, then back to the entrance and up the stairs.

Nedra noticed his agitation. She also noticed in the short period during which he had been missing, he had undergone some physical changes. He had lost weight. The ponytail he had once sported had been replaced with a short haircut that framed his face and made him look older, more conservative. His ears still sported two earrings, but the gold hoops had been replaced by gold studs. A five o'clock shadow covered his handsome face. He looked neat and clean, but there was a difference. Where he had always been fastidious in his dress, his stylish clothes now hung on him loosely and appeared rumpled.

Nedra watched as he walked back to the living room. "What in the world are you looking for?" His constant movement was getting on her nerves. "I told you Carla's not here."

He stood behind the sofa, watching her. Oh, she looked cool, calm and collected, dressed in her winter white slacks and sweater. White, the color of purity! The color angels wore, but everybody knew better didn't they? At least everybody but him! Yes, look at her, sitting there looking so superior, like she didn't have a care in the world. But she would have. She was about to have one big care in a minute. "Where's your boyfriend?"

Nedra started. "Where's my what?"

Richard snorted. "You heard me. I said, where's your boyfriend?"

No he didn't! Nedra couldn't believe what she was hearing. This woman beater, this fugitive from justice, had the nerve to come in here and join the other know-it-alls judging her! This was too much! Leaping from her chair, hands on hips, Nedra was ready to gave him a piece of her mind.

"I know you're not standing there trying to get into my business. I'd advise you to straighten up your own life before you start getting into mine."

Richard walked from behind the sofa, a sinister look on his face. The look unnerved Nedra for a second, but she gave no outward indication. He stopped in front of her, leaning down within inches of her face.

He hissed. "You whore! Who are you to give anybody advice?"

Nedra flinched, stung as much by his words as his delivery. Without warning he grabbed her by her upper arms and pushed her back into the chair. Shocked by his action, she struggled to get up. "What the—"

He pushed her down again, resting his arms on each side of the chair, effectively pinning her into it. "If you move again without me telling you to, I'll break your filthy little neck!"

Nedra froze as she caught the hard glint in his eyes. Anger turned into anxiety. "What's wrong with you, Richard? What is this about?"

He sneered. "What's wrong with me?" Then he laughed and shook his head as if unable to believe the question was asked. "What's wrong with you? That's the question here.
You go around acting all pure and innocent...making a man fall in love with you..."

"Richard, I—"

"Shut up, you slut!" His hiss descended into a low, guttural growl as he raised his hand to slap her. Nedra recoiled. The sound of the door chime stopped his hand in midair. Startled, his head jerked toward the sound.

Nedra's eyes flew to the front door, then back to him. She told herself to remain calm. She didn't want to show fear. It was obvious that he was high, but there was something else wrong, seriously wrong For the first time since he'd entered the house, she sensed real danger.

"That's Mrs. Wilson, Carla's next door neighbor, the one that bakes the good pies. She's bringing one over here for Carla. She knows that I'm here waiting for her. I was just talking to her on the phone when you came to the door. "

Richard's eyes narrowed at the sound of the chimes ringing a second time. She could see him thinking, but the gun that he slipped from his pocket caught her by surprise. She gasped.

"That's right, it's a gun and it's loaded. So don't try anything or there'll be two dead bodies."

Gripping her by her upper arm, he jerked her off the chair and walked her toward the front door. Harshly, he whispered. "I'll be standing behind the door. You take the pie from the old biddy, and keep the talk short." Releasing her arm, he stepped into the space behind the door.

With her mind working a mile a minute and her heart pounding out of her chest, she opened the door. "Mrs. Wilson, I—" She broke off as she stared in shock. Before her stood Sin.

Sin stared back at her, equally shocked at her presence. Obviously, he had expected to see Carla and not her.

Nedra was the first to recover, jolted by her awareness of the danger that faced them both. She started to slam the door shut, hoping that would at least give him a chance to escape Richard's insanity, but Sin's reflexes were quicker than her own. He moved swiftly toward her and stopped the door.

"Nedra! Baby!" His piercing black eyes caressed her as he searched her face anxiously. "Are you okay? I came by to see Carla...to see how you were doing... I never expect-ed...never imagined... Here, lets move out of this door-way. I don't' want anybody to see us."

Her startled, "No! Don't!" went unheeded as he moved the two of them into the house, where he pulled her into his arms. "Oh, God, Nedra."

His mouth found hers even as she pushed him away. "Sin!"

"Well, well, well. Look what we have here."

Sin stiffened in surprise and turned toward the sound of the voice. His eyes narrowed at the sight of Richard and the gun aimed at them both.

"What's going on, Nedra? Who is this?"

Richard laughed sarcastically. "Who is this? Do you mean, who am I? Or, do you mean, is this another one? Which is it?"

"Sin, this is Richard Ryan, Carla's brother."

Sin

"Richard Ryan?" Sin's mind raced, then recognition. Sharon's boyfriend! The one who beat up women! Why was he here?

Richard said, "Well you don't have to introduce yourself. We all know who you are, Mr. Reasoner, or should I say, Mr. Lover. There's no doubt about that, I see." Richard's gaze snaked down the length of Nedra's body. "You have definitely gotten some of that."

Insulted and angry, Nedra started to move toward Richard, but Sin's hand on her arm stopped her. She said, "Richard, I'm not sure what this is all about, but..."

"I bet you don't know what this is about." Richard spat. "Why should you know? When did you ever think that anything I did, anything I said was important. I was never good enough for you. You were too pure, too righteous. You never even gave me a chance!"

Gleaning the reason for his anger toward her, Nedra used it as leverage. Maybe there was a chance to talk him out of whatever he was planning. "You were a friend, Richard, and my best friend's brother. I never thought of you as a potential date or..."

"Or as anything at all! You made me fall in love with you. You led me on. I thought you were special, worth waiting for!"

"Richard, I—"

"I told you to shut up! I don't want to hear a thing you have to say. I wasn't good enough for you, but he was?"

He waved the gun at Sin and sneered at him contemptuously. "Some dope dealing gutter trash! This is what you want?"

Sin noted that Richard was high and becoming distracted as his agitation increased. He knew that he could take him. With a subtle movement, he placed himself between Richard and Nedra. "Man, I understand where you're coming from." He took one small step toward Richard.

Richard leveled the gun at him. "The hell you do! You don't know a thing about me, but I know at least one thing about you. You slept with this whore!"

Nedra saw Sin's eyes glaze with fury at Richard's reference to her, but his expression remained blank.

Richard chuckled menacingly. "And now you're going to die with her."

Richard moved from his spot near the door and walked slowly in a semi-circle around the couple. "You see, I decided that the scenario will be like this. You two can't live without each other. So, I think a murder-suicide will be more than believable."

The change in position brought Sin standing closer to Richard.

"You came over here looking for Nedra, upset with all that's happened," Richard droned on.

Nedra's eyes traveled nervously between the two men.

"You found her. You two fought."

She knew instinctively that Sin would try and charge Richard.

"You shot her, then killed yourself."

Richard shifted slightly in his stance, and Sin sprang into action, pushing Nedra to the floor. She looked up in time to see a blur of movement as Sin executed a rounded kick to Richard's hand. Stunned, Richard stumbled backward as the gun went off, the sound echoing loudly in the entranceway. It fell from his hand and skittered across the parquet floor, ending up on the living room rug.

On her knees, praying silently with every move she made, Nedra scrambled into the living room to retrieve the weapon. Picking it up, she raced back to the entranceway just as Sin smashed a fist into his opponent's chin. Richard fell like a log.

Nedra stood in the entranceway, her eyes fixed on Richard's unconscious form. Shaken, she placed the gun on a nearby table and joined Sin, who stood, looking down at Richard's crumpled form.

"Carla said that he was sick. I don't think anybody knew how sick he was."

Turning, Sin started walking toward the living room. "I've got to sit down."

Nedra's eyes went to his face, which showed no visible signs of the physical battle he'd just endured. Yet he looked ashen.

Nedra followed him, concerned "Yes, you do that, I'll call the... " Sin swayed. Nedra clutched his arm. "What is it? Are you okay?"

Her eyes swept the length of his body, and ice swept through her veins. A spot of blood was spreading rapidly on the front of the yellow knit sweater Sin wore under his leather bomber jacket. She opened her mouth to scream, but no sound came as he slowly sank to the floor.

"Sin!" She reached out to catch him, trying in vain to support him. His weight brought her down with him. Terror filled her as she clawed at his jacket. "Sin, honey, you're hurt! Do you have your phone? I've got to call 911!" With shaky hands she punched in the numbers, looking at Sin as she did so. "Don't close your eyes, baby, please!"

Tears streamed down her cheeks, onto his, as she smothered his face with kisses. "You're gong to be fine, sweetheart. Listen to me, everything's going to be fine."

His breathing grew shallow, his eyelids began to flutter, and Nedra watched in horror as the light started to fade from his dark piercing eyes.

"Oh God! Sin! Please! Please! Don't close your eyes, baby! Don't close your eyes!"

She cradled his large body to hers and prayed, desperately, as she screamed into the telephone, "Answer! Answer!"

With effort, Sin raised a hand and touched Nedra's damp cheek. He whispered, "Nedra...love..." before closing his eyes.

Chapter 22

Nedra hated the smell of hospitals. No matter how many times she went into one, that stench always assailed her senses. Hospitals held an antiseptic smell which fostered the illusion that everything was clean, pure, fresh, when in reality it wasn't. In hospitals death was a constant companion, and each day death hovered over Sinclair Reasoner .

On Day One, he went into cardiac arrest during the four-hour operation to remove the bullet that lodged only inches from his heart. Nedra prayed. He survived. On Day Two, in intensive care, his fever rose to an alarming level. Nedra prayed harder. His fever decreased. On Day Three, he slipped into a coma. Nedra's prayers went into overdrive and stayed there.

Her prayer was simple. Let him live. She wanted to make promises to God. She wanted to promise that if Sin lived she'd make the ultimate sacrifice and never see him again, but she knew that she would be lying. So, she kept her vigil by his side, and the only promise she made was to herself, that her face would be the first face he saw when he awakened.

She stayed at the hospital day and night. Carla brought her changes of clothes. She slept in the chair by his side and ate in the hospital cafeteria. Outside the world revolved, but it didn't matter to her. This was home as long as Sin was here.

Now Day Four was dawning, and through the night Sin had been making progress. He showed signs of awakening from the coma, and the ashen look that had settled on his handsome face had lessened. Nedra released a sigh of relief as her fingers caressed his jawline. He was going to make it. For the first time in days she could say those words with certainty.

Nedra glanced around the room, silent except for the steady bleep of the equipment which monitored Sin's vital signs. The room was bare except for the necessities, but when he was able to be moved into the private room reserved for him, she planned on filling the room with the many flowers and cards he had received from well-wishers. For a man who claimed that he had no one in his life, the past few days had proven he was not as isolated as he thought.

There were a dozen people who worked for his company in Oakland and each had called the hospital personally seeking information about his welfare. Mrs. Cosley, Sin's secretary, had spent the first two days of his confinement in the hospital waiting room. Forced by day three to return to Bayland to see to the business in her boss's absence, she continued to call frequently for updates on his progress.

There were calls from Bob Kirk and his son, Todd, who expressed deep concern for their friend. The Simpsons called, as did Arnella Cotter and Jason Rich, who remembered Sin's kindness as a chaperone at the amusement park. There were cards and letters from customers who had conducted business with Sin at Bayland, and a beautiful flower arrangement had arrived yesterday from the employees who worked for him in his east coast Bayland office. Each person had signed a gigantic card with personal notes included. Yes, Sin had touched more lives than he knew, especially the Johnson boys.

How Colin and Trevor found out about Sin's being shot wasn't hard to guess. Anyone living in the Bay Area knew, unless they didn't own a television, listen to a radio, or read a newspaper. The media was having a field day.

Nedra had answered a call at the nurses' station, which, the nurse on duty said, the caller described as "an emergency." To her surprise it was Colin on the other end.

No amount of bravado could conceal the fear in the young boy's voice. His tone demanded that he not be lied to about Sin's condition, and Nedra complied. Sin loved the boys and treated them with respect. She could do no less. She told the boy that Sin's condition was grave, but she had faith that God would pull him through. She asked Colin and his brother to pray for their friend. Colin hung up without a word.

Sin

The most mysterious visitor during Sin's crisis had been a tall, imposing man around sixty, with a head full of gray hair that matched his eyes. He identified himself to her as Mr. Tyler. That had been this morning.

She had been headed for the cafeteria to get something to eat when she passed the nurses' station and heard him asking about Sinclair Reasoner. Nedra stopped and introduced herself.

Mr. Tyler scrutinized her carefully, then with an approving gleam in his eye said, "I've heard about you, Ms. Davis, and after seeing you in person, I've got to say that Reasoner has very good taste."

Nedra eyed him warily. The compliment was given graciously, but there was something about the man that put her instantly on guard. The hospital had put extra security on duty to keep the press from disturbing Sin, or intruding on her privacy. Was this a reporter who'd gotten through?

"How do you know Sinclair?" Nedra didn't try to conceal the challenge in her voice.

He responded much too quickly, as if his answer had been rehearsed. "We're business acquaintances from the east coast. I just happened to be in the Bay Area on business and read about the shooting." He added in what sounded like an afterthought, "According to all accounts, my friend Reasoner is a hero."

He paused expectantly, as if waiting for Nedra to fill in the blanks. She didn't. He continued. "I wanted to stop by and see how he was doing."

His concern sounded sincere, but Nedra's senses were on alert. "Every day brings a new challenge, but today he seems a little better."

Mr. Tyler glanced toward Sin's room as if he wanted to see for himself, then drew his attention back to Nedra. The set of her jaw, the look on her face told him louder than words could have that her word about Sin's progress would have to be good enough. He would not be entering his room. A faint smile crossed his lips.

"I'm glad to hear that. Reasoner is a good man. A good man."

Nedra did not respond. Her uncertainty about his intentions kept her vigilant. "What company did you say you were with, Mr. Tyler? Perhaps you have a business card? I can give it to Sinclair when he gets better so he'll know that you came by."

Nedra noticed the slightest flicker of surprise in his eyes before he recovered and answered smoothly, "No, I'm afraid I didn't bring one with me. Just tell him Tyler from New York came by. He'll know who I am." He nodded his head and backed away. "Good day, Ms. Davis. It was nice meeting you."

Nedra watched him walk away, straight, tall, almost military in his stride. His presence had left her with an unsettling impression that there was more to Mr. Tyler's appearance than he had revealed. Forgetting her meal, she'd returned to Sin's side with the feeling that she needed to protect him. From what she didn't know.

Nedra's thoughts and her attention returned to her surroundings and to Sin. She started in surprise as her eyes were met by his familiar dark ones. He had awakened from the coma. Silently, she gave thanks to God. Fighting back tears of gratitude she laid her palm against his cheek and offered an emotional "Hello."

His smile was weak, as was his voice. She had to hover over his parched lips to hear his words, but they were the sweetest words she had heard from him in four long days and nights.

"Hello, yourself," he whispered.

The air felt good on Nedra's face as she took her first step outside of the hospital in four days. Sin's awaking from the coma has caused a flurry of activity among the medical team monitoring his progress, and she had retreated to the waiting room while they did their jobs. She called Carla to give her the good news, and her friend had convinced her to come home with her for a hot bath and a home-cooked meal. After assuring herself that Sin was resting well, Nedra had agreed.

As they drove along in Carla's car Nedra felt a mix of emotions, euphoria at Sin's medical progress and sadness about the events that had put his life in danger. The past few days had been a roller coaster not only for her, but for Carla and her family.

Richard had been locked up on a variety of charges, the worst being attempted murder. He had turned states evidence against Lynn Trellis but it didn't help reduce the charges. His bail was extremely high, and Carla's parents had refused to pay it.

On hearing about the shooting, Sharon had returned to Oakland. During the weeks that she'd been gone, she had faced the truth about herself and about Richard. She hadn't liked what she discovered. Not only had she allowed Richard to abuse her but she came to realize that her acceptance of his behavior helped foster it. She vowed never to make that mistake again. When he made a request for her to come to him in the lockup, she refused. His hold on her was over.

Nedra's arrival at Carla's house brought warm greetings from Sharon and Jacob. No expense had been spared to welcome her return to "civilization," as Jacob described it. The table had been set with their best crystal, china, and silver, and dinner and dessert were delicious.

After dinner, Nedra called Colin and Trevor and informed them of Sin's progress. As usual Colin received the news with restraint, but Trevor's cheers were so loud that they could be heard by the other occupants in the house. His exuberance brought much needed laughter to them all.

A call to the hospital confirmed that Sin was still resting comfortably and continued to make a remarkable recovery. Having received that news, Nedra was able to relax as the four of them settled in the living room to enjoy the rest of the evening. Her friends filled her in on the news she had missed during her confinement with Sin.

The media were now turning Sin the villain into Sin the hero. On one hand he was suspected of being a key player in the illegal drug trade, on the other hand he was the conquering hero who had saved his lover from a madman. The reporting was schizophrenic to say the least. They didn't seem to know what to make of the man.

Carla reported that Esther Costello claimed she knew what to make of him, and of Nedra as well. "Mount Peter is falling apart," said Carla. "They need you, Nedra."

Nedra listened calmly as Carla informed her of the campaign Esther was leading to replace her as the church's minister. The news did not surprise her, but she disagreed with Carla. The church wasn't falling apart. Mount Peter was stronger than most of its members realized and she had faith that it would survive this crisis as it had so many others. She was at peace with letting Mount Peter weather this storm without her guidance. The church's existence, its purpose was greater than one person's vision.

As for Esther, Nedra had plans for the woman that might not encompass the good book's definition of Christian charity. But being a minister didn't mean that she wasn't human. There were things that the woman was saying about her that were untrue and they had been repeated in the media. She would not stand by and allow her character to be attacked unfairly. Just as she was ready to accept responsibility for her actions, Esther Costello had to be held responsible for her behavior as well. She was going to see to it that she was.

She turned to Jacob. "I need to make an appointment with you in the near future, Jacob." Conversation in the room stopped as all eyes turned to her. "I've got some business to take care of and I need your advice."

Nedra meant to go back to the hospital that evening, but she made the mistake of taking Carla's advice and resting for a "little while". Carla was to wake her up in an hour. She hadn't. Nedra slept for eighteen hours. Despite her anger and frustration at her friends who had conspired to get her to take the much needed rest, she knew that what they had done had been for the best. She had been physically and mentally exhausted.

A frantic call to the hospital brought the good news that Sin had been taken off the critical list. His condition was upgraded to serious, and he had been moved to a private room.

When Nedra arrived at the hospital, she was surprised to see Mr. Tyler coming out of Sin's room. To her knowledge he was still allowed no visitors other than herself. Yet, here he was, this stranger, who claimed to be a friend, walking out of Sin's room as if he belonged there. Had he slipped past hospital personnel? If so, heads would roll.

Nedra planted herself squarely in his path as he turned toward her to head down the hall. "And just what do you think you're doing?"

Mr. Tyler started, surprised to see her, but he quickly regained his composure and offered a smile. "Ms. Davis. It's good to see you again."

Nedra tried, unsuccessfully, to keep the anger out of her voice. "I wish I could say the same, Mr. Tyler, but I'd like to know who gave you permission to go into Sinclair's room? Do the nurses know you're here? Does the doctor?"

Mr. Tyler ignored the questions. "Reasoner is doing much better today. I think seeing you will brighten his day."

With that he patted her arm indulgently and moved past her down the hall. Amazed at his audacity, an open-mouthed Nedra watched as he stepped into the elevator and the doors closed behind him. Recovering from her speechlessness too late to react to his insulting dismissal, she fumed. Now she was certain that he was a reporter! Who else would have the nerve? She meant to get to the bottom of this!

Spurred by anger and concern, she rushed into Sin's room, not knowing what to expect. What she saw stopped her in mid-stride. Although he still appeared weak, he sat propped up in bed supported by pillows. His face was gaunt, but some color had begun to replace the grayish tint his skin tones had taken during his illness. Best of all, the sparkle had returned to his eyes as he looked at her.

"Where have you been?" His voice was a bit raspy, but he sounded like a million to her. He reached out to her. "I missed you."

Amazed by his medical progress and moved by the tenderness of his words, Nedra moved to his bedside, took his hand and planted a slow, sweet kiss on his lips. He responded, and the joy she felt overwhelmed her. God certainly answered prayers.

Feeling bereaved of his warmth as her lips left his, she gave him her warmest smile. "Oh, I've been around, and that's where I plan on staying."

Sin smiled weakly, but a shadow fell over his features as he brought her hand to his cheek. "If only you could, then I'd know there really is a God, but, you really shouldn't stick around too long. Nothing has changed."

Nedra gave a frustrated sigh. Not this you-must-leave-me nonsense again. "Sin, don't even go there. How are you feeling? Did that guy, Mr. Tyler, disturb you? I ran into him outside your door. Who is he anyway? Do you really know him?"

She noted how his eyes became guarded at the mention of Tyler's name. Who was this guy?

"Yeah, I know him."

He offered no further explanation, and she decided not to ask for one. Why press an issue that wasn't that important. He still was too ill to be upset. Their conversation turned to other things.

Night was falling over the city, and the hospital had slowed its frantic pace when the orderly brought Sin his dinner. He still couldn't eat solid foods, and he resisted the soft, unidentifiable concoction, but she managed to coax him to eat most of it before she dozed off in the chair in his room. When she awakened she was in for another surprise. Colin was sitting on Sin's bed talking to him.

Nedra rubbed the sleep from her eyes to assure herself that she wasn't dreaming. Children his age weren't allowed on this floor. How had he gotten here? "Colin?"

The boy turned. "Hi, Reverend Davis. How you doin'?"

"What are you doing here? How did you get into this room?"

Sin continued looking at Colin, but spoke to Nedra. "He's a resourceful little man, that's how. He's just here to see for himself that I'm still alive."

He tweaked Colin's nose and was rewarded with a grin that lit up the boy's entire face. It was the first time that either of them had seen him smile.

With a satisfied sigh, Colin slid from the bed. "Gotta go now before they miss me at the Home. Trevor's waitin' to hear how you doin'. Couldn't work it gettin' him in here too. Maybe next time."

Nedra and Sin exchanged amused glances at his last statement. She said, "You don't have to run on my account, Colin. If you want to visit longer I can stand outside the door and watch out for the nurses."

Colin shrugged. "Naw, I been here a half hour already. You just been sleepin'. By my count, I got five minutes before the nurse comes by checkin' on things." He turned back to Sin. "So you really okay, man?"

Sin smiled at the boy trying so hard to be a man. He'd been so touched by his appearance that it had taken him a while to compose himself. Their chatter had been small talk mostly, but beneath the small talk was the child's unspoken fear that he might lose his friend.

Sin sought to reassure him. "I'm still in a little pain, man, but I'm feeling better everyday. You give Trevor the word from me that I'm going to live through this, okay?"

Reassured, Colin nodded and started toward the door. "Later."

"Hey, Colin." With some effort, Sin pulled himself higher in the bed. "Come here a second, will you?"

Sin

Colin returned to Sin's bedside.

"I want you to give Trevor something for me." Without warning, he hugged the boy gently to him and planted a kiss on his brow.

Surprised by the display of affection, the boy stiffened and backed away, holding Sin's eyes as he did so. For a moment there was no movement in the room as the adults waited to see what he would do. Sin suspected this was the first time in his life that the boy had been shown affection by a man. He knew it was the first time in his life that he had expressed affection for a child, but since being with Nedra there had been a lot of firsts in his life. He had discovered that love had no boundaries.

Still holding Sin's gaze, Colin backed toward the door, unsure of how to respond. He glanced at Nedra to read her reaction, and saw the same look of affection that he saw in Sin's eyes. His bewildered expression showed his dilemma. Love was a mystery to him. Showing emotions was unexplored territory. Yet, with these two people, maybe...

Backing into the door, he muttered, "See ya," and groped for the door knob. Opening the door, he made a hurried exit. Nedra and Sin exchanged smiles. "I think I'm jealous, Mr. Reasoner. I've got a rival for your affections."

She sat on the bed next to him. Sin cupped her chin in his hand as he looked into her eyes. "I want you always to remember, that no matter what happens there will never be anyone in my life who can ever be a rival for my affections for you."

His tone and the look in his eye was so serious that Nedra felt an involuntary shiver of apprehension. They kissed, and the apprehension vanished. A week later, he disappeared from her life.

Chapter 23

Six Months Later

The large Lincoln Town Car pulled up in front of the old red brick building and stopped. The front and back doors of the car opened simultaneously. Nedra stepped out of the front door of the car, while Colin and Trevor tumbled from the back of the vehicle. Dressed neatly in khaki pants, knit shirts, and brand-new designer sneakers, the boys carried themselves with the dignity their attire required as they looked at Nedra with eager expectation.

"Is this it?" Colin's eyes raced over the red brick building. It was old but well kept. The small lawn in front was freshly trimmed, with rows of bright flowers lining each side of the walkway leading to the front doorway. A colorful mural of African-American heroes and heroines was painted across the front of the building. Under the mural, in large, bold letters read, Pride Community Center.

"Is this where we gonna play basketball?" Trevor's voice was filled with awe, as if the building held the wonders of the universe.

Nedra smiled down at the faces of the two beautiful children who had become her whole world. "Yes, this is it, and I'm also enrolling you two in karate and swimming.

You're going to have a pretty full summer while we're in Kansas City."

She turned back to the car where the smooth brown face of Marva Davis peered up at her from the open window.

"You'll enjoy your visit here, daughter," she said, with a mysterious smile perched on her lips. "I assure you, there's something inside that you need." With that and a wave she drove away.

Entering the interior of Pride Center the three of them were pleasantly surprised. The contrast between the Center's exterior and interior was drastic. While the outside of the Center was neat and well kept, the brick building was over fifty years old and showed it. But the Center's lobby was exquisite. It was modern and awash with skylights, lush greenery, and floors so highly polished that Nedra could see her reflection. At the circular information desk in the center of the lobby an attractive young woman in cornrowed braids greeted Nedra with a warm smile.

"Good morning, may I help you?"

She returned her smile. "Yes, I have an appointment with your Executive Director, Grant Calen. My name is Nedra Davis."

A few moments later, Grant exited his office, his eyes shining with greeting. He and Nedra had known each other since high school. They had dated, exclusively, their senior year. He had been handsome then and he was still looking good.

His eyes swept over Nedra's tall, shapely frame. Clad in a sleeveless yellow sundress which complemented her rich brown tones, she wore her hair in micro braids, held back from her face by a colorful head wrap. The smile he bestowed on her was all male as he spoke. "It's so good to see you again." They exchanged a warm hug.

It was the word "Mommy" that drew his attention to the small boy standing beside her. Then a second child stepped into his vision. The children were handsome boys whom he hadn't noticed initially. But he couldn't help but notice the looks of disapproval on both their small faces as they looked at him. It was clear that they didn't like the appreciative appraisal he was giving Nedra. The oldest one placed himself between her and Grant then looked up at him defiantly. Nedra squeezed Colin's shoulder affectionately and drew Trevor closer to her side.

"Grant, these are my sons, Trevor and Colin. Boys, this is Mr. Calen. He runs this community center."

The boys shook Grant's hand politely, as they had been taught, but both pairs of eyes challenged his attention to their mother. Grant chuckled uneasily.

"In all the time your mother has been volunteering here, Nedra, she didn't say anything about your having children."

"Mama's kind of-old fashioned, you know. I'm still in the process of adopting them. So, she thinks if she says anything before it's finalized it will bring bad luck." Nedra shrugged. "What can you do but live with it."

Grant agreed. "Knowing Miss Marva, I'm sure you're right."

"When Mama dropped the boys and me off she insisted that there was something inside of Pride Center that I needed."

"Needed?" Grant looked puzzled. "What did she mean by that?"

"Who knows. Mama's been acting strange since we came to Kansas City." She glanced around the impressive structure then returned her attention to Grant. "You guys really have something going on here. So when do we start the tour?"

As Grant showed them around the building, Nedra was very impressed. Not only were there numerous educational, social, and recreational programs, but an extensive state-of-the-art computer lab was the center's showcase. A job training program that had placed hundreds of young people from the community into jobs was its most successful program. All of this was a far cry from the crumbling facility where she had volunteered so many years ago. She mentioned that fact to Grant.

"Yes, it all is amazing, isn't it? A while ago the Center really needed a new facility, but there was no land available around here, and we didn't want to build outside the community. Then, about five years ago, the Center started to get these anonymous checks in the mail every month. You wouldn't believe the amounts. They were enough to pay for renovations, and to build and equip the computer lab. One time we had a forty-passenger bus and two vans delivered to us to transport the kids. All paid for by our anonymous donor."

"Sounds like you had a guardian angel."

"No doubt about that, and the checks are still coming. As a matter of fact, our guardian angel established a very generous bank account in the Center's name, and we're able to run a lot of our programs off the interest alone."

"Surely, God is watching over Pride Center."

Grant nodded in agreement. "Amen to that. And how about you, Reverend Davis? I heard through the grapevine that God has been watching over you too. I don't mean to pry, but I heard you had some trouble sometime ago, something about your church trying to force you out as pastor. I was never quite sure what it was all about. You know how secondhand information can be. What was that about? Your mother wasn't talking. Is everything okay?"

He noted a brief shadow cross her face, then vanish as quickly as it appeared. "Yes, thank goodness, Mama was traveling out of the country when all of that happened. It was over by the time she got back. She was worried when she found out about it, but everything turned out fine, thank the Lord."

"I'm glad. So what happened?"

"Well, there was a move to force me to resign as pastor of Mount Peter, but the young people in my church rallied around me during our period of difficulty and staged a coup at the church to keep me as pastor. People who had been in power for years, didn't know what hit them. Unfortunately, I had to file a defamation of character suit against one of the church's members, or should I say, former members. She settled out of court."

"So, now you're back in the pulpit at Mount Peter?"

"No, actually, I resigned from there two months ago. Mount Peter has found its way. It's got a church full of leaders now. It's strong enough to stand on its own. My job there is done."

"Then what are your plans? Are you coming back here?" He sounded hopeful.

Nedra smiled at him fondly. "Like I told you on the phone, I'm just here visiting my mother. I've taken a new position, about two hours from Oakland, in a town called Seaside, on the Monterey Peninsula. I'll be working with the children of substance abusers." Her eyes went to the backs of the two boys walking ahead of them. "I've seen how devastating substance abuse can be on them."

Grant squeezed her arm as they walked along. "You're a great lady, Reverend Nedra Davis." He stopped at a closed office door. "Well, that's the end of the tour. You can sign the boys up for the classes they're interested in right in here."

Nedra read the red block letters printed across the painted white door: Volunteer Office. "I remember when I used to sit at a desk behind that door." During their tour she had related to him her stint as a Center volunteer.

"Well, we couldn't run this Center without them. Your mother works with the volunteer on duty now. He's one of our best. He showed up about four or five months ago. He's been tireless in doing whatever we ask him to do."

He tapped on the door, opened it and stuck his head in. The office was empty. Papers were scattered on the desk, and the radio on a file cabinet was playing softly. Grant glanced at the closed door leading to the room behind the office.

"Must be making copies in the workroom." He turned to Nedra. "You take a seat, and I'm sure you'll be helped shortly. Meanwhile, I'll take the boys back down to the basketball court to watch the game, that way you can fill out the forms without interruption."

"Thank you, Grant."

He nodded and closed the door behind him. At the same time the door to the work room opened and the volunteer stepped into the room.

"Hello, Nedra."

Crystal Rhodes

Her head snapped up with a jerk. Her heart skipped a beat. It was Sin.

Nedra's breath caught in her throat. Blood rushed to her head. For a moment she felt lightheaded. "How? Why?" She burst into tears.

Sin came to her and took her into his arms. With tears of happiness streaming down her face, she went willingly.

"Baby." His voice caught in his throat as he smothered her hair and face with kisses then drew away. "Are you all right? I didn't mean to scare you."

"I'm all right," she sniffed, swiping at her tears. "It was just such a shock."

Looking at his worried face, Nedra blinked, then blinked again. Could this be real? This man had been in her dreams day and night since he left, leaving only a letter behind. In it he told her that he was leaving so she could salvage what was left of her life. He said that he wanted to shield her from the turmoil surrounding them, turmoil he had caused.

He mentioned having heard the whispers of the hospital personnel and the gossip about them. Not only was her reputation at stake, but she was in danger of losing her position as pastor of Mount Peter. He felt the cloud of suspicion hanging over his head was dragging her down and it was breaking his heart. He didn't intend for her heart to be broken as well. The final written words on the letter had been: I'll love you forever.

288

Sin

Sin stood before her watching the play of emotions dance across her face. He was fighting his own emotions. His heartbeat was erratic. His hands were trembling. She was here. He could touch her. Hungry eyes roamed her body, the memory of the last time they made love still as vivid to him as his departure from her life.

He had signed himself out of the hospital against his doctor's advice. He told himself she had a destiny to fulfill and that he was in her way. He had sworn that he would never see her again. At the time he actually believed it.

Sin wet his lips as his eyes devoured her. What a liar he had been.

Seating her in a chair, he sat down beside her, drawing close to her but not too close as he caught a whiff of the perfume she was wearing and felt himself start to harden. All Nedra had to do was exist and he lost control. "I'm so glad to see you, Nedra."

Her eyes searched his dark ones. How could he appear so calm and composed after all that had happened between them? The shock of seeing him had almost been too much for her, but not seeing him over these past few months had been much worse. She exhaled shakily. "You don't seem as surprised to see me as I am to see you."

"I'm not. I've been waiting for you."

She tried not to look surprised. He knew she was coming? But, how could he know? Then comprehension dawned. "Are you the something inside here I need?"

Sin looked at her blankly.

She smiled. Thank the Lord for Marva Davis. "God works in mysterious ways."

Sin gave a long-suffering sigh. "Nedra."

She laughed. He still didn't like hearing sermons. "So you were in cohoots with my mother getting me back here to Kansas City?"

"Kansas City was your mother's idea. Pride Center was mine." He smiled. "This Center holds a special meaning for me and my connection to you."

Nedra frowned in confusion. "How so?"

"I'll explain it to you later. I want you to know what a wonderful mother you have. I see a lot of her in you. Marva and I have become very good friends since I've been here, but she still hasn't gotten me inside her church. I don't play that."

They shared a smile, then Nedra turned serious.

"I looked for you everywhere, Sin. I called your attorney. I drove down to your beach house. So tell me, why would you hide from me in my home town? Why would you volunteer at the same place where my mother is a volunteer?"

He shrugged. "Sometimes it's best to hide in plain sight."

He had a point. This was the last place she would have looked.

"Mama kept raving about this good-looking volunteer at the Center, but she would never mention his name. She said all the girls were crazy about you."

"Is that right? Well, I'm flattered but there's only one girl I'm crazy about." His eyes held hers as the heat emanating between them escalated. "I asked myself a million times why I settled in Kansas City but I couldn't explain it to myself. I knew it was crazy to come here but I didn't care. All I know is that I needed to be close to the places you had been. I've been miserable, Nedra. These past few months without you have been hell." His eyes caressed her. "I know you've got every reason to be angry with me but at the time I thought leaving would be best."

Nedra felt his caress even as she remembered her own misery. "You're right, I was angry and hurt. I read the letter you left me, and I tried to understand your reasons for leaving, but you never gave us a chance to take a stand together as a unit. For the second time you made a decision that we should have made together. I don't expect that to happen again."

Again! There was hope even in her reproach. Yet, there still were shadows. "Nedra, I...you...there are things that you need to know."

"Oh? Are you about to tell me that you were a government informant?" She noted that Sin's expression remained composed. He didn't appear to react. Anyone who didn't know him wouldn't have noticed the flicker of surprise in his eyes. She did.

"What would make you say that?" His tone was cautious.

Nedra watched him shift uncomfortably. Her eyes traveled down the sharp lines of his body, noting that he had regained the weigh he lost during his illness. He looked so good. He was dressed casually in a blue denim shirt and matching jeans that fit him well and hid nothing. Her eyes slid back up to his eyes, as she answered pseudo calm with pseudo calm. "You tell me."

Their eyes held as each telegraphed mutual desire. Sin was the first to break the spell. Closing his eyes, Sin rubbed his hands across his face. If he could have just exorcised her from his heart, from his every waking thought when they were apart he would have done it. But he couldn't. Now they were at the crossroads. It was time to put the past behind them and all secrets aside.

He exhaled wearily. "So you know. How did you find out?"

"I used reasoning and common sense," she grinned. "And of course, brilliant deduction."

Sin grinned back at her and shook his head in amusement. "Go on with your story, Reverend Modest."

"You remember my friend, Carla, her husband, Jacob— they just got married, by the way—well he's an attorney. I just happened to stop by his office one day to get his advice on a legal matter and guess who I saw coming out of his boss's office?"

"I'm scared to ask."

"Mr. Tyler, remember him?"

Sin remained silent.

"Anyway Jacob's boss just happens to be Oakland's District Attorney. So, casually I ask Jacob's secretary about Mr. Tyler and she tells me he's some high official with the FBI. Now, my girl can talk and from what she tells me this man is no street agent. He's way up there. So, I ask myself, why would a high ranking FBI agent come to visit some injured businessman in a hospital in Oakland? Not only did he visit him once, but twice. Could it be that they're more than just passing acquaintances? Maybe they're friends, friends who are also engaged in some kind of business arrangement. Why else would a high ranking FBI agent break through all security to get to him? And break through security without a hitch!"

Sin chuckled. "Breaking through hospital security, that's no accomplishment. Colin did that."

Nedra chuckled with him. "You got me there. But the secretary reveals that this Mr. Tyler—which by the way isn't his real name—was in town on federal business. Later, when I questioned Jacob about him and how you might be involved, he made the most unusual comment."

"Yeah, and what was that?"

"He told me that things aren't always what they appear to be."

"Sounds simple enough."

"Simple enough to make me suspicious. So, I went to the hospital to ask you what was happening, but you had disappeared." Her voice dropped to a whisper. "And that broke my heart."

Sin rose and hankered down before her, taking her hands into his. "I'm sorry Nedra. "The last thing on earth I wanted to do was hurt you. I wanted to protect you in every way."

Nedra looked at him with tears swimming in her eyes. She was touched by the sincerity she heard in his voice, but at this point more than sincerity was needed.

"So tell me, Sin. Tell me the whole truth."

He didn't hesitate. "My relationship with you was ruining your life in more ways than one, baby. Believe me, you only got a taste of how vicious the drug world can be. It's a world I know. It's a world I hate. It took my mother's life and separated me from the only security I'd ever known. And once I got myself together I was determined that it wouldn't destroy me. After college I joined the FBI and worked as an undercover agent for several years." He acknowledged Nedra's surprise at this revelation then continued. "I did my job well, quit and moved on with no problem. Then I went into business for myself and it was successful, successful enough to draw the attention of some fellow businessmen who approached me with a proposition they said could make me a fortune. I went to the friend of mine you met at the Bureau and told him what was up. The Bureau wanted me to go after the big fish for them, the ones who help support the drug trade in so-called legitimate ways."

"You mean people like the judges, the lawyers that were indicted."

"And bankers, other businessmen. The ones who make dirty money look clean by moving it through the system. They make the big bucks under the table and are rarely arrested."

"I see. How long had you been an informant?"

"Five years."

"Five years!" She paused, looking thoughtful. "That's a long time and these were some major players. That was so dangerous, Sin. Anything could have happened."

"I'd been well trained. Besides I had nothing to lose—no family, few friends, no lover..."

"Not even faith in the hereafter." Nedra squeezed his hand gently. "That's not living."

"I thought it was, until you came into my life. You changed everything. Everything." He brought her fingers to his lips. "The only time I felt alive was with you."

Nedra withdrew her hand from his and rose from the chair. Sin rose with her. "So prove it," she whispered in his ear.

No further invitation was needed. He kissed her fervently and she responded. There would be no more shadows in his life. From now on sunshine would rule his days. It could be no other way with Nedra beside him.

Finally forced to pull apart or suffocate, they continued to cling to each other as Sin planted butterfly kisses on her face. "I use an alias here because I didn't want your mother to know who I was at first. But when things cleared up in Oakland, I told her the truth about us and how much I love you. Her advice was to marry you."

Nedra drew back wide-eyed with consternation. "You didn't tell her everything about us did you?"

He chuckled. "I'm in love, Nedra, not insane. She'd kill me if she knew everything. And you're the only one outside the authorities who knows about my part in the drug bust. Now, since they dropped the charges against me last month in Oakland, and I'm cleared of all suspicion, I think we should follow her advice. Don't you?" He looked at her, his smile fading. "That is, if you'll have me."

Loosing his hold on her he planted himself on the desktop, then pulled her to stand between his legs. A pall replaced the smile on his face.

"Marva told me that you resigned from Mount Peter and I know I played a major part in that. Nedra, I'm sorry. That was the last thing I wanted to..."

She placed a silencing finger to his lips. "No. It was time. I take responsibility for my part too and I'm at peace with all that's happened. God has other plans for me."

Sin licked her finger, his mood improving. "I hope marriage is one of those plans."

"Among other things." She snaked her arms around him, drawing closer. "What else did Mama tell you? Did she say anything about the boys?"

His face dropped again. He had also left letters for Colin and Trevor telling them good-bye. He'd opened trust funds for both of them, knowing that money could never make up for his abandonment. Over the past months he had forced himself not to think about them and what they were going through in the foster care system. He sighed, heavily and said, "No. She hasn't mentioned them."

Nedra gave him a mysterious smile. "I'll tell you what, I've got some good news about them."

Sin brightened. "Really?"

"But I'll only tell you about it if you tell me something I want to know."

"You know that sounds a lot like blackmail, don't you?" His brow furrowed in disapproval.

"I prefer to call it an exchange of information." Reluctantly, she pulled out of his arms and took a seat on the desk next to him. She wanted to see the entire effect when she told him her good news. But first things first. "Like I said, I'm pretty good at deduction."

"No, you said you were brilliant." Sin teased.

"All right. I'll go along with that. Anyway, I was told today that the Center started receiving anonymous donations about five years ago. Was it you? Did you make some deal with the Feds that this Center would benefit, financially, from what you were doing?"

Sin looked astonished. "Now why would I do something like that?"

Nedra grinned. Her mother had been right. There was something that Nedra needed. A man called Sin in her life.

"Sinclair Reasoner," she announced, "Reverend Nedra Davis would love to become your wife." With that, she told him about the Colin and Trevor and watched as the look on his face changed to one of pure joy.

Epilogue

On the beach along the Monterey shoreline, Nedra Davis-Reasoner sat nestled on a blanket spread on the sun-drenched sand as her husband and sons explored the rocky crevices for marine life. Draped in colorful nylon wind-breakers that matched her own, the three of them maneuvered the rocks skillfully, stopping now and then to wave at her, or to exclaim in wonder at a new discovery. These hours, just before sunset, had become their favorite time. The four of them would walk the shoreline for hours marveling at its quiet beauty, enjoying the simple pleasure of being a family, of having found each other, no longer having to face the world alone.

Tomorrow they would drive into Santa Cruz , and their family of four would become five. Her name was Gillian, and she was three years old. Nedra had counseled her mother and promised the young woman on her deathbed that she would take care of the child. The woman died of hepatitis, contracted as the result of her drug addiction. She was nineteen years old.

Nedra sighed, her emotions a mixture of happiness and sadness. She had always wanted a daughter, but never at the cost that was paid. Yet, they were are all excited about the new addition in their lives. They had been a family a little over a year, and God's blessings continuously flowed. Sin had funded a non-profit organization which specialized in providing needed services for drug addicted parents and their children. It was named after his mother.

Nedra's attention was brought back to her men as the shouts of "Daddy" rang through the serenity of the evening and drifted into her consciousness. Excited, his face flushed and animated, Colin made his way across the rocks to Sin to show him his latest discovery. Trevor, forever his brother's shadow, followed him, not wanting to be left out of the hugs and kisses bestowed on them by Sin, no matter how big or small their accomplishments. He didn't disappoint either of them, and the looks of adoration on their faces brought tears to Nedra's eyes.

Yes, life was good, and God had been good to them. On Sunday they would go and give further thanks for their blessings. All five of them would be going to church, including Sin, whose faith had been gradually restored with the dawning of each new day.

THE END

INDIGO: Sensuous Love Stories *Order Form*

Mail to:
Genesis Press, Inc.
315 3rd Avenue North
Columbus, MS 39701

Visit our website at

http://www.genesis-press.com

Name————————————————————

Address————————————————————

City/State/Zip————————————————

1999 INDIGO TITLES

Qty	Title	Author	Price	Total
	Somebody's Someone	Sinclair LeBeau	$8.95	
	Interlude	Donna Hill	$8.95	
	The Price of Love	Beverly Clark	$8.95	
	Unconditional Love	Alicia Wiggins	$8.95	
	Mae's Promise	Melody Walcott	$8.95	
	Whispers in the Night	Dorothy Love	$8.95	
	No Regrets (paperback reprint)	Mildred Riley	$8.95	
	Kiss or Keep	D.Y. Phillips	$8.95	
	Naked Soul (paperback reprint)	Gwynne Forster	$8.95	
	Pride and Joi (paperback Reprint)	Gay G. Gunn	$8.95	
	A Love to Cherish (paperback reprint)	Beverly Clark	$8.95	
	Caught in a Trap	Andree Jackson	$8.95	
	Truly Inseparable (paperback reprint)	Wanda Thomas	$8.95	
	A Lighter Shade of Brown	Vicki Andrews	$8.95	
	Cajun Heat	Charlene Berry	$8.95	

Use this order form
or call:
1-888-INDIGO1
(1-888-463-4461)

TOTAL _____
Shipping & Handling _____
(\$3.00 first book \$1.00 each additional book)

TOTAL Amount Enclosed _____
MS Residents add 7% sales tax

INDIGO *Backlist Titles*

QTY	TITLE	AUTHOR	PRICE	TOTAL
	A Love to Cherish	Beverly Clark	$15.95 HC*	
	Again My Love	Kayla Perrin	$10.95	
	Breeze	Robin Hampton	$10.95	
	Careless Whispers	Rochelle Alers	$8.95	
	Dark Embrace	Crystal Wilson Harris	$8.95	
	Dark Storm Rising	Chinelu Moore	$10.95	
	Entwined Destinies	Elsie B. Washington	$4.99	
	Everlastin' Love	Gay G. Gunn	$10.95	
	Gentle Yearning	Rochelle Alers	$10.95	
	Glory of Love	Sinclair LeBeau	$10.95	
	Indiscretions	Donna Hill	$8.95	
	Love Always	Mildred E. Riley	$10.95	
	Love Unveiled	Gloria Green	$10.95	
	Love's Deception	Charlene A. Berry	$10.95	
	Midnight Peril	Vicki Andrews	$10.95	
	Naked Soul	Gwynne Forster	$15.95 HC*	
	No Regrets	Mildred E. Riley	$15.95 HC*	
	Nowhere to Run	Gay G. Gunn	$10.95	
	Passion	T.T. Henderson	$10.95	
	Pride and Joi	Gay G. Gunn	$15.95 HC*	
	Quiet Storm	Donna Hill	$10.95	
	Reckless Surrender	Rochelle Alers	$6.95	
	Rooms of the Heart	Donna Hill	$8.95	
	Shades of Desire	Monica White	$8.95	
	Truly Inseparable	Mildred Y. Thomas	$15.95 HC*	
	Whispers in the Sand	LaFlorya Gauthier	$10.95	
	Yesterday is Gone	Beverly Clark	$10.95	

* indicates Hard Cover

Total for Books _____
Shipping and Handling_____
($3.00 first book $1.00 each additional book)